BROKEN-DOWN HEROES OF THE WESTERN NIGHT

STEPHEN KOZENIEWSKI

Copyright © 2021 Stephen Kozeniewski
Copyright © 2021 French Press
manuscriptsburn.blogspot.com

Are you really reading this? My God, you must be bored. I mean, I'm honored, of course. But it's boring, isn't it? Who *actually* reads a copyright page? All rights reserved. This book or any portion thereof may not be reproduced or used in any manner whatsoever without the express written permission of the publisher and author, except where permitted by law.

This novel is a work of fiction. Names, places, characters, and incidents are the product of the author's imagination, or are used fictitiously. Any resemblance to actual events, locales, or persons, living or dead, is purely coincidental. If you've read this far wondering if I plan to have an open casket funeral, the answer to that is: remains to be seen.

ISBN: 9798450236438
All rights reserved.

Important Note!

Broken-Down Heroes of the Western Night does not contain any elements of science fiction, fantasy, or horror.

If you like my writing voice and caustic style of humor, you'll enjoy this novel. But if you came for things that go bump in the night, check out my back catalog instead.

On the other side of the coin, if this was your first introduction to my writing, please carefully read the descriptions of my other books before diving in. Some of them may not be for you.

In short: this one is a departure.

For all redlegs, past and present.

"...war blows..."
- Shakespeare, Henry V: Act 3, Scene 1, Line 45, Words 6-7

1

The biggest mistake 1LT Bickham Deth ever made was wearing scarlet socks to a funeral.

The trip was supposed to be three days: two funerals and a travel day in between. To be safe, Deth had packed all five pairs of black dress socks that he owned and threw in the red pair for kicks. That three day trip, though, had already ballooned into two weeks on the road, pinballing between Norman, Muskogee, OKC, and all points in between.

They had done ten funerals in that time, and Deth had cycled through all of his black socks twice. He had already done his laundry once at one of those quarter-devouring hotel Laundromats and he hoped against hope that Mortuary Affairs would finally call him home to that miserable den of iniquity known as Lawton, OK.

The Coalhouse funeral put paid to that dream.

"They've got another one for us, sir," SFC Bela Packs advised Deth with a sigh, hanging up his cell phone on the casualty center.

"I think I've figured out why they put me on permanent funeral detail, Sergeant," Deth said, not bothering to grunt his acknowledgement of the Saturday engagement.

"There's no such thing as permanent funeral detail, sir," Packs replied with absolutely no conviction.

"It's because of my name."

"Deth?"

He nodded. "I think they mixed up my file with the Grim Reaper's. Somewhere, right now, on the front lines in Iraq a guy in a black bathrobe is leading a platoon that's supposed to be mine."

Packs scowled a little bit, but only a little bit. He had been at the depressing business of folding flags at veterans' funerals off-and-on for over eighteen months. Of course, over the length of his career he had also been to Iraq, Germany, Korea, Texas, California, and Washington. Deth, on the other hand, had spent every day of his two-and-a-half years in the army in Oklahoma (excepting the occasional Arkansas runs) and every minute of those days on funeral detail.

When it came to the army, Packs was the expert. When it came to planting bodies, Deth was king.

Not relishing the prospect of having to don even the least crusty of his five pairs of dirty socks, Deth suddenly gladdened that he had packed his scarlet pair. He was expected, required even, under certain circumstances to don his red socks (along with red suspenders) and attend balls, dining-ins, dining-outs, and formal ceremonies of all types. Scarlet being the branch color of the United States Field Artillery Corps, it had become, in some peculiar fashion, customary for redlegs (also, probably a nickname that had evolved as a result of the branch color) to wear red socks.

At least, it was for the officers. Bela Packs swore up and down that the NCOs never did, had never, in fact, heard of such a preposterous notion. Deth, though, hadn't made it up. He had once been chewed out by the battalion XO for *not* wearing his scarlet socks at a St. Barbara's Day ball. At first he had assumed the XO had been playing a trick on him, but when he got back to his table and took a look around he saw that all of the officers were, indeed, decked out in scarlet socks.

Not mentioning what lay beneath his footwear to Packs, Deth piled into the car, a white 2002 Ford sedan some four years out of date now but by no means the worst Government-Owned Vehicle he had ever set foot in. On a run to Little Rock, Deth had once found himself inexplicably stuck in a 1992 Taurus. There hadn't even been a CD player. Stopping at a lone and dusty way station, he had purchased the first cassette tape he had owned in ten-odd years just to have something to listen to that wasn't the brand of irony-free, downhome country the local DJs were obsessed with.

Packs fired up the radio.

"...but I've been to Oklahoma," the speakers on either side of Deth in the passenger's seat blared, leaving the part about the singer never having been to Heaven implied.

Deth slapped the knob for sweet relief. Packs waited not even thirteen seconds before he sang of his own accord. "Proud to be an Okie from Muskogee..."

Deth slapped the knob on the radio again, not sure whether he was hoping it would turn Packs off or merely summon a louder, more primordial noise to drown him out. When Packs did not, in any case, shut up, Deth slowly turned up the knob on the radio and with his other hand slowly wheedled through the stations searching for something that was not country and western. Giving up, he settled on a nice white noise that lay in between stations and in no way discouraged Packs from his off-key caterwauling, until he had inveighed the entire song for his (nominally) superior officer.

"Got any CDs, sir?" Packs asked when he was finished, as though nothing had just taken place and the radio wasn't still tuned to nothing and blaring at maximum volume.

"Yeah," Deth said, grabbing at his compact disc sleeve.

He had not yet converted to the iPod. There was something about it he just didn't trust. Uppity like Tamagotchi, pretending like it was a turntable. He didn't trust it, somehow, like a cat that barked. He flipped through sleeve after sleeve of music. Classic rock, some '90s puss rock he had thought was good at the time, modern artists more attractive than they were talented, which he had bought mostly for the liner notes.

"Got any country?" Packs asked, following the "quip" up with the peculiar silent yukking that he sometimes did at his own jokes.

"How about Green Day?" Deth asked.

Packs shrugged, indifferent. Deth had gathered that he knew some country but didn't particularly like it. Nor did he particularly like any song or artist they had ever sat and listened to in their interminable hours in the car together. Packs seemed to have no feelings one way or the other about pop culture, being completely of a mind about the army. And cheese. He was obsessed with cheese.

"That's us," Packs said after the first song began playing, "A couple of American idiots."

"Two broken-down heroes of the western night," Deth intoned softly.

Packs took his eyes off the road to look Deth in the eyes. "It ain't even noon."

Deth said nothing.

They picked up the flag from the undertaker and asked to change in their bathroom. It was unusual, but sometimes the cemetery site had nowhere to change. Deth had once changed behind the seeming privacy of a tree in the graveyard only to turn and find kids in the backseats of cars on the highway waving and pointing at his flopping junk. Doing that once was enough. Now he always asked to change at the funeral parlor.

Once they were dressed in their Class A uniforms, Packs and Deth went on to the cemetery alone. They never drove with the funeral procession. They were not part of the funeral, only props at the funeral, like the casket, the green Astroturf carpet, or sometimes the caisson.

The February morning was cold and crisp. Before moving there, Deth had never imagined such weather possible in Oklahoma. Like most people, his only experience with the Sooner climate had been hearing the Weather Channel report some triple-digit travesty that made him feel better about his own little corner of the U.S.

Standing there by the graveside, Packs produced three rifle cartridges from his seemingly boundless supply of brass. Two seams of superglue fused the cartridges together into a single entity. As was his custom, Packs began polishing them furiously.

"You rub much harder and you're going to break those damn things apart," Deth said.

Packs, reminding Deth of nothing so much as an assayer from the Old West, held the cartridges up to the light of the sun to check their shine. "Gotta make 'em gleam," Packs said.

"They already gleam."

Deth tried to snatch the fused cartridges but grasped only air as Packs deftly dodged. "What difference does it make? No one's ever going to see them."

Packs stopped polishing to look Deth full in the face. "We'll see them," he said, "We're seeing them right now."

Deth was unable to respond. Some men had to do everything the right way, no matter what. He flipped a Lucky Strike, unfiltered, into his mouth. He preferred filtered, the kind he had smoked in college, but those could only be found in Europe. Deth either did not know or had forgotten that the company had stopped making his preferred brand of coffin nails stateside and always blamed their absence on the backwardness of Oklahoma.

He proffered the pack to Packs, who refused with a wave of his hand, instead producing his own packet of cowboy killers and chewed on the filter of one, unlit, for a few minutes.

"You know, sir," Packs said, in between polishing his brass and chewing on his cigarette tip, "You're the only ossifer I know who smokes."

"Yup," Deth said.

They had gone through the motions of this conversation dozens, if not hundreds of times.
At this point the words just blurred together into a mush, like a favorite rerun playing in the background vaguely remembered.

"Usually NCOs smoke and officers dip," Packs continued, hitting the usual talking points with no more vigor than usual.

"I'm a queer duck, all right," Deth added, without gusto or even irony, a rarity for him, even when he was deadpanning.

They smoked together silently for a while. The cold morning warmed up gradually. In a moment, Deth would feel obliged to seek shade. "What was it like Over There?"

"In Eye-rack?" Packs pronounced the first part of "Iraq" the same way he pronounced the first part of "Italian." Deth nodded.

"Hot."

That was the standard answer. Not just from Packs but from anyone Deth had ever asked, under any circumstances. Whether they elaborated further or not, that was always the first thing they said. He waited. This was the first time he had asked Packs about his wartime experience, although he had heard all about his time in Germany and Korea. Deth wasn't exactly sure what had prompted him to ask about the desert today.

"I ever tell you about Major Brannigan?" Packs asked, squinting out of his left eye as though he had smoke in it.

Deth perked up. "I don't think so," he said.

Packs nodded and tapped ash off his cigarette in time to each individual nod. He raised his arm, palm horizontal, as high as he could reach it.

"Son of a bitch was about as tall as a Georgia pine tree," Packs said, "Excuse my French, sir, especially about a superior officer, but it's deserved. He was a real son of a bitch."

"Not at all, Sergeant," Deth said, "I asked."

"Eyebrows you could rappel off of," Packs continued, "And a stupid expression on his face, no matter what he was doing."

"Like a troll," Deth mused.

"Huh?"

"Oh, uh, well, did you ever see The Lord of the Rings?"

Packs shook his hands in the air as though warding off an evil spirit. "I don't go in for that kind of stuff."

Deth shrugged. He should have known better. He hoped he hadn't thrown Packs off his story. Judging by Packs's vacant stare, he had though. "Major Brannigan..." Deth prompted.

"Right, right," Packs said, nodding copiously and taking another drag from his cigarette, "So this big dumb buffoon, I don't know who gave him a gold leaf, but he couldn't lead his way out of a paper bag."

Deth scowled, but only internally. He knew exactly how this Brannigan, and every other major, for that matter, had earned the rank. The army had been in Afghanistan for almost five years now, Iraq for three, and Deth knew that merit promotions would have made a huge difference on the battlefield. But the decade or so of peacetime before that had all but drummed the idea of merit out of the officer promotion system. Seniority trumped almost nothing else now.

Eighteen months after he joined, Deth had been promoted to O-2, just like every other lieutenant in the army. Eighteen months after that, he would pin on his railroad tracks. Eight years after that (give or take a year in pretend deference to merit), he would get major. Ten years after that, if he stayed in that long, he would pin on O-5. It was gospel, written in stone, like the Ten Commandments. Bad evaluations didn't do shit to your career. In fact, up to O-3 all evals, good or bad, were masked. The simple fact was that if you stuck with the army, you moved up. In a way, it was reassuring, but in a deeper, existential way, it made Deth fear for the future of his beloved army.

Packs continued. "Best thing for him would've been to stick him behind a desk a million klicks away from the nearest joe and set him to work making a PowerPoint about...Port-a-Johns or something."

Deth nodded, in a perverse way wishing that he had met this exemplar of bad behavior.

"The fucked-up thing is," Packs said, not bothering to beg pardon for his "French" this time, "You know he's going to be a general one day."

"Let me guess," Deth said, "He gets 300 on his APFT?"

Unconsciously, Deth ran a hand along his stomach, knowing that his tiny little gut betrayed his less-than-stellar physique. 300 was a perfect score on the Army Physical Fitness Test. Deth had never scored above 242.

Packs stared at the lieutenant like he had a third eye sprouting out of his forehead. "Hell no, sir," Packs said, stretching out the first word for three solid syllables, "I once saw the man fall out of a brigade run."

Deth snorted. He was no fan of exercise himself, and had never done much better than a seven-minute mile. But in the army, unit runs were not designed to be tests of physical endurance. They were team-building exercises. A battery run was at a very slow trot, and someone who fell out of that was a piece of shit. In a battalion run, no battery could run faster than the battery in front of it, and someone who fell out of that was an unusually big piece of shit. In a brigade run? Well, there practically had to be something wrong with a person to fall out of that. "No, you didn't."

Packs held up his arm solemnly as though he were swearing an oath in a courtroom. "My hand to God, sir. He was even in command at the time."

Deth shook his shoulders in confusion. "What happened?"

Packs rolled his eyes. "LTC Fink was out of town for some reason. Leave, I guess. I forget. But there was this brigade run on the schedule. So our mighty XO decided to step up to the challenge.

The day before, MAJ Brannigan issued strict orders that no one would fall out of the brigade run, because it would make the battalion look bad."

"No shit," Deth said.

Packs shrugged. "Yeah, no shit. Come the day of the brigade run, the major is nowhere to be found. All the other battalions are lined up with their commanders out front, standing strong, waiting for the brigade commander to arrive. And our battalion? One of the staff captains had to step up and assume command. Then, just as the brigade commander starts speaking to wish us well and bless our legs and shit, MAJ Brannigan comes running up, yelling at the captain who had 'stolen' his place." Open-mouthed, Deth just shook his head. Packs nodded. "All that's before the run even began. A few minutes later we all pass this hulking form doubled over on the side of the road, hacking and coughing and generally acting like a pathetic mess. I didn't recognize him at first but later FirstSergeant told me it was MAJ Brannigan."

"It's a shame nobody gave him a speech about not shaming the battalion by falling out."

Packs laughed, that weird, half-barking laugh of his when he found something actually funny. "I will say, at least he had the sense of shame not to show up at the head of our formation afterwards. He just disappeared. That was what he did all the time, just disappeared when he'd done something shameful like fall out of a fucking brigade run, pardon my French."

Deth nodded. "So, in other words, a real stud when it comes to PT."

"Hell, that's not the half of it, sir," he said, leaning in towards Deth conspiratorially, "I once saw that man choke himself out doing sit-ups in his BDUs because he grabbed his own collar."

Deth retched a little at the memory of the Battle Dress Uniforms, the uncomfortable dark green affairs that had preceded the current greyish Army Combat Uniforms. No amount of starching and ironing on his part could ever get the BDU blouse and pants crisp enough, and when he inevitably caved and took them to the dry cleaner's he was rewarded with a uniform that wore like cardboard, particularly around the crotch. He had spent what probably amounted to full days of his life polishing his boots, and yet the next day he always ended up standing in formation next to someone who gave him a case of polish envy.

The new ACUs, by contrast, were as comfy as pajamas, with brown no-polish boots and Velcro patches instead of sew-on. The switch had been like going from a Pinto to a Ferrari, despite Deth's irritation at having to restock his whole closet on his own dime one year into his army career.

The idea of Brannigan choking himself out in any uniform, though, was laughable. Instead of putting his hands behind his head (as was the army standard) he must have crossed them over his chest and grabbed both of his own lapels until he had pinched his own collar around his neck. Deth briefly wondered whether the test administrator who had let him do that had been a buffoon, been terrified by the man's rank, or thought it would be funny.

"Man's never passed a PT test in his life," Packs continued, "He used to make the Ops NCO fake his score. No, I say he'll be a general because...you ever meet a general, sir?" Deth shook his head.

"They're all tall," Packs continued, "I don't know what it is. They intimidate you, I guess, and then you feel like you have to give them a star."

While he would never admit it, Deth was enjoying hearing Packs dish the dirt. The man was usually so taciturn, and when he wasn't being taciturn, he was being professional. Deth assumed that if they hadn't spent so many days together on the road doing funerals, he never would have known Packs's feelings about the war, or anything else for that matter. But boredom will drive even a quiet man to talk.

Deth realized with a start that his question had yet again derailed the conversation. "What were you going to tell me about Major...Brannigan, was it?"

Packs nodded to excess, as though he had not allowed a break in the conversation, but merely a measured pause, and had been intending the entire time to continue speaking, when it was obvious that his thoughts had simply trailed off. "A lot of my job Over There was basically to be a travel agent," Packs said, "Catfish Air...well, I'll tell you about that another time. Anyway, one time I scheduled a flight for Major Brannigan to...I don't know, it might've been Normandy."

Deth furrowed his brow. "France?"

Packs shook his head like a mare just a little irritated by a horsefly. "FOB Normandy."

Iraq was awash with Forward Operating Bases or FOBs (not to mention COBs, COPs, LSAs, camps, firebases, and at least one palace) so Deth wasn't surprised he had never heard of Normandy in particular. Every conversation with someone who had been downrange seemed to feature a whole litany of new names.

"Anyway, I don't remember where it was to, but that's not important. What's important is that he came back and he looked me dead in the eye and he said, 'Sergeant Packs, how many flights have I been on since I got here?' I said I have no fucking idea, only I said it nice-like, because he was an officer. And then he says to me, 'How many do you need for an Air Medal?'"

Deth laughed unexpectedly, snorting smoke out his nose unpleasantly. When he recovered from his brief coughing fit, he cocked his head and slowly, slowly turned to face the unusually garrulous NCO full in the face. "Did he think it was like Frequent Flier Miles? Like, you fly around enough and then they just hand you an Air Medal?"

Packs nodded with a look on his face that said, "You're fucking brand new to the army and you already get it."

Deth was sure there was something he still wasn't getting. "You said he was just a passenger, right?" Packs nodded. "Did he think they should give Air Medals to the cargo, too?"

"That fucking guy."

"What'd you do?"

"Well, I explained to him as nicely as I could without busting my britches laughing that the Air Medal was supposed to be for air crews, and not just for being a lump of shit, but for actually doing something. I thought that was the end of it, but I can't even tell you how this guy was, sir. He always had his eye on the wrong thing, like, you know, getting scrambled eggs on his chest instead of taking care of his men. I can't even explain it, he was like the Rembrandt of doing dumb shit.

"So a few days later...days, he didn't even wait that long, he comes back from a flight with a big smug smile on his face and says, 'I think I earned that Air Medal today, Sergeant Packs.'"

"No, he didn't," Deth breathed. Packs nodded.

"What did he do?" Deth asked, "Jump into the machine gunner's chair when he got shot dead?"

"Oh, no, sir, it was way more above the call of duty than that. Apparently they couldn't get the bird to take off, some kind of mechanical failure, but all the passengers were standing around waiting for it to get fixed. And only our fearless leader Major Brannigan had a red flashlight. So he shined it around and spotted the cherry juice spilled all over the pad. And Major Brannigan was the one who pointed out the broken tube to the crew chief. So he asked me to put him in for an Air Medal."

Deth was sure his jaw was hanging in the dirt. "Did you?"

Packs dropped his cigarette to the cold ground of the cemetery and crushed it under his chlorofram. "Here comes the procession," he said, "Better get the stereo ready."

2

Deth tucked the boombox, likely a relic of the 1980s, behind a gravestone marked "DOBSON 1877-1910." The hearse pulled into the circle first, followed by a broken-down convoy of jeeps, jalopies, and at least one of what Deth would've sworn was a Model T. Laws being what they were in Oklahoma, a car only had to be entirely covered with paint, not necessarily car paint, and so a number of the vehicles were touched up with spray-paint where the dust and shit of the road had scraped away the original layer.

Deth had been to enough funerals in Oklahoma (Lord knew he had been to enough) to see the shitkickers in their cowboy boots and jeans and maybe, just maybe, a black button-down, but it still always rubbed him the wrong way. It wasn't that every funeral was that way. Usually it depended on the area. Places like Tulsa and OKC usually had more folks in suits and ties than just the funeral director, but the little double-digit population shitholes (and just as often as not even places like Muskogee or Broken Arrow) ended up wearing Alabama formal.

Deth stood at parade rest when the pallbearers began their weary trudge to the graveside. Packs, of course, had already been in the correct position, spine stiff, to Deth's left. They waited, not out of sight, but out of mind, for the moment, except for the occasional stage-whispering of family members commenting on the "army guys."

The preacher spoke first, in a Southwestern cadence and style that, no matter how many times Deth heard it, he still associated only with movies and not with real life. He rarely used a capitalized pronoun when he could say "Jesus" instead and he placed an overwhelming emphasis on the name every time he said it. One of Coalhouse's grandchildren stood up to speak next, a red-headed middle-aged man. Based on the fact he was wearing a tie, Deth guessed he was from out-of-state.

The funeral director sidled up alongside Packs, his hands still folded in a clump in front of him, and shaking his head in mock grief as if every word the grandson said was the end of a Shakespearean tragedy. "The woman in the center..." the funeral director started to whisper in an appropriately morbid voice.

Packs merely jerked his head toward Deth, not breaking his hands out of their parade rest position in the small of his back. The mortician nodded and scuttled around to whisper in Deth's ear instead. "See the woman in the center with the big jangly earrings? On her right, your left, the younger blond lady with the baby."

"Widow?" Deth muttered, although it was pretty obvious from her age that she had to be.

Deth tried to keep his lips from moving obviously in case any of the mourners were watching them. In fact, a few were: one who had excused himself to talk on a cell phone and at least one kid that Deth had spotted earlier sitting under a folding chair instead of on it. The kid was staring at them, in awe of their uniforms, and utterly disinterested in his great-grand-uncle's funeral.

The funeral director nodded in answer to Deth's barely asked question. The red-headed grandson was wrapping up his remarks, so the mortician quickly scampered away. Alas, that was not to be the last of the mourners to speak. A blue-eyed woman wearing a string of pearls came on next. She appeared to be no relation, making Deth briefly wonder if Old Man Coalhouse had been seeing a mistress some thirty years his junior. Whatever her relationship was with the deceased would remain an unsolved, uncared about mystery for Deth, as a son in a wheelchair, a niece or possibly an ugly nephew, and a cowboy of some sort each eulogized Coalhouse in turn, the last of whom attempting to do so with a guitar.

Finally the preacher stood back up and nodded solemnly to them, an agreed-upon signal that nevertheless all of the mourners immediately picked up on. They turned to stare at Deth and Packs. Deth's heart no longer fluttered at this moment as it had during his first few funerals, although he did fear fucking up. He strode boldly forward to the coffin, and the heads of the mourners, like meerkats, followed him.

Their eyes, now thankfully off Packs, left the crusty NCO free to press the button on the Reagan-era boombox. Slowly, mournfully, using up the entirety of the three seconds he had in which to execute the maneuver, Deth raised his hand to his eyebrow in salute as the haunting melody of "Taps" filled the air. Technically, he was saluting the flag draped over Coalhouse's coffin, but he never divested the family members of their assumption that he was saluting the dead man for his service.

"Taps" concluded, Deth slowly lowered his salute, this time milking it on purpose. He had to give Packs time to turn off the tape player (nothing worse than the recording starting over again) and hurry down to the foot of the coffin. So, vamping for time but attempting to appear not to, Deth slowly walked to the head of the casket, smoothed out the still-banded flag, removed the rubber band that held it in place, smoothed it out again, took the blue corner in his left hand and the red and white corner in his right, and waited.

All that accomplished, Packs was already at the foot of the wooden box. Only once or twice before had Deth had to stand there, looking solemn, waiting for Packs or another of his NCOs to arrive. Trouble with the boombox, for instance, or a bit of mud on the chloroframs that simply couldn't be ignored. Things like that. Usually, though, after "Taps," they were so deep into the solemnity of the ceremony that none of the grieving ones spoke, often assuming (Deth guessed) that the prolonged pause was all part of the mournful ceremony.

Counting out numbers in their heads (they had long since gotten past the point of needing Packs's whispered commands), they lifted the flag up, stepped to Deth's left (Packs's right), folded once, twice, then thrice. Then Deth's part of the folding was done; he just had to stand there.

Packs, meanwhile, made a tight, elegant paper football out of the flag, folding triangle after triangle from the foot of the casket towards Deth, and smoothing after each fold. Finally they were left with only a blue-starred triangle and a small flap of extra cloth. Packs slipped the brightly polished brass shells into the flag and tucked the flap into the triangle proper. (As Deth had pointed out, unless someone unfolded the flag in the future, as families rarely did, no one would ever see the brass.)

Packs then dutifully stood, pointing first one point of the triangle to Deth, then the next, then the next. Deth made a show of straightening and tucking to form a perfect triangle, but as so often happened at their level of experience, Packs had already executed the retirement so deftly that the lieutenant didn't really need to do anything.

Nodding his approval, Deth saluted, somewhat faster now that they weren't waiting for anything but theoretically still taking his full three seconds. Though it had felt odd to Deth at first to salute an NCO, of course he was not really saluting Packs but the flag, just as he had not really been saluting Coalhouse earlier. Packs handed him the flag, executed his own salute, did an about face, and marched off smartly.

Now came Deth's real time to shine, the moment of the ceremony when he felt like he was doing a real service to the country. Executing sharp left- and right-faces, he came around the casket, under the tent, and knelt down before the woman the mortician had indicated as the widow. It was then, with one of his knees on the ground and the other pointed skyward, that the mourners in the front row spotted his scarlet socks.

Sometimes the next of kin cried. Often, Deth had found, it was the younger NOKs who cried, not yet understanding life, perhaps. Older women, widows especially, and in this case, Mrs. Coalhouse, sometimes didn't.

"On behalf of a grateful nation," Deth said, neither whispering nor shouting but looking the widow Coalhouse dead in the eyes, "I present to you this flag, as a symbol of the sacrifices and service of your husband."

Deth had carefully rehearsed this, his personal version of the speech that he gave at every old timer's funeral. On his first funeral (how long ago that seemed now) the mortuary affairs civilian had told him that there was a sample speech in the manual, that it was not mandatory, that it was terrible, and that he had better make up his own, one that could come from his heart the first time and from his memory the hundred times after that.

"And never say 'loved one,'" mortuary affairs had told him, "For the love of God, don't say 'loved one.'"

Mrs. Coalhouse stared at him, as the widows sometimes did, like he was an alien from a distant galaxy. After a moment that encompassed an eternity, she took the proffered flag. Deth stood and again executed a three-second salute, which he again knew from long experience (but if he hadn't, he would've known instantly from the chittering of the other mourners) that they assumed he was saluting the woman instead of the flag.

A few sharp turns later and Deth was back at parade rest, standing to the right of Packs, out of sight and out of mind for the rest of the ceremony. Deth knew better than to chit-chat with Packs. "How'd it go?" Packs whispered gruffly.

Deth nodded. No issues. The preacher wrapped up the last little bits of the funeral, directions to the reception and the like. Then, like a football team breaking a huddle, the mourners dispersed. "Here they come," Deth whispered out of the side of his mouth.

The mourners were about to pass by the servicemen like a wave over a rock. Sometimes they were lucky. Sometimes the whole crew passed, Deth and Packs breathed a sigh of relief, changed, and hit the road. But sometimes a family member would want to speak to them. The NOK if it was a man or a young person. (Rarely did the widows want anything to do with them - too much of that old baggage from the old "knock at the door" during Vietnam and World War II, Deth guessed.) Or sometimes a very young kid approached and asked about their medals and what-have-you.

And if one mourner stopped, then a few others, cousins and rivals and the like, would feel obliged to stop, too. Then the funeral detail would be stuck there for ten, fifteen, twenty minutes having the awkwardest conversations in the world.

And they always wanted to talk to Deth. The type of person who wanted to stop and talk to them was usually the type of person who knew just enough about the military to know ranks. And they might know just enough to think that a sergeant (three stripes) was a scrub and a lieutenant (one bar) was a champ. They would never, of course, know that a Sergeant First Class was actually a champ and a lieutenant was a scrub in the real army. It was just the fictional world of rank unattached to responsibility, experience, or *de facto* power that civilians understood, as though the ability to command emanated from a metal chunk on your lapel instead of a whole variety of factors. So they always wanted to talk to Deth and ignored Packs, in spite of the chest full of metal Packs wore and the paltry three "I joined the army" ribbons Deth wore.

Packs fucking loved it that way.

Deth held his breath waiting for the wave of mourners to pass as though it were a literal wave. Yes. Home free. Someone was helping Mrs. Coalhouse to her car in the opposite direction and the rest of the crowd followed. That was it for the mourning party, except for an older lady who sported wild red hair and was easily the breadth of the two of them combined. Of course she came trouncing up to talk. Her face was wild with an excited smile, something that Deth had honestly never seen before at a funeral, even from the kids who usually knew enough to at least pretend to be sad.

"I LOVE your socks!" the lady practically shouted.

At least five or six of the mourners who had made it halfway to the car apparently heard crazy Aunt Carlotta shouting and turned around to circle the funeral detail. Either they wanted to hear what was going to be said or they were waiting for their own chance to address the Soldiers, which they hadn't known they were allowed to do until someone else did it first.

(Mentally, Deth always capitalized the "S" in "Soldier." For reasons known but to God and the Secretary of Defense a memo had been issued about two years ago ordering that particular violation of sense and grammar in all army correspondence. As stupid as he found it, Deth couldn't shake the habit, not even in his own brain.)

Deth heard Packs cough, ever so slightly, a minor violation of military customs and courtesies while standing at parade rest so out of character for Packs that Deth instantly realized he was suppressing a savage laugh. Deth swallowed a lump in his throat. "Ma'am?"

"Let me see, let me see!" she said, pointing at Deth's pant legs.

Mortified, Deth reached down and slowly lifted his right pant leg, revealing one of his scarlet socks. The wide lady clapped in delight. "I love them," she said, then, turning to Packs, "Are you wearing red socks, too?"

Packs gave another chirping cough which Deth recognized as a choked guffaw. Nevertheless, he was straight dignity and all drill sergeant when he spoke. "No, ma'am," he said, "I'm afraid I'm not allowed to. I'm not an officer."

Deth knew that Packs normally spoke so little in this sort of situation that this veritable tide of words was intended to get her to stick back on Deth like a remora. He even managed, somehow preserving his non-commissioned dignity, to raise his pant leg and reveal his ordinary black socks, as if to provide a striking contrast with the parti-colored buffoon next to him.

"Ohhhhhh, you're an oooooofficer," the lady said, turning back to Deth and stroking his lapel as though they were lovers, "So tell me, what do they mean?"

The other mourners who had gathered to circle like buzzards were talking amongst themselves. Had this been an outrage? Had their father/grandfather/uncle/dear friend been somehow degraded, given a less than perfect funeral honor due to those damn non-regulation socks?

Deth looked to Packs, though he knew there would be no help forthcoming from that arena, and Packs did not fail to not deliver. Packs would have his back if a proper fistfight broke out, Deth had no doubt, but it was up to the young Soldier to talk his way out of things before it got that far.

The options ran through Deth's mind. He could plead ignorance and beg for forgiveness, but he doubted the gathering mob of angry mourners would accept that. He could try to Jedi mind trick them into believing the socks were regulation, but Packs had already proven that false. He gritted his teeth. There were only two options left to him: tell the truth or attempt to bullshit them. So he could either explain about not being able to do any laundry or...

"Ma'am, I was told that Corporal Coalhouse was an artilleryman." Deth hadn't been paying attention during the funeral to whether anyone had mentioned Coalhouse's actual rank, but these old guys were always either CPLs or PFCs. For some reason he never seemed to bury sergeants or PV2s.

To Deth's delight, the woman appeared absolutely ignorant about her loved one's rank or branch. "Was he?"

The others, the vultures with clenched fists, began to chatter amongst themselves. No one quite seemed sure what grandpa had done in the army. More importantly, no one knew what the hell an artilleryman was. "Forgive me if I was misinformed," he continued, locking his eyes on hers, "But before we left Iraq last week to conduct honors at this funeral, the brigade commander pulled me aside."

"Is that a general?" one of the ill-wishers asked.

"A bird colonel, yes, sir," Deth replied, not breaking his death lock on the red-headed lady's eyes, "And do you know what he said to me?" She shook her head, her eyes now becoming somewhat misty. "He said, 'Lieutenant Deth, I understand you're going to be presenting the flag at the Coalhouse funeral. Coalhouse, as you know, was an artilleryman, and one of ours, and famous in the brigade for his exploits during the war.'"

Deth simply said "the war" because he had forgotten whether it was Korea or the Big One. "I nodded because I had indeed heard that. And he said that I was to make a special tribute to our fallen comrade, a fellow gun bunny, cannon cocker…a fellow redleg."

"Red…leg?"

Deth worried he may have been laying it on a bit thick, especially with the bit about flying home from Iraq, but the woman and, more importantly, her bruiser cousins were eating it up with a spoon. "Ma'am, as you know, scarlet is the branch color of the United States Field Artillery Corps…"

Now the woman was crying, full on. She held up her arms, shaking them at him. She embraced him tightly, cracking every vertebra in his back all at once and very nearly lifting him off the ground. "Say no more," she said, "I understand, young man."

The cousins or whatever were now nodding their approval. Some of them shook his hand after the redheaded woman had moved on. One of them even mentioned that he seemed to recall grandpa mentioning being a jeep driver for a general or something. "Oh, yes," Deth said, "Probably General Jones. A very famous field artillery general."

Packs laugh-coughed ever so softly at the mention of the made-up term "field artillery general." The mourner had no idea, of course, but generals sloughed off their branches with their first star, like a snake getting rid of its skin and finally being able to order all the other snakes around. More importantly, though, the mourner was mollified. That Packs didn't fall to the floor howling in hysterics prompted Deth to make a mental note to nominate him for an Air Medal.

Later, dressed like civilians again, Deth in his only change of clothes, they slammed the doors on the Ford closed. The day had grown hot and Packs fired up the air conditioner before he even put the car in gear. Deth pulled the release catch on the passenger's side seat and lay horizontally backwards over the back seat. "Hey, sir," Packs said, checking over his shoulder as he backed out.

"Yeah, Sergeant?"

"Next time maybe just wash your socks, huh?"

3

The Texas Roadhouse was fine, albeit crowded, although that was to be expected on a Saturday night. "I hope they don't think we're queers," Packs said as they walked in.

Deth gave him a sidelong glance which he was too distracted to see. Where Deth came from they were a little more...well, actually "tolerant" didn't seem like the right word. Maybe "circumspect" was more accurate. Packs probably didn't think anything of it. He probably didn't even hate gays, come to think of it. But he was blunt almost to a fault.

Deth opened his mouth, trying to bring himself to chastise the older man for his churlishness. "What?" Packs asked, finally noticing that Deth was looking at him.

There was no point. It would've been hypocritical to say anything, anyway. He had often thought the same thing about sitting and eating dinner with another man. "We could wear our uniforms next time," Deth said, a little bit ashamed of his own cowardice.

Packs dismissed the idea with a wave of his hand. "The hell with that," he said, "I spend enough time in uniform. I bet you don't even hate yours yet." Deth smiled. Of course he didn't. It was still a novelty. "Wait until you've been in as long as I have. I'll bet I've spent more time in a latrine in my boots than you have doing anything in yours. Scratch that, I'll bet I've spent more time in a latrine downrange in my boots."

By this time they had been seated. The waitress had been listening to them talk about their uniforms. "Are you boys cops?" she asked, popping her bubblegum.

"Paramedics," Packs said gruffly, knowing he looked nothing of the sort.

They had gotten the full "Soldiers in a restaurant" treatment before. Deth had even gotten sick afterwards once. He assumed it was from shaking so many hands while eating, although he couldn't rule out all the free drinks as a culprit. "Oh, that's neat, I guess," she said, as they knew she would, before proceeding into asking for drink orders.

They didn't order beers: Packs because he was driving and Deth because the government credit card wouldn't cover it and he was cheap. Scanning the menu, Packs asked, "How much have we got left?"

They had been wise to eat the continental breakfast at the motel and to only stop at Mickey D's for lunch. Deth had eaten a chicken sandwich for lunch in preparation for the evening's hot beef injection, but Packs had done nothing of the sort, ordering a Double Quarter Pounder then and probably a 20-oz steak now. Deth pulled the receipts out of his pocket and rifled through them, knowing better than to try to do it by memory. His memory had betrayed him way too many times in this regard. "Nothing for breakfast, sixteen for lunch, that leaves us with...thirty-eight apiece."

Packs nodded. Not bad. Not bad at all. As expected, he ordered a 20-oz ribeye. Deth moderated the amount of raw cow he tried to consume, but being as he had been careful with his per diem that day, he decided to splurge and have a filet mignon, albeit a smaller one. They still had a little money left over, so they got some blooming onions and rattlesnake bites and the like to share. Deth wouldn't be able to have a whole lot of appetizers, but he knew Packs would leave nothing on the table, up to and including Deth's own steak rinds if he would let him chew them like an animal.

As they were waiting for the appetizers, Packs, unsurprisingly, took a big handful of peanuts from the eldritch bucket on the table that contained them. He smashed them all at once between his hands and began picking through the mess, sweeping the shells onto the floor as he identified the meats here and there. Deth suddenly remembered something he had been meaning to ask. "That major you were talking about, Brannigan." Packs rolled his eyes and swept some more peanut crumbs onto the floor. "Did you really write him up for an Air Medal?"

Packs's hands made wild patterns in the air in a fashion that Deth recognized meant he was so dismissive of the idea, he felt he had to gesticulate to indicate exactly how dismissive he was. "No, no, no," Packs said, "I wasn't putting my hands on that crap. Not to mention that I didn't witness shit, so if I had written something, I would've been lying."

Deth nodded. "Too bad," he said, "I would've liked to have known how that turned out."

Packs had a rare, devilish smile on his face. "Well," the NCO admitted, "He did put himself in for it."

Deth goggled at the man. If this had been a cartoon instead of real life, he would've spit a torrent of Coke all over the booth. "What?" Deth said after he had regained his composure.

Packs seemed so ashamed of this story that he hung his head. "He thought he could be his own witness and recommending officer, so he put himself in for the award."

"So what happened?"

"What do you think, sir? It came back with everything but 'What the fuck?' stamped on it in red ink."

"You're shitting me."

Packs was shaking his head. "That's just the way this guy was. Wouldn't take 'No' for an answer. Especially wouldn't take 'Don't be a dumbass' for an answer. I wish he would've, even just once. God, the problems that guy caused. You know, I think the war effort was more hindered by his presence than aided."

"I can believe it," Deth said. Deth had to admit he was intrigued, but he didn't want to push Packs to tell him more. The NCO was obviously scarred by his experiences with this other officer, which to Deth was especially telling. A man he had seen swallow nails and shit bullets was so coiled up about this one dumbass officer it almost beggared the imagination.

Deth resolved not to press him for more information, but to his surprise, Packs began speaking again of his own accord. Perhaps it was cathartic for him. Or perhaps they had simply covered every other topic of conversation under the sun in their weeks together. "I met that guy my first day in this battalion," Packs said.

"Oh, yeah?"

"Yeah." Packs grunted a word of thanks as the waitress delivered their snake bites, loaded waffle fries, cups of chili, and other per diem wasters.

Packs ripped into the appetizers like a man who hadn't had a Double Quarter Pounder and XXL fries for lunch. Deth was a little more dainty, grabbing a nacho here and there and cursing himself for the paunch that he was already growing, comparing it to Packs's perfect washboard. When he had eaten enough to take a breath, Packs spoke again.

"First day in the battalion, new platoon, some old buffoon for a platoon leader. I thank my lucky stars for you, sir. You've got no experience, but at least you listen. Not thinking you're god-damned Patton and Jesus all rolled up into one."

Deth accepted this as neither compliment nor insult but merely Packs's measured opinion of the matter. They got along very well inasmuch as Deth saw no need to prove he was in charge and Packs saw no reason to undercut him. That granule of mutual respect made them perversely the strongest platoon leadership team in the battalion by far. Too many of the other teams felt the need to get into pissing matches about which was more important, rank or experience.

"Anyways, I says to this guy I was working with at the time, what was his name? Ostrich or something? Doesn't matter. Anyway, I says, 'Hey, sir, how's about we do a release run and if anyone can beat me, they can have the day off.' This is my first day, first PT session, so yeah, so what, maybe I had something to prove."

Deth nodded. At his own first PT session at the battalion, he had been happy to do a nice, easy battery run, even if it had taken them until practically 0745 to finish. He liked to think he could hold his own running, but he was no Packs, not even in the same league.

"So we run two miles out to Geronimo's Grave, and I explained to them as we're coming up on it that when we get around the tree, break formation and run back. So I take off and leave old Ostrich in the dust. And except for Anderson...you remember Anderson, he just left."

"Oh, Sergeant Anderson?"

Packs nodded. "Yeah, except he was PFC Anderson back then, but still a good enough guy. Anyway, he's the only one who can keep up with me. But then I leave him behind, too. And what do you think happens?"

Deth shook his head. "I have no idea."

The steaks arrived then, and they had to move around the remaining appetizers, combining what they could onto a few platters and letting the waitress bus the rest away. She asked them to cut into their steaks, which Deth refused to do, because he hated letting the juice out of his steak because some asshole waitress wanted to know if it was all right. What was he going to do? Send it back, wait another forty minutes, and most likely get it back with saliva *au jus*?

To placate her, though, Packs cut into his own steak, severing the centimeter of lightly browned crust and revealing the red, bloody, almost pulsating interior and telling her it looked magnificent, which Deth had to admit it did. Coming up, Deth had always taken his steaks well done. Then, out here with Packs, he had tasted his first medium. He didn't take them mooing the way the older man did, but he had discovered the joy of red meat still being red instead of grey.

"So what happened?" Deth asked, placing a delicate piece of filet in his mouth, knowing that there was an art to eating it slowly enough to savor but fast enough that all the juice didn't leak out and it became cold, "Sergeant Anderson beat you?"

Without closing his mouthful of meat, Packs said (with a modicum of difficulty), "Well, yeah, but back the boat up." He swallowed, grabbed some of the cold, congealing fried onion from the appetizers and threw it on top of his next hunk of steak. "Here I'm running, leading the pack, the whole platoon's not closer than a mile behind me (except ol' Anderson) when who comes out from pissing behind a tree but Major Brannigan, who was a captain at the time, and who I didn't know from Adam."

Deth liked that phrase, "I didn't know him from Adam." He had never heard it before joining up.

"But, ohhhh, he knew me. He had seen me at the last hail and farewell. You know how it is, the difference between having to memorize everyone's name because you're new, and having to just memorize the new guy's name?" Deth nodded, but nevertheless Packs said, "Well, you will once you've been in the army a minute and PCSed a couple of times."

Deth liked that term "a minute" meaning "a god-damned long time," too. Come to think of it, he had learned a lot of phrases in the army, perhaps more than a fair amount from Packs himself. "PCS" of course, meant Permanent Change of Station – a transfer.

"So he comes yelling and waving his arms," here, Packs illustrated by flailing his own arms Kermit-style, and catching the attention of everyone in the restaurant, including the entire wait staff which had lined up to dance to the Watermelon Crawl, **"SERGEANT PACKS! SERGEANT FIRST CLASS PACKS!** Just like that, like I was a marine and he needed to use my whole god-damned rank to flag me down."

Packs took a long sip of his water and made a face. "Wish it was a beer," he said.

"We can go for one later," Deth replied, desperate to hear the rest of the story, but attempting to appear casual, "On our own dimes."

Packs nodded. "So he pulls me off the road and out into a copse of trees and he says, 'Don't stop running, Sergeant, we'll run in place.' So we're standing there, in this grove of trees, running in place, and I've got a look on my face, I know I did, because my whole platoon was in a release run."

"Didn't you tell him what you were doing with your platoon before you left formation?"

Packs fixed Deth with a stare of contempt, but Deth sensed that the contempt was more for Brannigan, or perhaps for Deth'sfailure to appreciate Brannigan's incompetence. "He wasn't my commander. I was in Alpha Battery."

"What battery was he the commander of?"

"He was on staff. I think he was the A3."

The assistant battalion operations officer? That didn't make a lick of sense. "Wait, wait, wait..." Deth hung his head trying to get a handle on the situation, "He was just a staff pogue? Not only was he not *your* commander, he wasn't even *a* commander?" Packs shook his head. Deth shook his own head as well, though somewhat slower, in amazement rather than answering a question in the negative. "What did he say to you?"

Packs rolled his eyes back in his head. Incredibly, he seemed to have been put off his food with a solid five ounces of ribeye left. He pushed the plate away and leaned back in the booth. "He said, 'Sergeant Packs, do you know who I am?'"

This was perhaps the first time that Packs had taken the pains to attempt to replicate Brannigan's voice. Previously he had only related Brannigan's words matter-of-factly, though. Now, he spoke in a nasal, unusually high-pitched voice, a buffoon's voice, but Deth could tell he was not exaggerating for effect. Almost every word was scooped and the accent was unidentifiable by location but instantly recognizable as pure white trash. "I says 'no' and he says, 'Don't you mean "no, sir?"' puffing out his chest like this."

Packs demonstrated. Deth rubbed his temples. These were the kind of officers that gave him headaches and made it so hard to do his job. PT uniforms consisted solely of grey t-shirts and black shorts (and warm weather gear in the winter.) Expecting a stranger to know your rank in PTs was...Deth didn't know how to describe it.

"I snap to attention. Why not? He's an officer, right? Then he asks me where's my platoon. So I point, way off in the distance, where the sun is coming up, and I says, 'Way back there, *sir*.' He got all flustered and he said, 'I thought you fell out.' 'No, sir, it was a release run and I was way out in front. Up until you stopped me.'"

Deth covered his face with his napkin. The stories about this man just sounded too farcical to be true. And yet, in even his brief time in the army, he had met characters who had stretched the boundaries of belief. A "reformed" neo-Nazi supply sergeant who used to fight with the EEO officer about the meaning of "hate group." A private who had gathered every stray dog and cat in Lawton into his backyard for charity's sake and then forgot to feed them. Even the lieutenant (now captain, *shudder*) that Packs had been calling Ostrich, Deth's predecessor as platoon leader, who had been unable to send an e-mail, not from lack of access to machinery, but from lack of wherewithal. Surely a picaresque, unable-to-do-right major was not an impossibility. "Not even your battery commander?"

"Not even my fucking battery commander, if you'll excuse my French, sir. So he gets real serious-like and he says, 'Well, Sergeant Packs, you understand why I wouldn't want you to fall out, right?' I just looked at him. Didn't even respond, just looked at him just like this. And he says, 'Well, I'm glad we had this chat. Go try and catch up with your men.'"

Deth couldn't even hide his laughter behind a napkin any more. Between his sobs and guffaws came the words, "catch up" and "your men." Packs waited for him to stop, his appetite seeming to have returned, and dug into some as yet uneaten crab legs and finished off his steak and potatoes, dipping the crab legs in some of the remaining brown gravy. "What happened then?"

"I had to let half the flipping platoon have the day off. I sprinted the whole rest of the way and I still only barely beat

Menendez. Ostrich never let me live it down until I beat his ass at combatives."

"This guy Brannigan sounds like a Looney Toon."

"Yeah, well, Bugs Bunny wasn't a war criminal."

"War criminal?"

Packs threw his napkin down on the table, his massive athlete's hunger finally sated to some extent. "I've got to go pinch a loaf, sir. You pay and I'll call mortuary affairs."

"It's Saturday night," Deth said, furrowing his brow in agitation.

Packs shrugged, his back already to Deth. "Gotta call."

Deth shrugged and called for the check. They hadn't ordered alcohol, so they didn't have to separate it out of the check. They did, however, have to pay for the tip out of pocket. Deth checked his wallet. All he had was twenties and while the server had been good, she hadn't been THAT good.

When Packs returned, Deth held up a green portrait of Andrew Jackson and said, "Can you break this?"

Silently, Packs shoveled a fistful of ones and fives onto the table. With a feeling of alarm, Deth recognized the import of Packs's unmistakable scowl. "No," Deth whispered. The scowl did not abate. "You can't be serious." Packs's face remained as immutable as the sea. "Really?"

"Better wash your socks tonight, sir."

Deth threw his wallet down on the peanut shell-laden floor in frustration. "Who the fuck gets buried on a Sunday?"

4

The March funeral was a solemn affair, all beyarmulked men and women weeping behind black veils. March himself had seemingly only been in his sixties, a Vietnam veteran who had volunteered for a second tour, according to the funeral director.

"Tough as nails," Packs had said when he had been polishing the brass for the Marches, "That's not like doing two tours today."

"You must've known some Vietnam guys back when you first joined up," Deth had said, immediately cursing himself for phrasing it that way.

Packs had nodded, not seeming to notice. "They were on their way out, mostly," Packs had said, examining the brass for shininess.

"Although I suppose there are still a few today. Generals and sergeants major and what-have-you."

Packs had nodded. "I got a Vietnam-era MRE once in basic."

They had then discussed the relative merits of the various stages of packaged army food, even Deth having been in ROTC long enough to lament the passing of the ham slice from his fare.

Now they were standing waiting for the rabbi to finish his words. Sometimes Deth ran over conversations in his mind, word by word, wondering if there were better words he could have used and wondering if he had made an ass of himself. He was doing that now, ruminating over whether he had said something wrong about the MREs. Nothing sprang to mind, but it didn't stop him from thinkfucking it.

The rabbi finished and gestured for them to do their piece, which they proceeded to do with unusual rigidity and solemnity. The occasion seemed to call for it; even the cold, sunless grey of the sky seemed to demand a special amount of reverence for March. Deth knelt before March's eldest daughter, said his usual words, gave his usual misinterpreted salutes, and returned to his place at Packs's side, confident that this would be a post-funeral where no one would speak to them. No one spoke even as they filed out.

Deth even went so far as to nod to Packs to indicate that it was time to come to attention and break ranks when a child approached them. The boy was wearing a sweater, and not even a black one. Deth seemed to recall as a child being forced into an ill-fitting suit for funerals, but no doubt some combination of parental love and Southwestern lack of formality had spared this child the same fate.

The boy stared up at them, his finger hooked into his mouth as though he were tugging on his lip or pretending to be a caught fish. Deth stared back, expectant, his desire to leave suddenly vanished in a puff of curiosity. "Hello," the boy said, waving to Deth.

"Hello, young man," Deth replied.

"Did you ever kill anybody?"

Inwardly, Deth smiled, but he didn't want to show it to the kid. He had figured out how to pay Packs back for yesterday. "Well, I'm new," Deth said, "I haven't been to war yet. But Sergeant Packs has deployed. You should ask him."

The boy turned away from Deth and looked up at Packs, looking for all the world like one of those little dolls with the gigantic eyes. "Did you ever kill anybody, Mister?"

Deth pictured Donald Duck sputtering as Packs made an attempt to gain his composure. He smiled. He had never been able to put the old boy so off balance before. He really had to credit the cherubic little kid. That shit was disconcerting.

"Well, son, that's not...that's not really what we set out to do. That's not our intention. We're peacekeepers. I mean, sure, sometimes people have to die, but they're bad guys."

The kid nodded like he understood. He started to walk away and Packs breathed a visible sigh of relief. Then the kid turned back. "So, like a hundred?"

Packs turned to Deth for succor.

"Red socks," Deth mouthed and Packs's eyes narrowed.

"No, son, I don't really count..."

The kid's eyes were shining, and if it hadn't been a sunless, windswept day, Deth would have sworn the stars were reflected in his pupils. "You killed so many you lost count?" the kid asked breathlessly.

"No, son, it's not like that..."

"Wow!" the kid shouted and then went skipping off, no doubt to tell his 'rents.

Deth slapped Packs on the shoulder. "Now, why would you go and tell a kid something like that?"

Packs returned the love-tap with an unmitigated hate-punch that sent Deth legitimately reeling. "That's not funny, sir," Packs said, although he wasn't really that upset.

As they walked back to the car, stepped inside, and buckled their seatbelts, Deth turned to Packs. "It was kind of funny."

Packs white knuckled the wheel as he drove to the hotel. (They had already gotten a call for a funeral Monday morning.) "Not if you've ever fought before, it isn't."

Deth suddenly felt low, lower than a slug. Packs had really had nothing to do with Deth's embarrassment the day before. He had made his own bed and been forced to sleep in it, and all Packs had done was not bail him out because it was kind of funny. But today Deth had thrown his NCO under the bus. He had practically sicced the kid on him.

The truth was Deth had no idea what war was like. His whole Officer Basic Class had been like him, except for the occasional prior service guy who didn't want to talk about it. Deth's roommate had gone to sleep every night with headphones in his ears watching *Black*

Hawk Down because he claimed the battle sounds were soothing (probably because he wanted to seem hard.)

Deth had never thought of himself as quite that sad or desperate, but he still wanted to see the big show. He had joined ROTC in 2000, so it wasn't exactly like he had signed up the day after 9/11, but he hadn't quit after that, either. He had known for years now what was coming. The wars held a mystique for the uninitiated, and Deth envied the matter-of-factness that the veterans displayed about it.

"Did you ever kill anybody?"

"Nope, sorry, kid."

That would've put an end to it. Instead, he had laid bare whatever Packs's issues were. Who knew if he had PTSD? Or if nothing was clinically wrong with him, maybe he just didn't want to talk about it. Everyone who had been was that way: either they were matter-of-fact about it or they didn't want to talk about it. No one who had really been was eager the way Deth and his cohorts were.

Deth had gotten an e-mail from his OBC roommate not too long ago, the one who had listened to *Black Hawk Down* every night. Son of a bitch was in Kabul. A tanker in Kabul, which meant he was probably really just pounding pavement, getting into firefights, earning his red badge of courage, and all that other bullshit that Deth envied so sincerely.

The fucked-up thing was he wasn't the only one. Almost everyone he had known in OBC had been Over There by now, most to the Sandbox, but a few to Afghanistan, at least once. A solid 25% of his peers were already on their second deployments. And only

Deth, as far as he knew, had still not been. No, he was needed for funeral detail. Endless, endless funeral detail.

Light-on-the-right. That's what they called it sometimes. Every Soldier in the army wore the crest of their current unit sewn (or, nowadays, Velcroed) on their left shoulder. Those who had been deployed wore the crest of the unit they had been in a war zone with on their right. For most Soldiers, those two patches were the same. It had become stylish lately to wear a different combat patch than your current unit if you had one, as it proved that you were an old warrior (or at least that you had been through at least one PCS.) Deth even knew NCOs who switched out their three or four combat patches daily now that they could be Velcroed on.

The only real issue was when you were light-on-the-right. If you didn't have a combat patch, even privates didn't take you seriously. It was almost like there were two rank structures in the army: one for combat vets and one for pogues like him.

They pulled into the hotel parking lot and stepped out. It had been a quiet ride. Before they reached the sidewalk, Packs put his hand, palm-first, on Deth's chest. "I'm sorry, sir. I was a little nasty."

"No, Sergeant, I was the nasty one."

"Nah, nah, you haven't been, and I remember what it's like when you haven't been. It's frustrating. And besides, it wasn't like you did nothing. How about that freaking kid, though?"

Deth smiled. No harm, no foul. He was still light-on-the-right, but at least he wasn't a son-of-a-bitch anymore. "What a crazy-ass question," Deth said, "Who raised that kid?"

"Nah," Packs said, "They're all like that. Here, let me show you something."

Packs reached into his pocket and pulled out his wallet, which he called a "billfold." Packs's billfold reminded Deth of his dad's. It was thick and old; the leather was worn and shaped to the various things that had been kept in there, untouched, through a quarter dozen presidential administrations. "Here it is," Packs said, uncovering what he had been looking for.

It was an old, folded-up Polaroid, which Packs attempted to uncrease to little avail. Deth took it with a knowing grin. Leave it to Packs to use something so old fashioned. It was 2006 and the man didn't even own a cell phone. The back of the photo gave a date in mid-2004 and the inscription "WTF?"

Now Deth had to laugh at himself. Some things were old, some things were new, but everything old was new again. He always thought of WTF as internet slang, but Packs had probably been saying it for decades and pronouncing it, "whiskey tango foxtrot."

He flipped to the photo side, which was a somewhat blurry picture of a child's hand-drawn card, tacked to a wall in perhaps a command tent or maybe even a vehicle. The picture was nothing in particular, a triangle with a green stripe. It was signed by "Matthew S." who apparently attended "3 grade" at "St. Patrik's Elem." What was truly fascinating, though, was young Matthew S.'s message, which was all in caps and read: "HAVE A GOOD VICTORY OR DEATH!"

"Kid should've been a poet," Deth said.

5

The prices weren't right. Packs turned away from the front desk with a scowl. "It's too much," he said.

"How much?" Deth asked. He told him. Deth pulled out his cell phone and ran the numbers on the calculator. "That's with the government discount or without?"

"That's with it."

"Hmmm..." Deth scowled, too. "What are our other options?"

"There's no other hotels in town," Packs said.

"We could go back to that Motel 6 we passed on the way here," Deth mused, "I'm sure the price is right, but it's 20 miles in the wrong direction. And the Bloom funeral starts at 0800."

"I'm not staying in a motel," Packs said flatly.

Deth knew Packs would be unconcerned about having to get up early. He routinely got up at 0400. However, Packs had a strict "no motels" policy. Supposedly he had once slept in a motel in Georgia on TDY (temporary duty.) Going to sleep he had found a half-smoked cigar behind his pillow and upon waking up, he had crabs. Or so he claimed.

Deth tapped his cell phone against his teeth. "Well," he said, "Then the answer's simple. We'll share a room. They have two beds anyway. That'll save us...more than enough."

Packs's eyes lit up when Deth showed him the calculator screen. "We could have steak dinners for lunch AND dinner."

Deth smiled. He might have chicken for one of those. "We sure could."

Deth flopped into bed with a bottle of purple Mad Dog in his hand. He knew "purple" wasn't technically a flavor, but he didn't look at the flavors. He only knew his MD 20/20s by color.

He was of the opinion, right or wrong, that a single bottle of fortified wine was the perfect amount of alcohol to get pleasantly drunk in a hotel room without being too hung-over in the morning to perform a funeral. He had long ago discovered the dangers of buying a bottle of hard liquor and promising to "only drink enough to get drunk." The problem with that was that the bottle just sat there, even if you only intended to drink a certain amount. With Mad Dog, when it was gone, you were done, regardless of your feelings on the matter.

Packs, being older and a much more capable drinker, had purchased a couple of six packs of Lost Lake at $1.50 a six. It was entirely possible that Packs had spent less than Deth on booze. Packs was already a six pack in when Deth cracked the twist-off top of his fortified wine. An old rerun of *King of the Hill* flickered on the TV.

"Boy, that steak did me right!" Packs said contentedly, after censering the air with a brutal wave of flatulence.

"Which one?" Deth asked.

Packs chuckled and cracked another brew. "Either one. That much meat always gives me gas. Not like cheese, though! It's too bad we can't smoke in here."

"I'll bet we could've smoked at the Motel 6," Deth replied, a thought which Packs waved off angrily with his hands, "Cigarettes, cigars, whatever."

"Not even a deck?" Packs said, surveying the room, "And considering what we paid for it!"

Of course, they hadn't really paid a dime for it, it was all Uncle Sam. But the principle stood. "So stick your head out the window," Deth said, who was a much lighter smoker than Packs and could probably go without the rest of the night if he had to, "Or go down to the fire escape."

"Bullshit Kuwait stuff," Packs muttered, "Go smoke in this god-damned gazebo. Fucking MPs."

Deth noted that Packs had not begged pardon for his "French," meaning that even he was beginning to feel the effects of the alcohol. "Kuwait was bad, huh?"

"Ten times worse than Eye-raq," Packs replied, lighting up a cigarette in total disregard of the no-smoking sign, "The whole place smelled like garbage. And it was twenty degrees hotter. And fucking MPs with nothing better to do."

Deth rose and opened the window. Not that he objected to the smoke, but the credit card was in his name and he didn't want the hotel people charging him extra. They had already used up the per diem going to steakhouses for lunch and dinner. He sure as shit wasn't paying out of pocket for "smoke damage.""Eh, yeah, yeah!" Packs called, grunting as he rolled off the bed and onto his feet, to join Deth at the window and blow the smoke out. As long as they were both there, Deth lit up a Lucky.

"How can you smoke those unfiltered things?" Packs asked.

Deth shrugged, taking another puff. "I can't find the filtereds around here for some reason," he said, "Fucking Oklahoma."

"Yeah, fucking Oklahoma is right."

Packs was from Iowa or Indiana or somewhere that Deth also considered as backwards as Oklahoma, but he didn't press the issue. At least they were united in their hatred of this state. Missouri and Arkansas were only spared that hatred because of the rarity of their visits there. It was almost like a breath of fresh air crossing the border and doing funerals in another state. "That guy Brannigan," Deth said, taking another puff, "Why'd you call him a war criminal?"

Packs nodded knowingly without taking the cigarette away from his lips. "Well, he was," Packs said, "You know me, sir, I try not to exaggerate."

Deth nodded. He was a straight-shooter, all right. Packs sighed loudly. "So we had this plan to send men to Normandy..."

"France?"

Packs disregarded the recycled joke. "FOB Normandy. And when we gave our presentation to the general, he told us, no, absolutely not, Normandy didn't have the food, water, or resources to support the men we wanted to send."

"It was a lot?"

"Over a hundred. And at this point, Normandy was a little hole in the desert with some barbed wire around it. So when we got back, Major Brannigan told me to start arranging to send all the men by ones and twos to Normandy so the general wouldn't catch wind, like if we had sent a hundred all at once."

Deth gaped. He snapped his jaw shut when he realized what he was doing and took another pull on his cigarette. "What'd you say?"

"Well, I told him we would be violating general orders! And he said, 'Sergeant Packs, you have my orders. You can either follow them or I'll write you up.'"

"Or you could have gone to the general," Deth said.

Packs gave him a look. "He knew I wasn't going to go to the general. Get egg on the unit's face?" Packs angrily tossed his half unsmoked cigarette out the window. At least he had the good sense not to toss it on the floor. "I feel like an asshole," Packs said, "All the times I let that buffoon do something because I didn't want to hurt the unit. Send a hundred men into the desert to starve. That's why I call him a war criminal."

"Well, it's not like it was My Lai," Deth said.

"No, it's more like if My Lai had been full of Americans," Packs said, lighting another cigarette because he was obviously getting agitated, "That fucking guy."

Deth stroked his chin thoughtfully. "Where was Colonel Fink this whole time?"

"That's the thing," Packs said, "Battalion was back here in the rear. Stateside, I mean. We had a battery out there first, then two batteries, and me and Brannigan were supposed to be LNOs." Deth wracked his brain for a second. He didn't know the acronym off the top of his head. Then it occurred to him: liaison officers. "But then one day the major just decided he was in command. He wrote up command orders and declared the two batteries to be a Task Force, and himself the Task Force commander!"

Deth breathed deeply of the last drag of his butt. "Correct me if I'm wrong, Sergeant," he said, "But isn't a Task Force..."

"...An infantry battalion with an armored company! You can't just make up what a Task Force is! But he did!"

Packs was more agitated than Deth had ever seen him. Deth cracked a beer and handed it to him, not sure if it was the right thing to do. Packs took a long drink and seemed calmer, so at least it had not made things worse.

"So, anyway, we basically had Colonel Kurtz out here deciding he's in charge of a bunch of shit. And he was just supposed to go sell our rocket systems to the big divisions. That's it. Just an LNO, but then he declared himself commander, and the real battalion commander wasn't forward and no one outranked him and...we didn't report to anyone."

"How do you not report to anyone?"

Packs shook his head in dismay. "Sir, I've been in the army a long time. Things slip through the cracks. I've seen it. You ever meet a sergeant major who's never deployed? Or a finance officer who's been in the same post and the same position his whole career?"

"Or someone who gets stuck on funeral detail for two years?"

Packs pointed a finger at Deth and nodded. "We were supposed to report to battalion back home. Battalion didn't care because we were forward. And nobody in country wanted to deal with us because...would you want to be in charge of somebody else's orphans? It was one of those Mila-18 things."

"Catch-22."

"What?"

"Nothing. Well, the army is crazy. But didn't you guys ever try to...do something about him? Like, I guess I understand not wanting to talk to the general, but there's always the IG."

Packs smiled wanly. His second (or rather one-and-a-halfth) cigarette was finished. "I wrote an IG complaint," he said, rolling the spent butt between his fingers, "I never sent it. You know why?"

"The good of the unit?"

"That...and my own career. Nobody wants a whistleblower. They tell you you're protected but...whistleblowers don't get promoted. I just want to get my E-8 and retire. Maybe be a First Sergeant sometime. I don't want to become a, you know, a pharaoh."

"A pariah?"

"That either. You know what my biggest regret though, is?" Deth grunted for continuation. "He threatened to resign once and I talked him out of it."

"Really?"

Packs nodded.

The ground was writhing, as though the entire floor were alive. Deth opened his eyes but found himself in the state of near-paralysis that seemed to slip in during the grey hours of the early morning after a late night. He stared at the ceiling, and though he knew that, theoretically, he could move anytime he wanted to, the idea of sitting up seemed like an impossible task.

His bladder felt hellaciously full, and he feared a light poke with his finger would make him piss the bed, something he hadn't done since he was six, and even as a child not very often. The desire to pee made him want to get up, but something not quite there held him back.

He was aware of the wriggling mass on the floor, even though he couldn't move his head to look down at it. As though he were a spirit floating on the ceiling he felt like he could see himself in bed, and past himself to the mass of reptilian flesh. Now he really wanted to move, and it wasn't that he couldn't, but he absolutely could not bring himself to will his body into action.

A lone snake, green but unlike any color found in nature, and utterly featureless except for its lithe body, began to slither up the bedpost. Deth grew alarmed, but knew that something was wrong because he shouldn't have been able to see the bedpost. Dream logic was in full effect.

This time he opened his eyes for real. Looking down there were, of course, no snakes on the floor. His right arm was under him, already asleep. That was going to become an issue if he didn't do something about it.

Here in the real world Packs drowsed gently on the other bed, whereas he had been entirely absent from the dream. Deth's bladder still felt full, but not so uncomfortable that he didn't close his eyes and instantly find himself back in the room of horror, another snake working its way into his bed. He hadn't even rolled off of his arm. He wanted to reach down and slap the serpent-thing away, but found himself unable to move again. He swore that as soon as he felt it against his leg, he would immediately summon the will to move and shimmy away from it.

He opened his eyes. Or maybe he didn't. For what felt like an eternity, but probably was only a few minutes, he shuttled between wakefulness and snake-haunted dreams so quickly and randomly that he was sure the snakes were real, even when he was sure he was awake.

Deth awoke, finally, fully, with a snort. His right arm was now dead, dead to the world, absolutely empty of blood. He silently shrieked, taking care not to alert the world to his condition by making noise. He stood, cradling his cold, numb arm, and looked across the moonlit room at Packs, gently dozing, though snoring like a swine.

What a baffling, frustrating dream. He sat on the edge of the bed, trying to move his dead arm manually with his left, knowing that it would be some time before his muscles worked, and there would be much pain as the blood flow returned. That would happen soon, too, as his heart was pounding a mile a minute.

He lay back down on the bed with a sigh that was loud enough to make Packs snort and roll over.

He snatched the empty bottle of Mad Dog out of the bedside waste bin with his good arm and shook it. Just a tiny film of purple liquid remained at the bottom of the rectangular bottle.

"This is your fault," Deth whispered hoarsely, and turned to make sure Packs hadn't woken up.

He gently released the bottle into the trash.

"Never again," he vowed, then he rolled over and fell asleep on his left arm.

6

"Oh, hello," Packs crooned lightly to the amber-colored plastic shelf which contained the biscuits for the hotel's continental breakfast.

Bleary-eyed, Deth tried not to trip over his own feet as he grabbed a plate still sweating with steam. He stared on in something approaching horror as Packs split his biscuit and dumped about a solid cup of sawmill gravy over each half. Deth had never eaten biscuits and gravy before joining the army, but since then had at least encountered one at every army-provided breakfast, if not necessarily selecting it for himself.

Packs glanced at him. "You want one, sir?" he asked, proffering his plate in Deth's direction.

Deth practically leapt backwards, arms flailing in front of him. "No, ah, no, thank you, Sergeant."

Packs grinned, clearly having his fun with Deth's hangover, then shrugged, as though the offer had been genuine.

"Say," one of the hotel staff, a short lady in a polo shirt, said, "Are you two by any chance military?"

Packs and Deth exchanged a glance. Deth was way too exhausted to come up with a dodge. "No," Packs said.

The woman frowned. She eyeballed them. Their haircuts. Their demeanors. They were all but in uniform. Packs seemed to realize he wasn't going to get away with just a denial, and the other hotel workers were beginning to swarm around like gratitude vultures, preparing to shake their hands and hassle them for the rest of the morning.

"That is to say," Packs said, "Not real ones, anyway. We're a couple of those..." Packs paused, desperately searching for the right words, though none would come. "You know, we're a couple of those, um..."

He mimed a gun with his arms. Deth watched on, not amused, and not wishing to get caught up by the staff either, but not sure where Packs was going with this. He made an unusually hard recoil with his imaginary gun, and Deth suddenly got it. "Civil war re-enactors," Deth supplied the words, "That's ah, yup. That's the explanation for why I was calling Bela here 'sergeant' just now. Got to get in character, you know?"

It briefly occurred to Deth that Civil War battles had probably been few and far between in the Southwest, an inconvenient fact which might have endangered their cover. But the woman, probably not a history buff, simply nodded and scurried away, so intense was her disappointment. There was no audible groan as the almost-crowd dispersed, but Deth would not have been surprised to hear one.

His own plate was still empty. He double-checked the amber drawer containing Packs's beloved biscuits and gravy, as though hoping that in the few seconds which had elapsed since his right arm had gotten his own meal it would have transmogrified into something less repellant. Deth quickly closed the steaming drawer before it made him retch.

The next drawer contained bacon, even at this early hour still somehow as dry and dark as jerky. He'd never cared much for bacon anyway, and quickly closed that as well. Moving on to his last possible chance, he found a drawer full of rectangular, Hot Pocket-shaped lumps of egg which the hotel had rather unilaterally declared omelettes. No, there was no hope for him here.

Sighing, he snagged a blueberry muffin sealed in a plastic wrapper and filled three cardboard cups with orange juice, water, and coffee, respectively. Before he had even joined Packs the man had already messily devoured his first plate and was jumping up to grab another round.

"Be right back, sir...er, Bickham," Packs said, pronouncing the other's first name with deliberate, obtuse slowness. It sounded equally wrong on his lips to both of them, but they could see the ears of the hotel staff flattening, as if hoping to hear them trip up and prove themselves to be Soldiers worthy of the peculiar form of veneration which almost all civilians seemed to insist upon.

Deth drained his water and picked at his muffin as Packs returned. "Do we really need to be up now?" Deth muttered.

Packs was hardly listening, so enticed was he by what appeared to be a giant pile of nothing but bacon. "0600?" he asked. "That's practically sleeping in for the army."

Packs, like all real Soldiers, eschewed the singularly civilian construction of "oh six hundred" in favor of "zero six hundred." Occasionally, in reference to early PT sessions particularly, NCOs would say "oh dark thirty," but Deth had taken that to be a joke at the expense of people who said military time incorrectly.

Deth sighed. "Yes, that's true. But we don't have PT today. And we don't have a damn funeral until 0900."

"Don't want to be late," Packs said, verbally wagging his finger. Deth nodded and slouched down, barely touching his food and only occasionally sipping his fluids. "You seem out of it today, sir," Packs said. A few more guests had at last entered the dining room so that their conversation was less the only source of interest for the staff and they could feel a little freer to speak about their mutual vocation.

"Yes," Deth agreed.

"I meant that as a question. You hung over, sir? You know, you're really not supposed to drink within four hours of duty."

Deth was still young and healthy enough that he had never actually taken that rule particularly seriously. In college he had regularly stayed out drinking until 3:00 am (back then he had even called it "3:00 am") and still showed up for his ROTC PT. It had never been much of an issue.

In fact, a lot of ROTC cadets (and, he had learned later, regular Soldiers) preferred to show up to the PT test drunk so that they wouldn't feel the pain of exertion and could push themselves to a higher score. (Presumably that was a decision they would regret terribly upon sobering up.) Deth had never pulled that trick himself, being sure that, despite personally witnessing it work for numerous young men, he would surely be the asshole who got caught.

In fact, he had already gotten in trouble twice by showing up to formation, and neither of those times had he been drunk, so he already considered himself cursed. Once, during NALC, he had gotten in from a ruck march very late and been exhausted. He had made the less than optimal decision not to shine his boots, and this had been a few years ago before the rollout of the tan ACU boots, when boot-shining was a non-optional type activity.

No sooner had he not shined his boots than the platoon had been called into formation. He had hoped against hope that no one would notice the status of his footwear, gradually convincing himself as no one called him out minute after minute that he would be fine. But then, of course, the company commander, a brokedick JAG officer who couldn't even accompany them on field exercises, of all things, had called him into her office and proceeded to issue him a negative counseling statement, or yellow card.

"We can't be having officers with unshined boots in the army, *Cadet*," she had said with the usual insulting inflection on the word "cadet" that cadre used when upset, "We just can't."

Somehow, now that boots didn't need to be shined at all, he wasn't sure what the point of all that had been. Something about discipline, he supposed, but sometimes it was hard to really draw those lessons out when the learning material was so damn pointless.

The other time, during his sophomore year of college, he had realized on a Wednesday morning that his razor (back then he had still shaved with disposables, rather than electric as he did now) was blunt almost to the point of giving his face a rash. Weighing his options, it had occurred to him that it was dark outside and his Professor of Military Science probably wouldn't notice if he didn't shave.

The ROTC detachment had shown up for PT, and, as Deth had suspected, the sun had not yet risen, and the lights were not on at the football stadium where they did PT. Nevertheless, about halfway through the session, his PMS had pulled him aside. "Did you shave this morning?"

Shocked that he could tell, Deth had said, "Uh, no, sir."

The PMS had stared him down, but Deth still knew to this day that had he been enlisted and been caught by a drill sergeant, the ramifications would have been dire. "Don't let it happen again," was all that his PMS had said.

Briefly, Deth related that last story to Packs, clarifying that he wasn't presently drunk or hung over, but just hadn't slept very well the night before. He declined to explain that it had been due to a semi-fugue state of wakeful dreamingness which featured snakes crawling in and out of his bed.

Packs chuckled. "Well, you've got one thing right."

"What's that?"

"If you'd been at Basic, I would've demolished you for that."

"Oh?" Deth asked, perking up slightly. "What would you have done?"

The shit-eating grin on Packs's face was unmistakable. "Well, I'll tell you one thing I used to do back when I was a hardcharging young drill sergeant. I'd walk around after wakeup and check to see who hadn't shaved. There were always a few who thought they could get away with it, you know. Then I wouldn't show up to lead formation. Instead I'd climb up on the roof and yell down, you know, 'Thompson! I see you didn't shave this morning! Twenty push-ups, dickwad!' You know, 0500 in the morning, pitch black, it would fuck with them for days. Then I'd make them shave with the platoon razor, which I sanitized every day, but hadn't been replaced in years."

Deth smiled, finally, slowly emerging from his fog of sleep deprivation. "You know, Sergeant, you never did tell me about how you had to convince MAJ Brannigan to stay in the army."

Packs rolled his eyes. But then, glancing around, his face turned to a mask of stone. Deth felt his heart drop into his stomach and looked around to see what had spooked Packs. Half the guests in the hotel lobby were staring at them. Packs had, in fact, shouted "Twenty push-ups, dickwad!" at the top of his lungs as though he were really on the roof of that Basic Training billet.

"Uh...let me tell you about that later...Bickham."

Deth checked his watch for what had to have been the hundredth time. He still wore a watch, even in the era of cell phones, even though he now owned a cell phone, because it had a stopwatch he used for PT. The Bloom funeral was getting off to a terribly late start. They had arrived, quick, fast, and in a hurry, at 0800. Now it was closing in on 0945.

"The lady did say 0900, didn't she?" Deth asked. Packs nodded. When they had gone to the funeral home, the undertaker had been out, but his secretary had checked and double checked the schedule, even showing Packs where it said "Bloom" on her day planner before the old NCO had been satisfied. "I'm so glad we got up at 0600," Deth said, leaning back against his designated tree.

Packs gave his standard barking laugh. "Oh, sir, you're still such a short-timer you worry about that kind of stuff, huh? I miss those days."

"You really don't care about waking up at bullshit o'clock?"

Packs shook his head and glanced around. Deth could tell the older man was thinking the same thing he was. He was already nic fitting for his standard *après* funeral cigarette. But the funeral hadn't even started yet. And since they were past the time when it was supposed to have started, there was no guaranteeing that they could light up and the procession wouldn't suddenly arrive. Deth wasn't as huge on military discipline as Packs was, but he sure as hell wasn't going to be caught stamping out a cigarette in a flurry in front of a grieving widow. "I've been in the army fifteen years, sir. Ain't nothing bothers me."

Deth stared at the old man for a moment. It wasn't just that. Packs liked to put on a grizzled display, but the truth was he loved the army. Loved it in his bones. Not long after he'd arrived at Ft. Sill, Deth had attended the post Command Sergeant Major's retirement ceremony. The CSM had been 55, mandatory retirement age. He had been in the army for 38 years. Most Soldiers couldn't get out fast enough after 20 years, the minimum retirement age, unless their careers were really on the fast track or they needed more time to get their best retirement pay or something. The outgoing CSM had looked harder and tougher than the next ten drill sergeants combined. And up on that stage, being forced to leave, he had actually cried, broken down and cried in front of half the post.

Packs was like that. They'd have to throw him out before he left. And then he'd probably become a contractor, teaching Field Artillery to young lieutenants like Deth at OBC, just so he could be on post and surrounded by Soldiers and soldiering all day.

"Well, actually that's not true," Packs said, "There is one thing that bothers me even after a decade and a half."

"Oh?"

"Yeah. I fucking hate wearing a reflective belt for PT."

Deth grinned. The eternal refrain.

After another ten minutes had passed, even Packs was growing restless. He knew it was too much to hope that Packs's immeasurably studious discipline had eroded to the point of allowing them to have a quick cigarette, but he still dared to dream.

"Want to burn one?"

Packs shook his head just once, considering a single shake sufficient to shoot that suggestion down.

"Man, when are they going to get here? Oops, sorry, sir. I wasn't calling you 'man.' I just meant..."

"I know what you meant, Sergeant."

A low rumble finally filled the air. Unnecessarily, Packs tapped him on the shoulder, but he was already standing at ease.

They came to attention and saluted as the hearse passed, then settled in to wait for the funeral procession.

A small, pasty bald man exited the driver's side of the hearse and scuttled up to them. He took Deth's hand in both of his and did the same with Packs. "Hey, fellas, thanks so much for coming out. I'm Humbert." That was the name on the side of the funeral home.

"Nice to meet you," Packs said.

Humbert scurried around to the back of the hearse and opened it up. "Could you strapping young lads give me a hand with this?"

Deth and Packs exchanged a glance. "What do we do?" Packs growled.

"I don't know," Deth responded, just as low, "I guess he wants our help."

They didn't need to mutter much longer like that before the undertaker called out for their assistance again and, not yet seeing the procession, they reluctantly walked to the back of the hearse. "Okay," Humbert said, "I know it looks heavy, but if you stand there and you stand there, I'll climb in the back, and it should just slide out of there. Ready? One, two, and...three!"

Without waiting for their consent or say-so, Humbert clambered inside and pushed the coffin out of the back of the vehicle. Although the Soldiers had been caught flat-footed, he had actually been right. With all of the straps and contraptions that made the coffin slide in and out of the back, it actually basically just slipped into its cradle above the grave more or less by itself. They just had to very lightly guide and push it.

When they had finished, Humbert stood back, clapping his hands against each other like a dealer at the casino after the last hand in a shoe. "Thanks," he said, "Well, you want to do your thing?"

If stares could kill, they both would have slaughtered the man right there. "Uh, yes, sir," Deth said gradually regaining his composure before Packs did, "Normally we wait until after the preacher has said his piece."

Humbert shook his head.

"No preacher. Mr. Bloom's an agnostic. Er, well, he was an agnostic, I should say. And Chief Bloom, I suppose I should say. That's what you call a Chief Warrant Officer 2, isn't it? Chief?"

"Uh, yes, sir, it is," Packs said slowly, taking his turn with the bewildering undertaker at last, "I guess what Lieutenant Deth means to say is, when is the family getting here? And who's the next of kin?"

"Yeah, yeah," Deth agreed, "I need to know who to give the flag to."

In a single gesture, Humbert simultaneously held up his hands and shrugged.

"Nope. No family either."

"The family's...not coming?" Deth asked.

"As far as we can tell Mr. Bloom didn't have any family. At least, none that were interested in flying out to Norman, OK for his funeral. I mean, presumably he must have a second cousin twice removed somewhere. I'm not saying his entire genealogy died out. But none are coming."

Deth planted his hands on his hips. "Well, who's the next of kin, then?"

"There is no next of kin. I just told you. He doesn't have any family. Parents are dead, no siblings, never married. I guess the state gets all of his stuff. I don't know. I'll have to hash it out with my attorney."

Packs's face lowered from what had been a slowly developing grin of frustration to a truly dejected grimace. "This old guy died without anybody?"

"I don't know what to tell you, fellas. It's just you and me."

Deth felt a low sinking feeling in his chest. That was sad. He'd been to some sparsely attended funerals before, but never an unattended one. Not even a preacher. Deth wasn't the most religious guy in the world, but it sure felt like CW2 Bloom wasn't just going to be forgotten, he wasn't even going to have anywhere to go after he was forgotten.

He scratched the back of his neck, which was warm with an unpleasant admixture of shame and sorrow. "Well, no offense, Mr. Humbert..."

"Please, my friends call me Humbert. Just Humbert."

"Humbert," Deth halfheartedly corrected himself, "But if there's nobody here to receive the flag, what are we even doing here? Who even called for us?"

"That was Mr. Bloom's only request in his will. He didn't even bequeath anything to anybody. He just said he had been in Vietnam and he wanted an honors team at his funeral. So, there's really no funeral, but we can at least make sure the old man gets his honors team."

7

"That was fucking depressing," Packs said, "If you'll pardon my French, sir."

"I won't just pardon it, I'll second it: that was a fucking depressing funeral."

"Weird that we have to say it like that. Aren't all funerals supposed to be depressing?"

"Not when it's your job, I guess."

They drove along in silence for a bit. Nobody wanted to die alone, Deth supposed, but it seemed like a whole other level of fucking depressing to have nobody show up to your funeral. He sortof hoped that CW2 Bloom had been a terrible person who had beaten up children and hanged cats, but even if that was the case why hadn't somebody showed up to dance on his grave? It was just as likely that he had been a little old man who had fed the ducks down at the pond every day and had simply never quite met the right woman to settle down and start a family with.

It was almost enough to make Deth desperately want to start dating someone, anyone, even the grossest of townies if it meant he wouldn't have to die alone. But that thought was interrupted by Packs and their passing into a town. "Remind me, sir, who's the next guy up on the docket?"

Deth shuffled through some notes. Up next on the docket was the Henderson funeral in beautiful Norman, Oklahoma. Norman was a college town, home to either OU or OSU (Deth neither cared which nor understood the difference.) Back when he had gone to college, it had been easy to tell what the local school was from the bumper stickers everyone had on their cars. In Norman, though, everyone just plastered an upside down Texas Longhorns logo, which Deth, being equally as unfamiliar with Texan schools as Oklahoman, had long mistaken for a semi-realistic depiction of the female reproductive system.

Why anyone would plaster *that* on their back window had long confused Deth, but Oklahoma being famously conservative, he had guessed that it had been more of a statement that the driver loved pussy than that they supported female reproductive rights. A car bearing another such sticker passed them on the right.

"Hey, there's another one of them, what-do-you-call-them, Fallopian tubes, sir," Packs said, nudging him in the bicep and chuckling. He had found Deth's confusion about the upside-down Longhorns hilarious.

Deth shrugged. "Hey, you explain to me why they give all that money to a school they supposedly hate just to hang their logos upside down and I'll admit it makes more sense than what I thought it was."

Packs scowled. "I never thought of it that way. You a college football guy, sir?" Deth shook his head. "You know, Norman becomes the third biggest city in Oklahoma during weekends when OU has a home game."

Deth furrowed his brow. "Is that true?" Packs nodded. "I'm not sure whether that should make me impressed by OU or disappointed in Oklahoma."

"Probably both. Where do you want to stop, sir?"

Deth sighed and glanced out the window. Lawton, depressing as it was, was only an hour and a half away. He could've gone home, jerked off to his own porn, watched a DVD instead of whatever was on cable (assuming the hotel cable wasn't on the fritz) and even seen a friendly face or two that didn't belong to the nearly perpetually scowling Bela Packs. But tomorrow was Henderson, and they certainly couldn't have woken up early to drive an hour and a half. A million things, from a freak tornado to some sort of Mad Max-style apocalypse could have intercepted them between now and then, at least according to mortuary affairs. So they had to arrive in town the night before.

"Well," Deth said, "This is a college town. There's got to be something interesting here." Then he spotted something out of the corner of his eye. "Hey, look at that," he said, "Matsura. You like Japanese, Sergeant?"

Packs grunted and shrugged. "I guess I could get some of that steak Teriyaki there."

He pulled the car into the restaurant, which was eerily empty. They walked inside and after what seemed like ten minutes, a woman emerged from the kitchen, greeted them, and seated them. "Man, this place is dead," Deth said, glancing around.

"Just the way I like it," Packs said, picking up his menu, "Nobody to hassle us. It'll be perfect."

Deth picked up his own menu. He had gotten so used to the laminated single sheets of the various Oklahoma steakhouses that he had forgotten what a leatherbound, tea-colored fancy pants menu looked like. This one didn't even use dollar signs. The prices were just numbers.

The same woman who had seated them brought them two glasses of water and asked if they were ready to order. "Uh...not yet," Packs said hesitantly.

The waitress/hostess/whatever nodded and disappeared again. Maybe she was the chef, too? Deth had noticed an uncharacteristic knock in Packs's voice but hadn't decided to call attention to it. Now, though, Packs was staring at him, desperation in his eyes, over the menu. Deth cocked his head. "What is it?" he whispered, as though the restaurant were actually full and he had to keep his voice down.

"Did you look at these prices, sir?" Packs hissed.

Deth glanced down and his eyes boggled. The cheapest thing on the menu outside the appetizers was more than their entire per diem combined. He glanced around the room. The lone woman they had seen since walking in was not present. For a moment, Deth wondered if they had stumbled into a haunted restaurant from a B-grade horror movie.

Slowly, he closed his menu and rose. Packs did likewise and they slowly backed out of the restaurant together.

"Here we go," Deth said, rubbing his hands together, "Pizza in a college town. Now I'm excited."

Packs still looked dazed. "I'm sorry, sir. I've never left a restaurant before. But I've never even heard of prices like that."

"Forget it, Sergeant," Deth said, dismissing his concerns with a wave of his hand.

"I mean, we won't get in trouble for skipping out on the bill, will we?"

"The world is a far darker place than I've imagined if we get thrown into debtor's prison for a sip of tap water."

Packs was still not fully mollified, but he seemed content to look over his new menu, laminated, on the front and back of a single large sheet. It was just like being back at a steakhouse. With their per diems combined they had already ordered a table full of calamari, mozzarella sticks, and jalapeno poppers. They were just now finally putting in their pizza order.

Deth had found pizza in Oklahoma to be a shockingly wretched affair. Where he had grown up, there had been a pizza parlor on every block, many with brick ovens, all offering some variation on a heavenly slice. If Luigi's down the block didn't make good pizza, it went out of business. Everybody back home had known what a good pizza was, and could get it anywhere.

In Oklahoma, though, there were no pizza parlors. At least, no mom and pop joints. There were chain stores, and the closest he could find to a decent pie in Lawton was Pizza Hut, which just depressed him in so many different ways. He was hoping against hope now that Norman, being a college town, had to have something akin to a real pizza parlor there. Now, for the first time since he had joined the army, his first real pizza was ordered and on its way.

Deth leaned back in his chair, always a dangerous habit, perhaps made doubly so by the tile floor and hollow metal chair he sat in. He cracked open a cooling mozzarella stick and dipped it in marinara sauce. "Well, you've been holding out on me, Sergeant."

Packs drained one of the beers in the six pack he had already bought with cash to make sure they kept it separate from their government tab. He cracked another. "Oh? How's that, sir?"

"Weren't you going to tell me about the time you talked MAJ Brannigan into staying in the army?"

"Oh, that." Packs rolled his eyes. "It was stupid. You remember I told you we took two batteries over, which the major called a task force for no good reason?" Deth nodded. "Well, at one point we were all in Fallujah."

Deth's eyes nearly popped out of his head. "Fallujah? Like, Fallujah Fallujah?"

"Well, yeah, I'm pretty sure there's only one Fallujah. I can't imagine two assholes in different parts of the world coming up with that name separately. But it wasn't what you're thinking. This was after that whole Phantom Fury thing. It was just another fucking place to occupy."

"Oh, okay."

"So MAJ Brannigan wrote all these rules on the chalkboard. Nothing useful. You know the bullshit officers come up with."

"Better than most," Deth said with a wry smile.

Packs half shrugged, half held up his hands in apology. "You know what I mean, sir."

"I do."

"'Fight for the common cause.' 'Always be a team.' Shit like that, that sounds good, but doesn't really mean anything. The thing is, we spent a lot of our time working around MAJ Brannigan. He'd come up with a stupid idea, and we'd just have to figure out a way to not implement it. And this was a perfect example.

"So, one day, we needed the chalkboard for something. I mean, something mission pertinent. The fucked up thing is, I can't even remember what it was now. A missile count or something. Something everybody needed to see. And Phillips, who was a specialist at the time, I think, or maybe a buck sergeant, asked me if he could erase part of what MAJ Brannigan had written up there so he could put it down."

"And you said yes."

"I said yes. I said, 'Hell, erase the whole fucking thing. It's not helping anybody.' You can probably guess what happened next.

Next time the major comes in, he calls loddy doddy everybody into the BOC. And when they're all there, he slams his fat fist against the chalkboard.

"'What is this?' he says.

"So nobody answers. It's completely silent. And I know what you're going to tell me. And I know I shouldn't have said it. But I did. 'A chalkboard, sir.'"

Deth snorted, trying desperately to keep his composure.

"That was the same reaction the men had, sir. Except they couldn't hold it in. He's glaring at everybody in the room, trying to burn laser holes in each of our foreheads. But the man is just so damn ridiculous looking it just makes everyone crack even more.

"So he starts shouting, telling everyone to shut up, respect his rank, 'I'm the commander of this Task Force,' that kind of thing. Finally the men start to quiet down, because, you know, they're professionals and they know they shouldn't be sitting there laughing at an O-4, no matter how damn stupid he is. And when the room is finally quiet he looks at me and he says, 'You know what erasing my orders is, SFC Packs? It's a mutiny!'"

"A mutiny?," Deth mused, "Because you were on a boat?"

Packs sloshed the liquid around at the bottom of his next beer. "That's almost exactly what Phillips must've thought. He goes 'Aaarrr!' like a pirate. And that sets the men to busting up again. And MAJ Brannigan is just getting madder and madder and his face is just getting redder and redder. And he shouts, 'Shut up! Who said that? Whoever said that had better stand up!'

"So Phillips, you know, I don't like Phillips much, but he's honest enough. He starts to stand up. But then I stood up, too. And all the men got the idea. We were like Spartacus that day, all of us in the BOC standing at perfect attention." By BOC he meant the Battery Operations Center. "Eh, but maybe that was before your time. You ever see *Spartacus*?"

"Yeah, I've seen *Spartacus*, Sergeant." The truth was, he hadn't. But he hadn't been born under a rock on Mars, either. He knew the famous scene Packs was referring to.

"So Brannigan starts walking up and down with his hands clasped behind his back like he's standing at ease. Except you're not supposed to walk at ease, any first day buck private knows that, so he just looks like a Nazi villain in an old World War II movie or something. And he's acting like he's inspecting us and we're locked and terrified of him. And he says, 'I want to know who erased my commander's guidance from the chalkboard!'"

"That's what he was upset about?" Deth asked.

"Jesus Christ, sir, I couldn't make this stuff up if I tried. And he's stamping his foot. Every word, stamp. 'I,' stamp, 'want,' stamp, 'to,' stamp, 'know,' stamp, just like that."

"A real Napoleon, huh?"

"A seven-foot-tall Napoleon, sure. I don't know how a man can be that big and that small at the same time. At this point, the battery commander comes hurrying into the BOC to see what the commotion is, but he can't start chewing ass because MAJ Brannigan's already there kicking up a fuss. So BC says, 'Hey, look, sir, why don't you and I and SFC Packs step outside and discuss all this?'

"But that's not good enough for Brannigan, so here comes his size 12 clodhopper and he goes stamp, stamp, stamp, 'This is an insurgency against my authority.' Like, ah, Phillips was a fucking terrorist or something. 'I put twelve lines of commander's guidance on this board and somebody erased all twelve of them.' He knew the exact number. 'I demand to know who it was.'

"So I kind of sigh and pinch my nose and he goes, 'Something to say, Sergeant?' Just like that. 'Something to say, Sergeant?'

"I said, 'Yes, sir, it was me. Is that what you want to hear? Or it was one of these Soldiers on my orders.'"

"You took the fall for Phillips?"

Packs shrugged. "I wasn't taking the fall for him. It's just what you do. And so BC tries again, 'Hey, sir, let's step outside, let's discuss this in private, all right?' But Brannigan's not having it. He wants to make a point in front of all these joes. So real loud like, he says, 'Am I not the Task Force Commander?'

"So BC takes a few steps toward him, you know, and kind of whispers so that no one else will hear. I mean, a few of the joes would hear, but they'd know well enough to pretend they hadn't. And he says, 'Look, sir, everyone here respects your rank, we appreciate your rank, but you're not in command. You're a liaison officer.'

"And instead of lowering his voice, MAJ Brannigan replies to the group again. 'An LNO? Oh no, no, no, I'm the commander.' Then he points at me. 'SFC Packs, why do you think I'm here?'"

Deth hoped he didn't look like a giddy schoolboy leaning in. "Did you let him have it?"

Packs shook his head. "Nah. I didn't have to let him have it. There was a room full of Soldiers behind me, sure, but I'm a non-commissioned officer. I wasn't about to lie to spare MAJ Brannigan's feelings, or anyone else's, for that matter. So I just said, 'I have no idea why you're here, sir.'"

Deth hissed in sympathy pain. "That's almost more brutal than letting him have it. Did he blow his top?"

"Like Elmer Fudd with steam blowing out of his ears. He starts yelling for BC and I to meet him in his office then he storms off. So I look at BC and I'm shaking my head and I say, 'Listen, sir, what are we gonna do with this guy? I mean, he's a major, nobody's disputing that, but what are we supposed to do when he acts this way?'

"And BC says, 'I don't know. I've never come across anyone half this bad before. It's all I can do just to keep him from fucking everything up.'

"'I'll tell you what they would've done in the old days,' I said."

Deth had heard similar sentiments before. In fact, once, in his ROTC days, an instructor who had particularly hated his guts had stopped him during a Field Training Exercise and told him that if this were still Vietnam, he would have fragged Deth. Although enlisted men had "solved" Brannigan-type problems since time immemorial by turning a blind eye to their mortal danger or even just outright murdering them, the process had become known as "fragging" in Vietnam due to the preferred use of fragmentary grenades, which couldn't be traced the way ballistics could.

Packs continued. "BC told me we don't do that anymore. So we headed for MAJ Brannigan's office. You could recognize it because it was the only office in the firebase without a sign. All the other officers and NCOs had really nice carved signs, crossed cannons and the unit insignia, you know, and the owner's name. The men got bored during all that downtime we had in the desert and carved them for everyone except MAJ Brannigan."

"I'll bet he loved that."

Packs nodded. "He used to sit around and comment how he'd love to have a sign like that. But he couldn't just ask, because it would have meant admitting that no one liked him enough to just do it the way they had for the rest of us. So the men just didn't make him one. So he pulled this plank out of the firewood panel and painted Task Force Commander on it with black paint. Looked like something a kid would have made."

"So he did have a sign, just a bad one."

Packs shook his head. "Nah, somebody just pulled it off his door and tossed it back on the firewood pile at some point." Deth laughed. "So we go in there and the major's back is to us. BC says, 'Look, sir, nobody's disrespecting you, that's not it. But you know, you call the men together to yell at them in a warzone about a chalkboard...I mean, respect is a two-way street.'

"So Brannigan slowly turns around and his lip is quivering, you know? And he says again, 'This is an insurgency against my authority. I'm the Task Force Commander.'

"So I feel like I have to set him straight. I say, 'Listen, sir, we've already got a battery commander. There is no task force. There's just the battery and your liaison section and you're the ranking guy, but that doesn't make you a commander."

"I figured he was going to lay into us both then. Instead he starts crying, talking about resigning his commission and going home. I was that close to getting rid of him. But he just wouldn't stop crying. He even at one point says, 'Why doesn't anybody like me?' So BC and I had to spend the whole night stroking his head and trying to convince him to stay in the army, even though we would have liked nothing better than to see him gone." Packs paused and a faraway look appeared in his eyes. "I sometimes think of how much suffering I might have saved other Soldiers if I had just let him go."

Finally their pizza arrived, Packs's half covered with sausage, meatballs, pepperoni, and every pig-derived meat ten thousand years of human agriculture had yet managed to conjure. Deth's was a solid two inches shorter, and just plain.

"Ah, finally," Deth said, "I haven't had decent New York-style pizza since I moved to the Southwest."

He took a bite and scowled in disgust. He didn't know what it was, but authentic New York-style pizza it was not.

8

It was pouring the morning of the Henderson funeral. Deth was reminded of the cinematic shorthand for funerals. For some reason it rained at every funeral in the movies, and yet Deth had been to dozens, if not hundreds, and it had only rained at a few. And these were old-timey, Greatest Generation vets. If the angels were going to weep at any passing, it would be theirs. No, Hollywood was all bullshit.

So the rain on the morning of the Henderson affair was a little odd, and a little irritating, and it was compounded by the fact that they couldn't do anything to keep the rain out of their eyes. "Are you sure we can't use an umbrella?" Deth asked.

"Come on, sir."

"I've got one in the car. It lights up like in *Blade Runner*."

"Who?"

"Never mind. Come on, these people don't know we're not supposed to have umbrellas."

"It's AR 670-1, sir."

"I won't write you up if you don't write me up."

"Come on, sir."

There was no brooking the admonition to "come on." Deth liked to think of himself as a rule follower, but Packs was a zealot. He'd never seen the man break the speed limit, although, to be fair, a lot of roads in Oklahoma were 75 mph.

"It's these god-damned berets," Packs said, perhaps an attempt to be conciliatory, "Pardoning my French. No brim to keep the water off your face. You can thank General Shinseki for that."

Deth furrowed his brow. The old boys complained about the black berets a lot. Like, *a lot*. More than seemed reasonable for the mild inconvenience they caused. Deth had come into the army with nothing but berets (except for patrol caps in the field or the motor pool) and he kind of liked them. But something else was bothering him.

That was it. He would've snapped his fingers if he hadn't been standing at parade rest. You didn't wear a patrol cap with greens. "But the old garrison cap didn't have a brim, either."

"Huh?" Packs said, "Oh, the cunt cap?" He giggled his odd, silent hissing giggle that he sometimes did at a particularly juvenile joke that he maybe knew he wasn't supposed to find funny. "Yeah, I guess you're right. Still hate these damn berets, though."

As the service wound down and the minister signaled for them, Deth stood to attention but spoke out of the corner of his mouth, attempting not to indicate that he was speaking, since everyone was looking at them now. "Who's the NOK?" he hissed. The funeral director had never come to tell them.

"I don't know," Packs said, covering his mouth as he passed behind Deth's back, "I'll try to find the undertaker. Just stall."

Shit. Sometimes they had to play this game. Deth could stretch out some of the saluting for a while, but there was a point where he could no longer fake the solemnity of prolongment and it became obvious something was wrong.

Deth went through his paces as slowly as he ever had. He even added some steps, everything he thought he could get away with, kneeling in front of the flag and pretending to say some prayers. The audience, at least, was receptive. Some crowds were more agitated, but these folks were willing to let him vamp for time, as long as they didn't know that's what he was doing.

Finally Packs joined him with a look of panic in his eyes that only Deth could see. The funeral director must have been off somewhere. Neither broke his façade of staid, professionalism and manliness, but the whole time they folded the flag, Deth's internal monologue was shrieking, "Shit shitshitshitshit shit..."

When they were close enough to kiss, and Packs was presenting each corner to Deth for inspection, he took the risk of speaking again. "What should I do?"

"Just ask who wants it," Packs replied out of the corner of his mouth.

Deth shrugged internally but didn't let it affect his performance. Luckily they had both performed this ceremony enough times to do it with their eyes closed, let alone distracted, so

Deth was pretty sure the mourners were none the wiser that they had been speaking.

Deth walked down the front row, in front of the mourning family members, and did a right-face so he would be looking at them. A gray-haired woman with a big mole on her face might have been old enough to be Henderson's widow, but then again, she could just as easily have been his sister. Then there was the woman whose ginger hair was obviously dyed, so there were at least two candidates for widow, if he had been married at all. Supposing he was married, though, there was a thirty-something man and a woman in her forties, either of whom could have been Henderson's son, daughter, son-in-law, or daughter-in-law, if he had had any of those. So no help there.

He swallowed deeply and scanned the back of the assembly for the funeral director. The bastard was nowhere to be seen. Perhaps he had wandered off to take a phone call or deal with some emergency at another funeral. They did that, sometimes, when the ceremony was in full gear and they weren't really needed.

"And who will accept this flag on behalf of a grateful nation?" Deth asked loudly, succumbing to what he hoped would only be a minor embarrassment.

Heck, maybe they would appreciate being asked. Maybe it wouldn't be so bad after all.

The woman with the mole, the one Deth had originally pegged as maybe possibly sort of the widow, slowly came to her feet. She had a cane, so it took her a moment. "I'll take Gene's flag," she said, her voice strong and proud in contraindication to her feeble appearance.

Deth breathed a silent sigh of relief and executed sharp cuts to turn and walk towards her. Then a raven-haired beauty Deth had taken for a grand-daughter or a girlfriend of a grandson due to her youth and sharp clothes, jumped to her feet. "Fuck you, Liz!" the young woman cried, "He was my husband!"

Deth clenched his jaw so tight he felt his teeth splintering. The woman with the mole (apparently Liz) turned slowly to face the young woman in the black business suit. "He was my husband first, you streetwalking hussy!" Liz replied.

"Well, he was my husband last!" the ostensible streetwalker replied.

The older woman with the dyed hair who Deth had initially suspected of being Henderson's sister stood and walked up to Deth, who didn't know which of the feuding women, if either, to proceed to. "Here, just give it here," the woman with the dye job said, "Eugene was my cousin. I'm blood."

Henderson's cousin pawed at the flag that Deth was still trying to hold, sandwiched between his hands, with all the dignity of his position. He was trying to maintain some level of composure, even though he knew his eyes were as big as boiled eggs.

Out of the corner of his left egg he saw that Liz was attempting to beat Henderson's second wife with her cane. The second wife seemed entirely prepared to pile-drive the older woman, but some of Henderson's other relations and well-wishers were physically holding her back, as her legs kicked out in the air.

Deth was just happy for an out, so he dropped to one knee in front of Henderson's cousin, cursing himself when he remembered that she was standing and the purpose of kneeling was not just to kneel, but to be eye-level with the flag recipient. He wasn't sure whether to stand back up or not. There really wasn't a script for this sort of thing. "On behalf of a grateful nation..." Deth started to say.

"Sit your ass down, Aunt June!"

Deth closed his eyes and cast them to the ground. The thirty-year-old whom Deth had taken for a son or son-in-law was on his feet now, his fists balled as though he was about to knock Henderson's cousin out if he had to. "If blood is what you're looking for, I'm more blood than she is," the man said, pounding his chest, "It should go to his son before it goes to his cousin." Young Henderson made the word "cousin" sound like a curse more vile than the R-word, the C-word, and the N-word combined.

"It should go to his widow!" Henderson's more recent widow screeched.

"Yeah, me!" Liz asserted.

"Well, who's it supposed to go to?" Henderson the Younger asked.

That, at last, cut through the commotion. Every eye in the crowd, fighters and bystanders alike, riveted on Deth. Deth opened his eyes and stood to his feet with as much dignity as he could muster. He looked to Packs who, if anything, seemed even more mortified than Deth did. He looked to the preacher, who had apparently been shouting on behalf of the first wife, perhaps not believing in divorce.

Deth scanned the crowd until he spotted a little girl, not older than three, who was wearing a white satin dress that was probably the only dress she owned and standing on a chair so she could see the ruckus. The little girl was crying. Deth hurried over to her as fast as he could while still maintaining something akin to a military bearing.

He knelt down and even though the girl was standing on her chair and holding her mother's hand, he was eye-level with her. "Is this your grandfather's funeral?" he asked quietly.

The little girl nodded between tears. "Will you please take this?" he said, proffering the flag to her, "It was important to your grandfather and it will help you remember him."

She took the flag, which was nearly as tall as her, from his hands. He stood and kissed her on the forehead, and looked around. The mourners appeared to have reached détente, and even Crazy Liz had folded her hands and begun watching quietly.

Deth slowly saluted the flag and happily extricated himself from the whole mess with as much dignity as he could retain. The one positive outcome, from the perspective of the funeral detail, was that all of the mourners were too ashamed to look at them, let alone come talk to them after the service.

Slamming the car door after changing behind a tree, Deth buried his head in his hands. The muffled words, "What a nightmare," wafted through his fingers.

Collecting himself, he sat back, ran a hand through his hair in deference to the days when he had had enough hair to run a hand through. He looked at Packs, who was sitting with his hands on the wheel and his seatbelt buckled, not making any motion. "Not going to bust my balls, Sergeant?"

Packs shrugged. "You done good, sir," he said. After a moment's reflection, he added, "Shit happens. Pardoning my French."

Deth waited. He felt for his seatbelt. It was also buckled,

although Packs didn't strike him as the type to refuse to drive unless everyone was buckled in. He had known a girl like that in college, who would literally sit and wait until everyone was buckled. "Where's the next one?" Deth asked tentatively, "Should I call the funeral home and ask for directions?"

Deth had always thought it might be nice to have a GPS for these trips, but they were so damn expensive and bulky, and he had never been into buying faddy gadgets. He hadn't even gotten a cell phone until 2004. Packs looked at him, though, and shook his head. He looked like someone had run over his dog.

"What is it, Sergeant?" Deth had come this close to calling him "Bela."

"They're sending us home."

Deth felt his heart literally skip a beat. He made a mental note to have a doctor look at that, but not an army doctor. They were all butchers.

"Home" meant "Lawton," but still, it would be oddly cathartic to finally go back to his apartment, look at some of the meager possessions he had amassed over the course of his twenty-four-odd years on the planet. Maybe watch a DVD, microwave a frozen chicken cordon bleu, and later jerk off to the internet instead of a Maxim, in his own bed instead of one a chambermaid would have to clean (or likely not) later. "Isn't that good?"

"It didn't sound good," Packs said, darkly.

Deth looked back at the scene of the debacle. Was it possible one of the angry mourners had gotten in touch with mortuary affairs to complain? How would they have even known the number? Oh, well, of course the funeral director would have known. He might even have complained on his own, without waiting for a mourner to prompt him.

Deth felt his heart freeze and the chunk of ice splash into the swirling juices in his stomach. They had never fucked up a funeral this badly before. They had never really fucked up before at all, scarlet socks excluded (because who would even notice that, seriously?) But if someone had complained, they might be in trouble. They might have to go see LTC Fink. They might even be pulled off funeral detail. "Drive!" Deth shouted.

Only the seatbelt he had so conscientiously buckled prevented him from leaping through the windshield with joy.

9

They stopped at the Wendy's in the center of the highway. They usually ate at Mickey D's because Packs preferred it. Deth preferred Wendy's for no particular reason, although also as a change of pace. Both agreed that the doors of a Burger King were not to be breached except in some sort of post-apocalyptic scenario where every other food source on earth had been contaminated. Likely the fact that there was a Burger King on every post in the army fed into their mutual hatred of it. Nothing spurred hate quite like availability.

"Not every post," Packs said between bites of his triple square-cornered burger, "There's a McDonald's in Ali." He meant Ali al Salem in Kuwait, but everyone just called it "Ali."

"Hmm," Deth muttered, "That must've been a welcome change."

"After the Balad Burger King, it was like a breath of fresh air.

Except for, you know, the garbage stink of just being in Kuwait. Shit, I'd eat at the D-FAC before I'd eat at the Burger King. Although there was a Pizza Hut, too."

Deth had noticed that men referring to a cafeteria overseas tended to call it a D-FAC (short for Dining Facility) while stateside they tended to call it a chow hall. "You don't usually think of all that shit as being in Iraq."

"It wasn't," Packs said, beaming with pride, "Until we brought it there."

Deth nodded in something between mock and genuine appreciation. Packs was tearing into his chili in between bites of his triple. The whole table was littered with wrappers already. They had to enjoy the last of their per diem, after all. They hadn't had breakfast and they wouldn't be having dinner (so, of course, dinner wasn't included, but still, double lunch.) It might be the last time they ever feasted in this fashion together.

Well, probably not. It wasn't like they'd be dead. There'd be barbecues at each other's houses and the like. But nights of devouring steaks and mornings of steak and eggs and lunches of steak burgers all on the road to some jerkoff octogenarian's funeral? Those days might well and truly be over. And the stories about...

"Brannigan."

Packs looked up, suddenly turned off his third Junior Bacon Cheeseburger. "I shouldn't have gotten cheese," Packs said, "It always sticks up my colon. What were you saying about Big Smell?"

"Huh?"

"Big Smell," Packs said, stretching first his right arm, then the left, "That's what we used to call him because he didn't wash."

"He didn't wash?"

"Nope," Packs said, reflectively, "Well, maybe he did. But no one ever saw him go to the shower buildings. And he always smelled like BO."

Deth rubbed his chin. He seemed to recall hearing once about a genetic disease that made you smell like fish even if you washed all the time. Although, not washing at all would also account for it, so there was no reason to assume that Occam's Razor wasn't in effect. "Big Smell, huh?" Deth mused.

"Big Douche," Packs said, "The Jackass. Big Hooah. Sir Doucheington. Major Steele called him Daffodil Dave and they got into a sissy slap fight over it once."

"Seriously?"

"Yup."

Packs squinted his eyes. "There were others. Everybody called him something different. It was kind of funny. You'd never know what somebody else's nickname for him was until you talked to them about him. But everyone always had one." Packs ruminated a moment before picking up his sandwich again. Apparently the cheese didn't disagree with him so badly that he would not eat it. "But why'd you bring *him* up?" Packs asked before taking a bite, implying by syllable stress that "him" was a demonic entity of some sort.

Deth felt a wave of embarrassment pass through him. "I just...I was just thinking how we might not have lunches like this anymore."

It was the closest to an assertion of unencumbered sentiment as either of them had ever shown. Packs smiled. "You really like hearing about him, huh?"

"It's like a car wreck," Deth said, "You want to look away but it's just right there, a guy's coconut splashed all over the road."

Packs shook his head sharply, first right, then left. "It's not that," he said, then finished the burger before continuing with mashed beef patty and pork posterior in his mouth, "You're an officer. And you want to be a good one. And the only way you can tell..." Packs swallowed the whole pulpy, bunny mess. "...Is by comparison. Don't worry, sir. You're good as far as I can tell. Not the best I've ever seen, but I worked for Jesus when he was a corporal. Still, you could stand to work out more."

Deth grabbed his paunch reflexively. "I'm not the one that eats a whole cow every day."

"I'm not the one scoring a 181 on the APFT, either."

"Hey, 181 is exceeding the standard."

Technically, that was true. 180 was the minimum passing score for the PT test. Unperturbed, Packs prised the lid off another large chili, scraped off the raw onions, and dug in with the overwide plastic spoon.

"All right, I've got one last story for you," Packs said, "It's not like we're going to be dead or anything, but you know I'm not going to talk shit about a major in front of the joes."

Deth nodded in agreement with this verbal contract. Packs nodded knowingly as well. "All right, so one day, Big Smell came into work at 1600..."

"For the night shift."

"No. We didn't run a night shift. We were a liaison section, remember? He just came into work at 1600."

Deth ran his fingers across his lips. "What?"

"You're just going to have to believe me on this, sir."

"I believe you, Sergeant."

"Now, actually, now that I think about it, this was the first time he came to work at all for about a week."

"Let me guess," Deth said, "He wasn't on pass."

"Nope. Just sitting around. Sometimes he would get depressed and just sit in his can all day. And, hell, we didn't care, it was nice not having him around. Half of what I did when he actually came to work was to put out his fires. So when he just didn't show up, I could get real work done. Now this particular time, if I remember correctly, he was depressed because his request to go home early had been denied."

Deth ran his hands through his phantom hair. "How's that?"

"Oh, well, he wanted a six-month tour."

"I thought only marines and air force get six-month tours."

The truth that both of them knew was that marines had seven-month tours and airmen got four, but neither of them was in a hair-splitting mood that day. Soldiers deployed for twelve months at a minimum, but these days that was typically extended to fifteen or eighteen, depending on the needs of the army. Deth had even heard horror stories about twenty-four month tours, but those were rare enough to be possibly apocryphal.

"And malingerers. Well, actually, if I really think back, Big Smell wanted a thirty-day tour. That's the bare minimum to get a combat patch."

"Holy shit."

"Yeah. No one was having his thirty-day business, but he just fought and pissed and moaned non-stop to be let go after six months. Hell, we didn't care. I would've signed the orders myself if I was a O-6. Except, here's the thing, sir: he just pulled it out of his ass. No one had ever told him that he was going to do a six-month tour or a thirty-day tour or any of that. He just sort of figured he'd be able to weasel his way out of it."

"How so?"

Packs wiggled his fingers in the air. "The power of the ring."

He was referring to the West Point ring. Being ROTC himself, Deth did not have a ring, and while he had witnessed the occasional ol' boy preference shown to Pointers over OCS and ROTC, he was generally of the opinion that your commissioning source counted for shit. People who went to West Point however, he had noted, expected that their rings would take them places.

"So, since he had been talking about going home since we had arrived in theater," Packs continued, "No one was surprised when he started talking about going home after ten months. But this time, he really talked about it. He said he was going home, and it wasn't his choice, and if the choice was his he would've stayed with us and the Soldiers, but, by God, he had to go back to the States. He talked about it so much and even called back home to talk about it, that Colonel Fink even put an O-4 on call to replace Big Smell. Major, ah...Rupert, if I recall correctly."

"Oh, I know him," Deth said.

Packs nodded. "Major Rupert even went on two weeks leave to see his family before deploying. That's how much Brannigan had everybody spun up about him going home. And when 10 months finally came, Big Smell went and for the first time brought up going home with an O-6 in theater. (Being as you need O-6 approval to cut any orders going home.)"

"Sure," Deth said, as though he had already known that, which he hadn't.

"What do you think that colonel said?"

"Pound sand?"

"He said, 'Bullshit, you've always claimed you were "the commander" and a commander stays with his troops. You have absolutely no reason to go home, so I'm denying your request.' So he screwed over his replacement Major Rupert, who had already squandered leave time getting ready. And when he heard the news his request had been denied, he went and hid in his room for six days and never came out."

Deth leaned back in his chair, stunned. "That's a hell of a story," he said.

"Oh, that wasn't the story I wanted to tell you, sir," Packs said, "That's just, you know, the setup."

Deth wasn't sure whether laughter was appropriate. "Okay..."

"Anyway, we were all pissed off because we had been real excited about him leaving. And then the day before his replacement was supposed to get here, some bigwig in theater put the kibosh on the whole thing. Heck, we were all excited to see him go. But, ah, he was depressed, and we didn't see him for a week, and then when he finally came back to work we were expecting a nervous breakdown or something. We had this mission, where it took two hours to clear the airspace. And, sir, I know you're new to the branch and the army and all, but do you know why we clear air before we fire rockets?"

Deth wasn't sure if the question was meant to be facetious or not. "So you...don't hit any friendly airplanes?"

Packs snapped his fingers and pointed at Deth as though he were the smartest kid in the classroom. "Anyway, we had to cancel a mission because it took over two hours to clear air. Sucks, I guess, but like you said, better than blue-on-blue. Not to mention could you imagine what a debacle it would be if we shot down a damn helicopter! What if it had a general on it or something? We'd all be in Leavenworth.

"Anyway, Big Smell comes running into the main office from his office (you know, he insisted we set up a separate room for him, and we didn't care, nobody wanted to share the space with his stink anyway.) And he has this big smile on his face. We half didn't believe it because he had been so depressed about not going home. So he says, 'After that debacle where it took two hours to clear air, I'm worried no one will ever want us to shoot for them again. So I'm working on a plan where' - I'm not making this up - 'Where if ten minutes goes by and air isn't clear, we shoot anyway.'"

It took Deth a moment of working his jaw before he could form words. "So all the choppers and planes we down would just be...what, collateral damage?"

Packs shrugged and took a sip of his orange Crush. "What did you tell him?"

"I told him it was a great idea, and it was too bad I was an NCO because the writeup would need an officer's touch."

"No, you didn't."

"I did, and he said he'd better do it himself, because the colonel - the one that denied his request to go home - was super excited about the idea."

"Was it...was the colonel playing a practical joke on him?"

Packs shrugged. "I guess. I wish I could've been there for the presentation. I'll tell you one thing, though, sir."

"What's that?"

"Next time I'm late for work and my kid is playing in the driveway, I'm just going to gun it after ten minutes. It's his own fault for being in my way."

10

"Five miles a fucking hour," Packs said. Deth nodded. "Can you imagine going five miles an hour?"

Deth glanced at the speedometer. They were going just under ten and Packs was riding the brake. "Maybe if you had a stick shift?" Deth ventured.

Packs shook his head. "It's ridiculous," he said, "Look, I'm just trying to approach 5 and look how fast they're piling up behind me."

Deth glanced out the back window. Indeed, no one behind them on their way to the Cache Road Gate had been going as slow as they were until they had gotten caught in Packs's interminably slow wake. No one beeped. They were all angry, but no one beeped. They were all glancing up at the "5 MPH" sign. Deth glanced at it himself. It seemed so...pedestrian.

"It's impossible, I say," Packs said.

"Could be," Deth agreed.

"Look at how slow we're going," Packs said, gesturing widely at all the rolling beige fields of Ft. Sill, soon to be blackened by the first powder fires of the year.

Deth had started the fires himself one year, the one year he had actually been in town to fire and not out on the road doing funerals. SSG Phillips, one of his section chiefs, had gestured for him to jump into the launcher as they rolled out onto the firing point. He sandwiched himself in between Figueroa, the driver, on one side and both Phillips and the gunner (whose name escaped him after so long on the road away from his platoon) on the other.

"Have you got your gas mask, sir?" Phillips had asked.

"Gas mask?" Deth had goggled, "What do you mean? Why would I have that?"

All three of the regular crewmembers exchanged worried glances. "Sir," SPC Fig had explained as though to a mental deficient, "If the launcher starts leaking toxic gas and we all have to button up, you won't be able to breathe."

Phillips had slapped his driver. "Don't scare the sir, Fig," Phillips had said, "Sir, if an alarm goes off, just hold your breath. It probably won't happen."

They had then proceeded to the firing point, and no sooner had they reached it than an alarm had started blaring loudly. All three of the crewmen had reached for the gas masks at their sides. His eyes wide, Deth had taken a long deep breath. He had let it out when Phillips had slapped him on his back. They had all been guffawing loudly.

"Toxic gas," Phillips had repeated, wiping the tears from his eyes, "Yeah, right. Go ahead, sir, pop your cherry. Press that red button right there."

Deth had pressed it, unwittingly destroying his own patrol cap, which they had stuck to the back of the rocket to be incinerated and presented to him later as a symbol of his lost Field Artillery maidenhead. That rocket had started the fires that year, and no one else in the battery had been able to shoot for almost 24 hours while range control had come out to put them out.

Packs spoke, snapping Deth back to the present moment. "You think we can even do it?"

"Do what?" Deth asked groggily.

"Get down as low as 5?"

Deth looked at the speedometer again. The line behind them was piling out almost as far as Rogers Lane. In front of them, the MPs, or, probably, more likely, the civilian security guards at the gate, were gesturing and waving for them to speed up in spite of the sign. At their present speed it would take minutes and minutes to reach the gate.

"Rules is rules, Sergeant," Deth said with a smile, "They put up that sign, they must want us to go 5."

Packs nodded and clamped down infinitesimally harder on the brake, trying to slow the Ford down to 5.

They reached mortuary affairs at 1630. Deth had tried to convince Packs to drive slowly, or to stop by their houses first, or to stop and catch a movie, or something, anything, so that they wouldn't arrive before closing time. Packs's commendable and damnable integrity prevented any of that, though. "We get there when we get there, sir. If they're still open, they're still open."

They were, as it turned out, still open. They were spotted by a civilian in a white, pin-striped shirt and a loosened tie whose name Deth had never quite picked up, though the man had briefed them every time they had gone out. He was a transitory figure, whose name was unworthy of memory, the same as the others, who all constituted a single, fungible character in the mind of Deth as "Mortuary Affairs."

"You run into Westboro?" Mortuary Affairs asked, narrowing his eyes, which were still visible behind his giant glasses.

Deth and Packs exchanged a glance. "No, sir," Deth said, "We've been to Muskogee, Norman, Broken Arrow…"

"I'm not asking if you've been to Westboro," Mortuary Affairs said testily, "I'm asking if you ran into Westboro."

"Is that a guy?"

"What? Weren't you briefed when you left?"

Deth and Packs looked at each other again. "Yes," Deth said, "But we've been on the road for two weeks."

Mortuary Affairs flipped through some paperwork. "Oh, I guess we did add it to the warnings since then," he said, not quite contritely, "But you didn't run into them, did you?"

By silent gestures, Deth and Packs indicated once again that they had no idea what the civilian was referring to. As if explaining the matter to a pair of dummies on par intellectually with a monkey, Mortuary Affairs explained that a church in Kansas had just cropped up and they were picketing military funerals and nobody really knew about them yet and nobody really knew what to do about them, so just ignore them if they interfered with you.

"Liberals," Packs said as though the word tasted sour in his mouth.

Deth rolled his eyes at Packs's remark.

"No, quite the opposite," Mortuary Affairs said, "Loonies."

Deth wasn't sure if loonies were the opposite of liberals, but he would take it as a win.

"All right, well, now you've been briefed," Mortuary Affairs said, waving his arm dismissively, "Have a good one."

"Um, that's not what we're here for, sir," Packs said.

Mortuary Affairs fixed them with an angry glare. "What, then?"

"Well, you called us back in from the road and..."

"Who did? Me did?"

"I don't know, sir. Someone from this office..."

"Who?"

"I don't know."

Mortuary Affairs looked like a chunk of raw lemon was wedged uncomfortably in his throat. "Names?"

They told him. He flipped through some clipboards. "Ah. Here it is. I called you back in. Why are you trying to defraud the federal government?"

Deth jumped. Packs looked angry enough to go swinging at the guy. No one impugned Packs' shonor. Though he was stunned himself, Deth had the wherewithal to put his hand on Packs's chest. No more was needed to hold him back. (Which was good, because Deth was certain that neither he nor Andre the Giant could have successfully restrained SFC Bela Packs on a rampage.)

"We didn't," Deth said, "We never have. I've got receipts for everything. We never bought booze, paid all our tips out of pocket, never went over our per diem..."

"Oh no?"

"No," Deth said.

Deth was carrying the green and brown plastic folder that contained the car's fuel log. He also kept the receipts in there and the credit card when he wasn't using it. Every day he checked the financials, and Packs followed it closely enough to point out his occasional mistake and reel him in. They'd never spent a dime more than they were allowed, and they had come in under budget often enough (even with Packs's beloved steak dinners) that they had saved the government hundreds of dollars. Deth prided himself on it. Even when he had been brand new on funeral detail, he had never boloed a receipt.

"Explain this," Mortuary Affairs said, slapping down a computer printout triumphantly.

He crossed his arms and leaned back in his chair. Deth approached the man's desk like a supplicant and picked up the slip of paper to review. Their lunch bill from the previous day was highlighted and surrounded by bright yellow asterisks and exclamation points. Deth pulled a pen out of one of the three tiny pouches on the sleeve of his ACUs and drew a bracket encompassing the bills of the entire day.

Mortuary Affairs looked stunned, as though Deth had just attempted to tattoo his name on his wife's forehead instead of making a pen mark on a piece of paper. Deth muttered under his breath, going through the calculations again. He marked the total for the day on the side of the paper, to the left of the bracket.

"Yeah," Deth said, "It's all there and under budget."

Mortuary Affairs spluttered for a moment, then regained what passed for composure with him. "The hell it is!" he said, "You spent almost double what you should've on lunch."

Mortuary Affairs dropped a damning forefinger down on the paper, pointing over and over again at the highlighted portion that required no further emphasis. Deth took the sheet and turned it around so that the man could read it right-side up. He brought his BIC down on the area in question and tapped it over and over again with the cap still on the pen.

"Keep on looking," Deth said, aggrieved now that the man was doubting him, and forgetting all about his dreams of being kicked off funeral detail and what he would do when he saw his platoon again, "We doubled up that night. The hotel bill is almost half of what we were allowed. So we spent some of the balance on a nice lunch. Look, the per diem total is STILL under."

Mortuary Affairs angrily slapped the pen out of Deth's hand. "It doesn't go by day," Mortuary Affairs said stiffly.

"My Latin's a little rusty," Deth said, "But I'm pretty sure 'per diem' means 'per day.' Have you got a dictionary? We could look it up."

"*Carpe diem*," Packs added helpfully, "Seize the day."

Deth snapped his fingers and shot Packs with a finger pistol.

"I don't care what per diem means," Mortuary Affairs said, grinding his teeth, "DOD regulations state that you can't spend per diem allotted for housing on sustenance, and vice versa."

"I didn't know that," Deth said, "And I've been doing this for a minute. Did you know that, Sergeant Packs?"

"No, sir, sounds crazy to me," Packs said.

"Well, there you are," Deth said, "Honest mistake. But if you want to take us off funeral detail, I totally understand."

"Honest mistake, my foot," Mortuary Affairs said, as though Deth had never uttered the next sentence, "You're going to pay back the government every cent you overspent."

"We didn't overspend," Packs said, "We underspent. Are you going to pay us back?"

Mortuary Affairs opened his mouth, then shut it. "Hang on," he said, then scurried out of the room with the piece of paper.

By force of habit, Deth stood and took his place at the right of Packs.

"I really hope he comes back with pink slips," Deth said.

"I hope you didn't ruin this for me, sir," Packs replied.

"Sorry, Sergeant," Deth said, "I was defending your honor and all."

"Yeah," Packs said with a resigned sigh, "Yeah..."

Mortuary Affairs returned a moment later with pink cheeks and two typed pieces of paper. He put them down and pushed them towards Packs and Deth. "Sign these," he said.

Deth raised an eyebrow. Neither moved an inch. "What are these?" Deth asked.

"They're sworn statements affirming that you weren't trying to defraud the federal government," Mortuary Affairs said, "The boss said I can't charge you anything because you didn't overspend...but do it again and you'll pay a steep penalty."

Neither man asked what the steep penalty would be, and each stepped forward to sign his personalized affidavit in turn.

"Well, now that these are signed, we'll just drop the car off at the motor pool and..."

"Oh, no," Mortuary Affairs said, "You two jokers have got a funeral tomorrow in Little Rock."

Packs's eyes turned red and his lower lip quivered. "Little Rock? We'd have to leave now and drive all night!"

"Well, you'd better get going," Mortuary Affairs said, pulling some papers into a stack and straightening them, "Now that these are signed, we can put you back on the road."

Packs slammed his hands down on the man's desk. "You mean I can't...I can't even see my wife?"

Mortuary Affairs checked his watch as though it would make a difference. "Maybe for a few minutes..."

"You mean to say you pulled us all the way back here for this? I could've told you over the phone we weren't trying to defraud anybody. Or you could've faxed them to our hotel! We were halfway to Little Rock this morning!"

Deth put a hand on Packs's shoulder. "Come on, Sergeant," Deth said as gently as he could, "I'll drive as far as Ft. Smith and you can get some sleep."

Packs tossed his hands up into the air so that Deth's hand would fall away from his shoulder. He turned his back on Mortuary Affairs and stormed out of the office. When he stepped through the doorway, he shouted over his shoulder.

"Officers don't drive!"

11

True to his word, Packs wouldn't let Deth drive. He never had before, but Deth had never realized what a matter of pride it was to the NCOs. Officers did not drive them. They drove officers.

For the first four hours, they didn't speak. "Did I ever tell you about the raccoons?" Deth asked tentatively when they reached the state line, "Best Joe story you ever heard, your whole army career, I promise."

Packs said nothing, so he let the subject drop. It was really a quite funny story, but if Packs was not to be cheered, then Packs was not to be cheered. Deth had thought of himself as the most unhappy about being on funeral detail. But, of course, he had nothing waiting for him, no wife at home or kids or dog. Packs had the whole deal, and even though he was an NCO and hard as week-old bread, he was human, too, and didn't care to be jerked around, same as anybody.

They stopped for Korean barbecue, but Packs being in the mood he was, there was no jovial dinner, and they just got the food to go and ate in the car. "Hope we didn't overspend," Packs said after deliberately keeping the dinner bill to a minimum.

It was the first words he had spoken the whole trip. Even without stopping for dinner, they didn't reach the hotel in Little Rock until after 0200. Deth forewent his customary bottle of Mad Dog, knowing that it was way too late to start, even though he wasn't normally too strict about the "no drinking within four hours of duty" rule. He personally felt too exhausted to start, and he also didn't want to ask Packs to stop at a convenience store. The man remained in a black mood.

They easily afforded two rooms, and though Little Rock was not a bad town, they didn't take in any of it that night. Deth liked to sleep, and even Packs required his minimum 4 hours a night, as the army was obligated to give him. They'd be at the funeral soon enough.

"Where the hell is this place?" Deth asked, scratching his head.

It was customary for them to scope out the graveyard before reporting to the funeral home for the flag. Packs never stopped reminding Deth about a miserable, no-good debacle where the honor guard had gotten lost and hadn't shown up until an hour after the ceremony and made a laughingstock of his beloved army. To prevent that from happening to them, they always found the gravesite before the undertaker's, and they never arrived less than an hour early to the ceremony. Most days it was more like two.

For the third time, they passed the spot where the theoretical turnoff should've been. "It should be right there!" Deth said, pointing off to the left.

"I don't know what to tell you, sir."

They reached the next intersection, yet again, where there was no STOP sign but there was a street sign indicating that the cross-street was Povey Ave. Packs pulled the car over, yet again. Deth slapped the map down on the dash and pointed at the damning evidence. "Povey Avenue," Deth said, "Back there was Scales. It's supposed to be right here, in between Povey and Scales, down, what is this, unnamed route."

Deth gestured back towards where the boneyard theoretically was. Packs scratched his head and looked at the map. He glanced back in either direction. "We made the right turn..." Packs said, twitching at his upper lip with his thumb.

"It can't be that dirt trail," Deth said, reluctantly adding, "Can it?"

Packs glanced back. So far, the dirt path was the only thing they had spotted. The other option was to go back and ask directions in what counted as "town" in this rural Little Rock adjunct, which, as far as Deth could tell, consisted of a gas station and a farmhouse.

"Well, I ain't in my 'frams yet," Packs said, "It's supposed to be less than a mile."

Deth said nothing, tacitly agreeing by his silence. A few minutes later, walking along the trail, Deth spotted a huge plastic tank of some sort raised above the ground. "What the hell is that?" Deth asked, "A water tank? Don't they even have plumbing out here?"

Packs chuckled his barking, half-hissing laugh. "Nah, sir, that's...gas-o-line," Packs said, forcing himself to use the civilian term instead of "fuel."

Now that they had passed the tank, Deth had to look back to see that Packs was right. In fact, there were fuel hoses attached to one end of the tank, just like at a filling station. "What the hell do they need that for?"

"Tractors and such," Packs said, "It's a heck of a lot easier than driving to the gas station whenever they need to. They just have the fuel truck come out here and fill it up whenever they need more."

Deth had never heard of such a thing. City living. "I wish I had bought one of those Global Positioning things," Deth said after they had tramped along a while longer.

"Shit, sir, you're an officer," Packs mused, "You can afford it."

"Yeah, well, they told us not to in ROTC," Deth said, recalling the land navigation course at Ft. Lewis vividly.

"They told you not to? Don't they know we use PLGRs in the real army?"

"Well, I didn't know about that, either," Deth said, "They used to tell us that if the GPS broke and we didn't know how to do land nav, we would've, you know, failed the army."

"You still do everything they told you to do in ROTC?"

"Well, it's like $200, too. $500 for a good one."

They reached the area where the graveyard should've been and, to their disappointment, found that it was nothing more than a farmer's land, and not even cultivated land, just a rolling green meadow. For as far as they could see in every direction, there was grass and wood, and no damn gravestones. Plus the immense potential of an angry farmer who would probably mistake them for trespassers rather than an out-of-uniform funeral detail searching for a graveyard that didn't exist. "All right," Packs said diplomatically, "The map's wrong."

"Are you sure we've gone far enough?"

"We've gone almost two miles and it was supposed to be less than one. Let's go back and just check out what's in the opposite direction."

"All right."

As it turned out, the map *was* wrong. They went all the way back through "town," then in the opposite direction of where the map indicated, and, like magic, they spotted the elusive boneyard. There was a tiny chapel there where they considered changing, but it was locked and looked to be infested by hornets and hadn't been opened probably in years. Besides, they still had to go get the flag from the undertaker and they hated driving in their Class A's.

"GPS wouldn't have helped you with that, either," Packs said, "That was pure country instinct."

Reaching the funeral parlor, they did not identify themselves but merely asked to use the bathroom, which a dignified young secretary, unsure whether they were mourners, pointed them to silently.

Emerging from the bathroom fully decked in their greens, the funeral director, who wore a plate identifying his surname as BAINES, snatched them up. "Hello!" Baines said, shaking hands, "Welcome! Thank you for your service. Did you have trouble finding the place?"

Packs and Deth exchanged a glance. "Not this place," Packs said, "But we had a heck of a time finding the burial site."

"Oh, yeah?" Baines asked, smiling and putting his hand on his hip, "You boys aren't from around here, are you?"

"Oklahoma," Packs said, and though Deth hissed, he didn't correct him.

"Okies, huh?" Baines said, never hiding his pearly whites, "All right, well, we'll have you boys back in Sooner country soon enough."

Baines disappeared into a cupboard and returned with one of the hundreds of neatly folded American flags that every funeral parlor kept in stock and handed it to Packs. Packs whistled at the flag's ironed creases. "Look't that, sir!"

"Seems a crime to unfold it," Deth said.

"All right," Baines said, clapping the two Soldiers simultaneously on opposite elbows, "We'll see you fellows down there."

"You sure you know the way?" Packs asked, "You've been there before, right?"

"Sure, sure," the funeral director said, obviously not listening.

"Listen, Mr. Baines," Deth said, "If you've got the time, you should probably follow us down there. It's not the way it is on the map."

"Don't worry, gentlemen," Baines said, "Razorbacks don't get lost the way Sooners do."

Packs kicked a stone, unworried about taking the mirror-like shine off his chloroframs. The funeral procession was an hour late. "What's this 'My Place' all the joes keep talking about?" Packs said, "Should I be worried about it?"

Deth ran his finger across his left eyeball for the hundredth time. He hoped he wasn't scratching his retinas or anything. He checked himself in the Ford's outside rearview mirrors. The white of his eye was pink from being rubbed, but it wasn't pulsing with red burst vessels, so he felt okay to keep searching for the lost contact. "Huh?" Deth asked, "MySpace? It's just a website."

"Like Yahoo?" Packs pronounced Yahoo as though it were the first part of Yehuda, instead of like a cognate with the gross kid's drink Yoo-Hoo as most people did. Typical Packs. Deth lifted his upper eyelid and fished around gently. Where was that damn contact?

"Kind of," Deth said, "It's a big website where everybody has their own little website. So there'd be a Packs website and a Deth website and I could look at yours and you could look at mine."

"Like playing doctor?"

"I guess," Deth said, "There's *a lot* of porn on it. And most of it is Kenyan men pretending to be supermodels."

Although Deth knew that not every sexy girl on MySpace was a Kenyan man (surely some of them were Taiwanese or Ukrainian) one of the other lieutenants in the battalion had in fact very nearly married a Kenyan. Posing as a sexy Norwegian artist, the scammer had strung along Deth's colleague for some weeks. The hammer finally fell when "she" had been invited to an art festival in Nairobi, but sadly had been paid only in shillings, which, for political reasons, were impossible to convert to U.S. dollars. Deth had patiently explained to the naïve young man that he should not forward any money so his almost-fiancée could afford a plane ticket to the States, where he would surely get every dime back plus her eternal love.

"Well, now, how could you pretend that?" Packs asked.

"It's one of the wonders of the information age. God damn it!" Deth grunted in anger. He was right at the point where he would just take the right contact out and do the ceremony in glasses. He hated to do it, especially because it messed up the way he saluted, being as he was supposed to salute from the brim of the glasses when wearing them and from the eyebrow when not. But, more importantly, he hated being a four-eyes in uniform. He didn't wear the plastic Birth Control Goggles the Army optometrists always issued, but even with regular glasses he felt lame. And he wasn't enough of a macho jerkoff to make the men ignore his four-eyesedness and focus on his non-existent muscles with which he could beat any challenger that decided he didn't like his uppity lieutenant.

"What are you doing over there?"

"I lost my contact in my eye somewhere."

Packs hissed. "That's what you've been doing this whole time?"

"Yeah. If I don't get it out, it could really fuck up my sight."

"Why don't you just get that Lasik surgery?"

This time it was Deth's turn to hiss between his teeth. "Cut my eye open? I'd rather jam little plastic things into them every day for the rest of my life than go blind."

"Lots of guys get it and they don't go blind."

"It's got a 0.1% failure rate. Who do you know that's a bigger sad sack than me?"

"No one."

"No one. I'd be that 0.1%. Guaranteed. Not to mention, it hasn't been around that long. Nobody knows what happens after twenty years. Your eyes could just disintegrate. No one knows the long-term effects."

Packs shrugged. "So I shouldn't worry about Figueroa being on My Place?"

"Fig? Yes, I'd be worried about anything Fig does. He thinks he's a gangster now or something, doesn't he?"

"Oh, yeah, that 'Brown Pride' tattoo? I should submit an EO complaint, see if we could get orders to have it burned off."

"Well, you do that and Sergeant Phillips will have to get all his swastikas burned off."

"Yeah...yeah."

Deth fluttered his eyelids again. There was still clearly something stuck in there. The irritation was way too intense. Damn it. With a sigh he opened the car door and pulled out his glasses case, where he kept his spectacles and his contact container both. Cursing the lack of a place to wash his hands, he popped out the right contact, clenched his eyes shut until the burning from his dirty fingers went away, and threw his spectacles on. "Not too bad?" he asked.

"Better than having you scratching at your eyeballs the whole time."

"It's killing me not to be able to get this out."

"Yeah, well, just try not to think about it."

"Easy for you to say."

They leaned against the car, not caring how dirty it was against their uniforms. "You told him to follow us," Packs said.

"I know." Deth rubbed some invisible lint off the green sleeve of his dress jacket. "We should see if we can get these dry-cleaned after the funeral," Deth said.

"In less than a day?"

"Maybe it'll be an afternoon one tomorrow. Then we can pay for overnight."

"Just don't pay for it with the housing allowance. Or the food allowance."

Packs laughed at his own joke, his silent, almost Muttley-like chuckle. Deth was in no mood. The contact was still bothering him. He tried to silence the irritant with willpower, and his willpower was decidedly lacking. He glanced over Packs's uniform to distract himself. "Do you mind if I ask how you earned your Bronze Star, Sergeant? Is that rude to ask?"

Packs shrugged. "It's not rude to ask, it's just not a very interesting story."

"Well, you must've done something. Won a firefight or something."

"Nope. In fact, I never fired my weapon in anger. The only time I fired it in theater was at a berm in Kuwait.

Packs tapped his chest. "There's no V-device, sir. It's just for service, not valor."

Deth took a closer look at the blue, red, and white ribbon. It was, indeed, unadorned by a small gold "V."

"I just did a lot of logistical work, you know, moving platoons and batteries around. That was tough. And babysitting Big Smell is why I wasn't ashamed to accept it. But mostly I got it because I'm an E-7."

Deth furrowed his brow. "How do you mean? Awards aren't rank specific."

Packs grinned, a coprophage's grin. "You ever see a private get an MSM? Or a colonel get an AAM, for that matter?"

"No, I guess not."

"Well, there you go. There's rules and then there's rules, if you know what I mean."

"I do know what you mean." Deth had always been by-the-book, to a fault. As an officer, there was a mild expectation that he would dodge things, avoid formations, and disappear from PT and go fishing when work was light and the like. He had always tried to stick to what he was supposed to do and found that whenever he transgressed even in the slightest he was crucified. He hated watching other officers sham to excess and get away with it, and yet he envied them.

"But I guess you wanted a blood and guts story."

"Oh. Well, I wouldn't put it that way."

"I was the same way before I went. I'll tell you a story if you want. I almost died once."

"What happened?"

Packs sighed deeply. "I was flying on a Chinook. You been on a Chinook yet?"

"Once. At NALC."

"Then you know how the seats are just red ambulance stretchers. And not good stretchers either, like the bullshit M*A*S*H 4077 ones." Deth nodded, not really recalling, as his lone experience in a helicopter had been one of exhilaration rather than tedium. "Sometimes my ass has been sore before the Chinook even left the pad. But I blame the lead feet of the air traffic controllers for that. Sometimes we would just sit on the pad for hours and hours...but, anyway, it was dark when I boarded, 0300 local, I think, and I couldn't find the strap to my safety belt. I was thirsty, too, and I tried to take one of the bottles of water that they kept on board when some pissant lance corporal - did I mention this was the jarheads? - anyway, he yelled at me to put it back. Two cases of water and none for the passengers."

"They should've given you an Air Medal for flying without water."

"Yeah, well, he said it was in case they crashed. I guess that one bottle was gonna make or break our survival. Anyway, I'm tired, I'm thirsty, I'm unbuckled, I think I might've been sitting in between two seats because the bird was real empty. That might've been why I couldn't find the safety belt.

"So, anyway, out of nowhere, the whole bird does a half barrel-roll to the right. Port. Whatever bullshit they call it on a helicopter. Counter-clockwise. My ruck goes flying. I grabbed the seat and I was just about to shit my pants because I thought they would keep going and I would fall on my damn head twice on the one time I didn't buckle my belt. Probably break my damn neck and be a casualty. Maybe then they would've let me have some damn water.

"But they stopped and I relaxed, or, at least as relaxed as you could be when your seat just turned vertical and you're clinging to it for dear fucking life. But then instead of straightening out, they did another half-barrel roll all the way the other way, so this time my chair was vertical again but I was on the other side."

"Holy shit."

"Yeah, I guess. I had heard stories about birds taking small arms fire but I had never been in one before. I looked out the window or the porthole or whatever the fuck they called it, as best as I could, but I couldn't see anything. Then we straightened out finally.

"There was this Navy Corpsman sitting across from me. That's like, the jarhead equivalent of a medic. He just stared at me, and there was terror in his eyes, and his face was pale like the moon, even in the low light he stood out like a white rat's ass. I just hoped I didn't look that bad to him. Then, real calm like, like nothing was going on, he opened one of his own barf bags, puked into it, folded it up however you're supposed to fold it, and stowed it in his ruck."

"Did you find out what happened?"

"Not really. When we got on the ground I found my buddy the medic and asked him what he saw and if those Marine Corps assholes had just been doing barrel rolls for fun. He said he saw the flares go off, which I guess was what they do to try to set off RPGs and stuff prematurely, but he didn't see the RPG.

"When we walked into Catfish Air - that's what the airstrip in Balad was called - a couple of female officers walked up to us and asked if we'd been on the bird that got attacked. You know, all the birds fly in pairs."

"You mean the helicopters or the females?"

"Ha ha. Anyway, that was when I found out we had really been RPGed. Nobody saw it but the accompanying bird."

"That's a hell of a story, Sergeant. Man, I wish I had a story like that. I've got to get Over There."

"If all you want is stories, I can tell you stories 'til the cows come home. You don't have to go to war for that."

"It's not the same when it happened to somebody else."

"Maybe so. But you want to know what the real fucked up thing was?"

"What?"

"It was the only exciting thing that happened to me the whole fucking war."

Deth took another pass at trying to knock the lost contact out of his eye. He'd been unlucky for nearly two hours now. He'd just have to accept his spectacles and adjust his hand movements slightly.

When the funeral procession arrived, Baines stepped out of the lead car and smiled lamely at them. "Sorry, guys," he said, "I got lost."

After the service, when they stepped into the car, Deth spotted a tiny shriveled chunk of lint or something on the floor. He picked it up and examined it. "Oh," he said, "Here's my contact. It was on the floor the whole time."

12

Deth was worried about Packs. He never thought he would have been for a man all but twice his age, a man closer to a father than a peer. And yet, Packs was one of his Soldiers. He was his top Soldier, the Audie Murphy of Deth's brief military career, but a Soldier under his charge nonetheless.

The reason for Deth's unusual concern was that Packs was not eating. Deth had finally convinced the man to stop at a seafood restaurant - admittedly a dicey prospect in landlocked Missouri - but he wasn't entirely convinced that was the root cause of Packs's seeming dyspepsia.

Because, true to form, Packs had ordered the surf and turf, and though Deth wasn't entirely sure how Packs felt about the surf, he knew that the untouched turf signaled something dire in the man's mood. Something so dire he hadn't seen it in the last three weeks they'd been on the road together, nor in the two-odd years they had worked together prior to that.

Deth poked around at the catfish that he assumed had been at least somewhat locally sourced, filled with crabmeat that he was certain had not been flown in overnight from the Western seaboard. Something warred inside him, his priggish nature and his sense of common decency, he supposed. Or perhaps the priggishness of military protocol warred with the priggishness of putting one's Soldiers before oneself. Whether angel or devil, the side that suggested he should broach the matter won out. "Did you, ah...did you stop and see your wife when we were in Lawton?"

Packs shook his head. "That'd be worse than not stopping."

Deth nodded and went back to toying with his stuffed filet. "Say, do you want that lobster tail?" Deth asked, moving his fork towards Packs's plate in a threatening manner.

Packs threw his arms around his plate and raked it closer towards himself, though it hadn't been all that far from the edge of the table to begin with. That was enough to solve the symptom, though Deth doubted that it would make a dent in the underlying problem. He was thankful (for once) to be a lonely, spiteful little man. Being on the road didn't affect him one way or the other. But Packs was married, with kids supposedly, and...

Hmm. Deth furrowed his brow, though he hoped he wasn't furrowing it. Packs had been on unaccompanied tours (Korea, Bosnia) as well as his wartime deployment. He had left his family for months, in some cases years, at a time. What was so bad about three weeks?

"I suppose I'll have to get married," Deth said, considering how he might breach the walls another way, "They always say officers have to."

"Captains have to," Packs agreed, "It's okay while you're a lieutenant. But unmarried majors tend to be unsuccessful."

"Why is that, I wonder?"

Packs shrugged. "FRG meetings. Family Readiness Groups. You know, hens clubs."

Packs bocked like a chicken to Deth's mild disdain. (He had long since gotten over the urge to correct Packs's moments of political incorrectness. They were of different generations, and he had too much respect for the man anyway.)

"And you've got to have parties and box socials and stuff like that when you're a commander. Oh, and your wife shouldn't work. That'd be as bad as having no wife."

"Should she be barefoot and pregnant, too?"

"Ideally," Packs said, although he smiled, recognizing that Deth was joking.

"Well, the army's certainly not the ACLU," Deth said.

Packs shuddered at the mention of such a communist fifth column. "Nah, but it's just like the real world," Packs said, "You know, civilians think we all just listen to Rush Limbaugh and want to kill people. But the army's just like America. Statistically and every which other way. Like, take you, sir. I know you're an Ivy League snob."

Deth snorted. "I went to state school."

"Well, still, you hate when I talk about women and queers and that kind of thing."

"I don't hate when you talk about them," Deth said, "I just hate when you talk about them like they're second-class citizens."

Packs shrugged. "But we're not at each other's throats," Packs said, "We work together just fine, you and I. I don't kick Fig because he's Puerto Rican or Phillips because he's...whatever. My wife's Korean, did you know that?"

Deth smiled. So maybe he hadn't left her behind during his time in Korea. Maybe he had met her there. "I didn't think you were a racist, Sergeant."

"Well, I'm not," Packs said, finally at least cutting into his steak, which was still pink though almost cold, "That's what's great about the army, you've got to work with all types. All over the country. And we're all just green inside. It's very..."

Packs shrugged. Deth thought he might have wanted to say "democratic," or maybe he just couldn't think of a word. "Was Korea really as bad as they say?"

"You know the fastest way to make E-5?"

Deth shook his head. He found the enlisted promotion system arcane beyond belief. There were points and boards and it seemed a whole mess. He didn't find the largely seniority-based system of officer promotion to be superior, but at least it was easier to understand.

"Go to Korea as an E-6," Packs finished the old axe, which was brand new to Deth.

Deth laughed out loud. He had indeed never heard that one. "Is that true?"

"Everyone drinks too much," Packs said, "There's nothing else to do. And the MPs are all out to get you. Well, you know, there are some guys who take the opportunity to really buckle down and, you know, get their correspondence courses and maybe their associate's. But that's like...5%. 95% go over and either develop a drinking problem, or, if they went over there drunks already, get chaptered out."

"Not anymore," Deth said.

The tides were already changing. Drinking had always been accepted in the army with a wink and a smile. But now it was becoming all but impossible to even kick out drug addicts. Users were still being deployed, under the dubious logic that being away from the states would make it impossible for them to use. Deth had already sat on a board that had deployed two Soldiers who had tested positive for cocaine. They wouldn't get promoted, but they had probably been using to get out of the deployment, so their "punishment," such as it was, was to not be punished. Now that was some Mila-18 logic right there.

Otherwise, they were letting all sorts of undesirable types in. Two wars would do that to a volunteer army. Gangbangers (real gangbangers, not fakers like Figueroa), fatbodies who couldn't shit out two push-ups, guys with tattoos on their faces and hands. Anybody, really, that was willing to volunteer was being pushed through Basic and it was left up to platoon leadership like Packs and Deth to straighten out the grunts who should've been culled out the second they stepped into the recruiting office.

"No," Packs agreed, "Not anymore."

"So were you in the 95% or the 5%?"

"What?"

"You were saying some guys drank and..."

"Well, I can hold my liquor. I don't know if you know that about me, sir." Packs was grinning with pride.

"Well, shit, let's get the bill with the card so we can belly up to the bar."

"What's your wife's name?" Deth asked finally.

"Yu-Ni," Packs said.

They had been talking about Packs's exploits in Korea and Germany long enough that Deth felt it okay to meander back into the personal stuff. Packs either didn't notice or didn't care. He took another pull on his beer.

"Remember, Sergeant, that shit's not 3% like in OK."

Packs dismissed the young LT's concerns with a sloppy wave. The bartender approached them. "Say, you boys G.I.s?"

Shit. He had heard the word "sergeant" being tossed around. Deth blamed himself.

"Fire police," Deth said, "You know, as long as I've got you here, I've been meaning to ask you about that extinguisher."

"Oh," the bartender said, "Let me grab my manager. Hey, how about a round on the house, anyway, boys?"

As soon as the worried little man scuttled off, Deth and Packs clinked their glasses together. "Someday we should come clean to these restaurant jerkoffs," Packs said.

"Hell no," Deth said, "That's worse than telling them it's your birthday at TGI Friday's."

Deth didn't doubt that Packs had his own reasons for never wanting to reveal his military affiliation in bars and restaurants. Perhaps he'd just been around the block once or twice and found all the fuss exhausting. Of course, it was just as likely that Packs had a genuine sense of humility after all his years as a Soldier. Either way, Deth had to agree that all of the fawning and question-answering was not worth it for the occasional free drink.

Deth had a very specific reason, though, why he never said who he was to civilians. He had been put in fear for his life once. It hadn't been a terrorist threat or anything; in fact, it had been much more banal.

After his commissioning, Deth had been very excited and proud to say he was a Soldier, not to mention an officer, at every available opportunity. So many places had a 10% discount, and even if they didn't, he liked the fawning. Once he had mentioned it in a bar and not only had the waiter paid for a round of his drinks, Deth didn't pay for another drink the whole rest of the night. So there was that nice aspect to it.

But then there was the darker side to it. In the middle of OBC, Deth and a few of his friends had been caught at class late, just one of the hazards of school. His friends Vu and Sanchez had decided that they should all go to Outback for dinner directly. It was already 1900 and none of them felt like getting changed. Being as they were coming directly from work, there was nothing in the regulations stating that they couldn't eat in uniform, as long as they didn't drink.

All had gone well at first, and being as Lawton was a military town, the fawning and the uproar over their uniforms was more subdued than it had been back home. Which had been fine until Deth had gone to take a Class I download.

The stalls in the Outback men's room (it said "bruces" or "dingoes" or something stupid on the door) were not the tightly constructed, close-fitting kind that Deth and any reasonable person preferred. The gaps between post and door were so wide that full-on eye contact was possible with people passing outside, as Deth was about to find out. An old drunk stumbled in, although, really, he probably wasn't that old, just in his forties most likely, but was decidedly stinking drunk.

The man's eye filled up the whole of Deth's vision as he sat there, ACU bottoms around his ankles. "Yer a Soldier," the drunk slurred.

"Yes, sir," Deth replied, trying not to take too much offense at this breach of restroom etiquette.

"I was a Soldier once," the man said, "You guys are great for doing this, you know that?"

"Yes, thank you, sir," Deth said, breathing a sigh of relief.

It wasn't as though the man had stopped looking him full in the face as he attempted to do his business, but at least he didn't seem to be the type to call him a babykiller or decide he had to be beaten up to prove a point to his fellow gangbangers.

"Whatshur rank?"

"I'm an officer," Deth said, non-committally, trying to determine whether he could pull his pants up with his shit only half shat and still retain his dignity.

But that had been exactly the wrong response. "A *officer?*" the drunk intoned in a pained voice, "A officer? I knew a officer onesh."

"Oh?" Deth said, really starting to panic and wondering if there was any way he could get Sanchez's attention from this far away. Vu was a female, so she wouldn't be rushing in to help him. He decided there was no real way to call to Sanchez, except maybe to pull out his cell phone now, which would probably set the drunk off.

The drunk proceeded to unfurl a lengthy, semi-coherent story about why he had been put out of the service. Deth didn't really catch a whole lot of it, tensing as he was for the moment when the man inevitably busted into the stall and decided to engage Deth in what would be the first real fight of his life, at a distinct disadvantage with his dick flapping around and a still-shitty bottom. He prayed that Sanchez would walk in, or anybody, really, being as normal people would no doubt find this situation unnerving or at least the drunk would realize he was acting contrary to good human decency. For some reason, though, the good patrons of Outback were holding onto their shit like it was gold.

"And then, do you know what that *officer*tol' me?" the drunk asked, pronouncing Deth's chosen profession as though it were the foulest invective on this side of the solar system and snapping Deth back, unfortunately, into the "conversation."

"No," Deth said calmly, "What did he tell you?"

The drunk leaned in so that his leering red eye was no longer visible, but now his beherped lips were. A wave of hot, funky breath washed over Deth and chilled him to the bone. For the first time in his life he was certain that someone was going to do willing, unpleasant bodily harm to him. He just waited for the door to burst in.

"He said," the drunk explicated, "'Sometimes you're the bird. And sometimes you're the statue.'" He waited a moment for Deth to respond, but Deth had nothing with which to respond except a cold clammy pallor and a dry, defiant throat. "'Sometimes you're the bird!'" the maniac repeated, "'And sometimes you're the statue!' Son of a bitch said that to me. To me!" He pounded his own chest as hard as Deth had been thinking he would thump him. "*Officers*," he repeated one last time and then wandered off to another stall.

Deth hadn't wasted a moment wiping his ass, tugging up his pants, and running his hands under the sink just long enough to make them marginally clean enough to touch his food. He returned to Vu and Sanchez, who asked him whether he had fallen in before he related the whole story as the pounding in his chest slowly subsided.

Deth ruminated over all of this while the bartender they had told they were fire police poured out a round on the house. Oddly, he never did manage to find his supervisor. Deth had wasted some time trying to think of something to say about the fire extinguisher in case the manager did show, but instead of making up something about it being the wrong brand or something, he decided to just ask when the last time it had been filled was. It turned out to be a moot point. "You know, I've got to get Over There someday," Deth said after a while.

"So you keep saying."

"Well, how would you feel to spend your whole adult life training for war, and to have two wars on, and to have everybody you know be a veteran, and to never go yourself?"

Packs cocked his head, just short of a nod of understanding. "I guess I'd feel like a sack of shit."

"Rightly so," Deth said, "My mother is happy I haven't gone. She hopes I never go."

Packs rolled his eyes. "Telling ma was the worst," he said, "You'd think she was the one going to Eye-raq."

"Mothers," Deth agreed, "Mine *made* me go to college, then I got through my whole first semester and found out she wasn't paying a dime for it. Then when I got a ROTC scholarship, you'd've thought I broke her legs."

"I always figured you for a guy who joined up on September 12th."

Deth shook his head. "Nope. About a year before. But I didn't quit on September 12th. And that's more than I can say about a lot of guys I know. Scholarship guys, too."

"Bet they didn't have to pay back a dime."

"It pays to be a pussy. What about your wife, though, what did she say?"

"When I joined up? Hell, we didn't meet until I was a E-5."

"No, no, about going Over There."

"Oh, to the Sandbox? Or Grafenwoehr?" Deth shrugged. "Well, she could've come with to Graf, but she didn't want to learn a third language. I sent her home so she enjoyed it. Funny thing is, when I went to Eye-raq, she didn't want to go home. She wanted to stay in Hood. Friends and all that shit. She was a big wheel in the FRG, and there were enough Korean wives that she didn't feel left out."

"That's funny."

"Well, American living is hard to deny. A lot of those wives come over, and they stay in the house and do nothing but clean all day and bring your slippers and a martini at 1700. Then as soon as they step out of the house that one time..." Packs snapped his fingers and laughed.

"Regular fat Americans, huh?"

"Oh, in a flash. You know, she was really good about the deployment. Kept herself busy, took care of the finances, all that stuff. Never called me crying, even though I knew she was crying. Didn't want me to worry about the home front, I guess. She knew that if I was off my game, guys died and, you know, I guess she didn't want that on my conscience. Or hers."

"She really buckled down, huh?"

Packs nodded. "It's much worse now because she didn't buckle down for me to be gone for three weeks. She buckled down for one day, and then every day you get stuck out on funeral, it's like getting stung. She just keeps getting stung. I wish I could tell her I was going to be gone for a year, that'd be easier than calling her 365 times and saying I'll be gone for a day."

13

"Don't blink."

Deth looked up from his reverie and scanned the side of the road. Tree after tree went whizzing by, the ground was bare of grass and muddy, and only the occasional mailbox at the head of a dirt trail suggested human habitation. He saw no animals, or anything of note. "What am I looking for?"

"Just don't blink."

Deth's eyes rolled back and forth in their sockets, scanning. No tree looked very different from any other, and he made sure to step back and observe the forest as a whole so that he wouldn't miss it for the trees. Nothing jumped out at him. He checked the other side, the driver's side, too. Still nothing.

He pretended he was in Iraq, in the Track Commander's seat of a HMMWV, although he would've preferred being up behind the

50 cal, but his men had insisted that he sit down for his own safety's sake. He tried to spot IEDs, hidden in junk and invisible under phony rocks and carried sometimes by trained dogs and the like. Even people, strapped with suicide vests. But there were no people or dogs on this lonely stretch of Missouri highway, and the junk and detritus was unlikely to hide any home-brewed bombs here in the States.

"Did you blink?"

"Why, what'd I miss?"

"I knew you'd blink."

"What was it?"

Packs was smiling. "We just passed Ft. Leonard Wood."

Deth turned all the way around in his seat to look back. He still didn't see anything. "It's not nice to mess with officers. We have very delicate egos."

"I'm not messing with you, sir," Packs said with a laugh, "We just passed Ft. Lost-in-the-Woods. You must've blinked and missed it."

"Yeah, I guess so." Suddenly, Deth scowled as the full meaning of what had just transpired struck him. "You say that's Ft. Leonard Wood back there?"

Packs nodded.

"And you're not playing with me because I'm a dumb First Louey?"

"Nope."

"Then how come we're out here planting their dead? Why don't they cover Missouri?"

"Couldn't tell you, sir," Packs said, "Alls I know is, we cover Oklahoma, Arkansas, and Misery."

"Shit in my mouth," Deth said, not sure what else to say.

The funeral went flawlessly, no scarlet socks or feuding family members or anything. One of the mourners was even a ROTC cadet in a dress uniform of sorts that was a Frankenstein of current and previous uniform parts. (Deth's own uniforms had been much the same way when he had been in ROTC.) Deth was unsurprised to learn that everyone had agreed that he should present the flag to the cadet.

Back standing next to Packs, waiting for the funeral to end, Packs asked, "What's up with the little dots?"

Rather than any recognizable rank, the cadet was wearing a single silver pip in each place on his uniform where rank normally would have gone.

"Cadet ranks are bullshit," Deth said, "Rockers and chevrons are squared off for cadet enlisted ranks and cadet officer ranks are all dots and diamonds. Three dots is a captain, and a diamond is a major and two diamonds is a light colonel."

"So he's a Second Louey?"

"Yes. Well, maybe. Also, if you're not hanging around other cadets, like if you're a cadet but you're working with the real army, you're just supposed to wear one dot like that. So he could be anything."

"That's stupid."

"It is pretty stupid. An old guy looking for directions once called me captain when I was wearing one dot like that."

"Do I have to salute him?"

"Um...I think, yes. You're supposed to treat him like a third lieutenant. Higher than a warrant officer but lower than an O-1."

"I'm not going to."

"I didn't think you would. A specialist saluted me once and he told me he was going to ahead of time. That was it."

After all that discussion, Packs and Deth were astonished when the cadet walked right by them, flag in hand, and nodded at them. "Gentlemen," was all he said.

They exchanged a glance. "I would've put money on it he would've come to chat us up," Packs said.

"Cadets do love the real army," Deth said, "Oh, but, well, maybe he was prior service."

"You get a lot of those?"

"Well, I did, but I went to a state school. Expensive colleges, like our battalion headquarters, they don't usually have a lot of prior service. Which makes them dicks."

A skinny man in his late twenties or early thirties did walk up to them, though. "Gentlemen," he said, shaking each of their hands in turn.

"Sir," they each said, nodding gently and stiffening their backs.

He didn't move off. "So, what, ah, what are you guys?" he said, pointing to each of the Soldiers in turn.

Deth was tempted to say, "Males," but held his tongue. Packs was ready to speak.

"I'm an E-7," he said, "And Lieutenant Deth is an O-2." Deth wasn't sure whether Packs had done that on purpose, but civilians never responded to pay grade. Civilians all had it in their heads that ranks were the be-all end-all of military service, and couldn't quite wrap it around their heads that a 1SG had more power than a 2LT, even though the latter outranked the former. And they always wanted to hear "sergeant" or "general" and never E-5 or O-7.

So, true to form, the skinny man turned to Deth and said, "Oh, a lieutenant, eh? That's pretty high up there."

Out of the corner of his eye, Deth saw Packs was smiling. So he had done it on purpose. "I suppose," Deth said, not sure how to respond.

"And they had you out here doing Uncle Percy's funeral? Don't you have some privates or something who can do it?"

"Well, sir," Deth said, glad that at least he knew a concrete answer to this question, "The army is obliged to send someone of equal or greater rank to the deceased to serve as honor guard at a funeral."

The skinny man whistled loudly, appreciatively. "So if we were burying some, ah, colonel or something, they'd have a general or even a major out here doing it?"

Deth didn't bother to correct him. "Yes, sir, I believe so."

Nodding, the skinny man turned and then scratched his head for a moment with just his forefinger. "But Uncle Percy was just a corporal. That doesn't outrank a lieutenant, does it?"

"No, sir," Packs said, "But also sometimes when a funeral team is already on the road, they'll ask us to stay on the road rather than send out a new team. We were in Arkansas last night, and a new team would have had to come all the way from...Oklahoma City." Packs didn't bother to say Lawton. Nobody knew Lawton.

"Oh, yeah, that makes sense," the skinny man said, "And as long as Percy didn't outrank you, you're okay, right?"

"Precisely, sir."

The civilian then did something that Deth had never encountered before. He stood in front of Deth and executed what he seemed to think was a salute. Baffled, but too inured from receiving salutes in four years of ROTC and two of active duty, Deth returned the honor. When he moved on to Packs and did the same thing, Packs remained immobile, stony. It was improper to salute an NCO, but it was even more improper to deck a civilian for doing so, so Packs refrained from his obvious desire. When the man had gone, Deth said, "What was that all about?"

"Who knows?" Packs responded, "Civilians are weird."

14

A clang-a-lang-a-lang came at Deth's hotel room door, which had one of those little metal knockers. He snorted, awakened, glanced around. In one hand he held a bottle of Mad Dog (despite swearing off the stuff,) but luckily it was sealed and therefore not leaking all over the bed. He looked at the clock, which was the only thing in the room that wasn't blurry without his glasses or contacts, being bright red and shiny. 0315. "...Is it?" Deth grunted.

"Hey, sir, it's me!"

"Well, no shit, Packs," Deth grunted, although he wasn't sure if Packs's preternatural hearing would have allowed him to hear it or not.

Regardless of whether he did or not, Packs shouted, "Sir, I found something you've got to see."

Deth stumbled out of bed, scratching at his armpit through the brown, GI-issue t-shirt. He opened the door and looked at Packs, his eyes watering from the light of the hallway. "...Hell is it?"

"Come on, sir," Packs said, attempting to give a non-sexual version of the come-hither gesture, "Downstairs. You've got to see this."

Deth held up his arms in a shrug and let it drop. Sure. Why not. Whatever. He stumbled back into his room, found something approximating pants, and pulled them on over his boxers. (The army may have been able to tell him everything else to wear, but he sure as shit wasn't going to give up boxers for them.)

Packs led the lieutenant down the hall and into the elevator, rubbing his hands together and making various exclamations of unbridled and incomprehensible glee and excitement as they went. Finally, when they reached the lobby, Deth saw that Packs had been at the hotel's courtesy computer all night, a surprise if ever there was any, since Deth had doubted numerous times whether Packs even knew how to use a computer. "Don't give me that look," Packs said, seeming to read Deth's mind, "Who do you think typed up all those platoon memos?"

Deth shrugged. The walls of their offices back at the battery were indeed lined with memos signed by the Ostrich and himself and all the other platoon leaders who had come and gone over time. "What are we looking at?" Deth asked, sitting down in a chair facing away from the computer screen.

"Check this out." Packs pointed at the screen, which Deth leaned forward to peer at sidewise. He had called up his AKO account and had apparently been poring through e-mails all night.

One had a date stamp which Deth noted as towards the end of Packs's deployment in late 2005.

"IG complaint," Deth read sleepily, punctuating it with a yawn. Then he sat up sharply. He pulled the wrong-way-facing chair around and faced the right way. "Oh, you mentioned this before. I didn't know you still had it. It's against Big Smell?" Packs nodded. "Well, let's see it."

Packs clicked the attached file, which Deth noted with a little sadness was a Word .doc instead of a .pdf. That meant it was probably just a draft and had never been signed and scanned to be sent in formally. "You never sent it in?"

"No," Packs admitted mournfully.

"Why not?"

"Well, I've got a career, you know," Packs said, "They say they don't punish whistleblowers, but that's a lot of horseshit. And as a senior enlisted..." Packs kind of trailed off.

"You're just supposed to take it?"

"Yeah, basically."

"Okay, let's see it." Packs opened the file. While AKO was doing whatever AKO does, which incomprehensibly takes minutes instead of seconds where seconds would do in the civilian world, Deth stood and walked over to the all-night bar to get a cup of coffee. All they had was that powdered creamer that Deth hated.

Deth was an all-or-nothing kind of guy. Despite his time in the army, he still liked his coffee the way The Wolf from Pulp Fiction did: lots of cream and lots of sugar. Without both, he took it black, the way he knew he would have to learn how to take it to succeed in the army. He only ever drank it black in the field, and even then under protest, although he had to admit that over time he had developed a close approximation to what could be called a taste for it. He didn't spit it out.

Styrofoam cup in hand, he returned to the hotel computer and sat with Packs. The file had finally come up. It was only a few megabytes, and AKO had insisted on taking the entire length of time that it took a lieutenant to get a cup of coffee to open it. "No wonder we're losing the war," Deth didn't say out loud, for various reasons.

Deth scanned the letterhead and the subject line, recognizing his unit and smiling at the subject line "WRITTEN COMPLAINT AGAINST MAJ DAVID Z. BRANNIGAN." He scrolled down the first paragraph, which related the story Packs had already told him about Brannigan sending his men one at a time against general orders to a FOB that couldn't support them, although in a little better detail and in more professional language.

He took a sip of his coffee and instantly regretted it when he reached the second paragraph. He didn't quite go through with a Bugs Bunny-style spit-take, but he did nearly choke on his mouthful of hot black liquid, slam his palm on the desk, and swallow as fast as he could so that he could set down his Styrofoam cup and laugh between fits of coughing. "What?" Packs asked innocently, "What part did you reach?"

Although he had recovered enough to breathe, Deth remained too stunned to speak. He merely pointed at the computer screen, indicating the offending area. "'I personally witnessed as MAJ Brannigan downloaded games and racist pornography onto the SIPR net,'" Packs recited mechanically, as he might a risk assessment for a hearty morning run, "Yeah, that's right. What's so funny about that?"

"He put porn...on the secret drive?" Packs nodded. "I thought you told me this guy was a big time Bible thumper."

"Oh, the biggest. But you know what they say about Bible thumpers. They're always trying to cover something up."

"And what...pray tell...is racist pornography?" Packs rolled his eyes and nodded. He scrolled down quickly through the memo and Deth's eyes widened as he saw the list of attachments. One of them was titled "Very Sexy - Pornographic Word Document."

"Pornographic...Word Document?" Deth asked, wondering if Packs had made some kind of computer terminology error, but now, having seen him actually use a PC in person, somehow doubting it.

"Wait for it," Packs said. Packs scrolled down to where Packs had indeed copied and pasted an exceedingly foul and degenerate short story about a white woman who ended up fucking a black valet. It somehow never quite reached the production values of even the '70s style porn videos which Deth found laughable. Most compelling of all, perhaps, was the fact that it **WAS** a short story. Deth himself had, on occasion, been reduced to jerking off to a Maxim or a Playboy, but as far as he was concerned the hierarchy of porn went: video, nude photo, underwear photo. He had scarcely been aware that erotic fiction was a nascent genre.

"Blue-eyed black buck..." Deth read, barely able to keep his composure, "Is this for real?"

"Real as the nose on your face, sir," Packs said, "Let me tell you a story."

Deth got up to get another coffee, his head shaking like a pendulum. He knew there was no way he was going back to sleep at this point. "Go ahead, I'm listening."

"After we left Kuwait, we went straight to Balad and we hit the ground around midnight. Big Smell had left with the forward section, I think because he didn't want to have to qualify in Kuwait."

"Because he couldn't?"

"Most likely."

"Wouldn't he have been carrying..."

"A pistol, yes." Qualifying with a pistol was staggeringly easy. Deth still dreamt of the day - coming soon, hopefully - when he would move on from his position of platoon leader and as a staff officer or Battery OpsO he would finally get to qualify on an M9. He hardly even needed practice to do so. "So we dropped off our gear at the transient tents (which let me tell you, is not a place you want to stay,) and then Big Smell decided he wanted to take me and the BC and the 1SG and a couple of others to midnight chow."

Deth had not been fully aware of midnight chow until just that moment, but it made sense. Four meals a day meant that operations didn't really have to stop. Most joes would still be able to get three hots a day that way, whether midnight counted as breakfast or dinner.

"So we walk into D-FAC 3 and Bananarama is blaring over the speakers."

Deth was surprised that Packs knew who Bananarama was, but he was more interested in why. Then again, he was older, so maybe that was around the time his pop culture knowledge dwindled out. "Why...?"

"It's always like a party at midnight chow. I don't know why. I guess to keep the men's spirits up."

"Makes sense. I guess."

"Did you know our cooks don't even serve Over There?"

"What do you mean?"

"Well, there aren't enough cooks to go around, I guess. So there's one or two per D-FAC, mostly I guess to make sure the food's all cooked through and it isn't horsemeat or something. But most of the work is done by Pakistanis."

"The fuck? How does that work?"

"Oh, yeah, Pakistanis in the chow halls and Ugandans guarding the towers."

"Ugandans?" Deth didn't even know what to say to that. "Why were there foreign nationals on our posts? More importantly, are those guys even part of the Coalition?"

Packs shook his head. "They're all contractors."

Deth rolled his eyes. "Fucking contractors."

Packs held up a finger. "Now, now, not all contractors are bad. I knew some guys from Lockheed and Boeing Over There that were real stand-up guys. They deployed with us and they knew how to fix all our launchers better than I did. But...yeah, some of them are shitheads, too."

"That whole thing in Fallujah was started by contractors." Packs shrugged. "I'm sorry," Deth said, "You were about to tell me about the Pakistanis in the chow hall."

"No, I wasn't," Packs said, rubbing his chin, "I was about to tell you about meeting Big Smell my first night."

"Oh, yeah."

"But about the dotheads in the chow hall," Packs said anyway, "The way I figure it, Cheney hires one of his companies to run the chow halls. Then they say, 'Well, if we send Americans Over There to do it, we have to pay them 100 grand a year or whatever plus benefits. But if we send foreign nationals Over There, we can pay them circus peanuts and pocket the rest.' So they do. So that's how we end up with Ugandans guarding our bases and Pakistanis cooking our food and South Korean fairies giving us haircuts."

"South Korean..." Deth just kind of trailed off.

"We're getting off track. What was I talking about? Oh, yeah, the first night. We arrived after Big Smell had been there a little while on advanced party. I went and got an omelet..."

"No steak?"

"Well, a steak omelet. And we sit down to start, you know, talking about the future. What we're they're for. So you know how I told you we didn't really report to battalion and we didn't really report to anybody in theater?"

"You did tell me that."

"Well, we ask Big Smell, 'Sir, who do we work for?' You know what his response is?"

"America?"

"Close enough. He says, 'MNC-I.'"

Multi-National Corps Iraq. In other words, the headquarters of the entire war. Deth leaned back and took a sip of his coffee. "No, he didn't."

Packs gave him an eye that he was starting to get used to. It said, "I've already told you this much about this guy and you still don't believe me?"

"Well, what did you say?"

"I didn't say anything," Packs said, "I didn't want to be involved. You remember, I met Big Smell before, running. I thought, hey, maybe going to war would change a guy, make him realize what's important and make him stop being a dumb jerkoff, or at least knock enough sense into him to realize he was being a dumb jerkoff and just get out of everybody's way. I left it for the BC and the 1SG to deal with."

"This is the same BC who talked him out of resigning that time when they erased his guidance from the chalkboard?"

"Yeah, but that hadn't happened yet."

"Oh, sure, I guess I knew that. So what'd BC say?"

"Well, what do you think he said? He said, 'Well, sure, sir, we all work for MNC-I, but who do we work for directly?'"

"'MNC-I!'"

"Then 1SG tried. 'Sir, the general doesn't sign our NCOERs. What we mean is, who do we work for?'" Packs assumed the nasally, overblown tone he used when imitating Brannigan. Deth often wondered how much of it was an exaggeration and how much of it was Packs simply trying to be true to form. Either way, Brannigan must have sounded as stupid as he acted.

"'First Sergeant, who's the commander here?' Nobody answered. 'I'm the commander. And I'm telling you, we report to MNC-I!'"

"How'd that work out for you?"

"We found an Artillery colonel in Balad who was willing to sign our awards and shit. Then - oh, you'll love this, sir - guess what he started talking about?" Deth held out his hands palm-up in surrender. Every sarcastic guess he had been able to make about Brannigan's behavior had so far been totally outshadowed by the seeming truth of it. "He started talking about how much flight time he had logged in the, you know, two weeks he had been in country."

15

Cold, exhausted, and unable to stop yawning, Deth stood alongside Packs, who was handling himself a lot better than Deth was that morning. Packs never seemed to need more than the four hours the army allotted him for sleep at night, and Deth had certainly seen him functioning at full physical capacity with far less.

"Come on, sir," Packs said, punching his superior with an attempt at playfulness that felt like anything but to Deth's now aching arm, "It's not like you've been marching all night."

"How do you do it?" Deth moaned, rubbing his arms with his hands to warm up, "You don't sleep and you never look tired..."

"Exercise."

Deth scowled blackly. Everyone always told him to work out more than the mandatory five times a week. "PT is just team-building," the admonition usually went. Especially for an officer, expected to get a 300 on his PT test and set an example for his Soldiers, even if he was a buffoon at every other aspect of his job. Maybe he would have to start doing it, just so he could be bright-eyed and bushy-tailed every morning like Packs.

Sometimes joes spoke of lifting in Bosnia or Korea (or, more recently, in Iraq at places that had gyms.) Deth's Professor of Military Science in ROTC had described it as prison-lifting. "There's nothing else to do there," the PMS had explained.

Deth didn't believe that. He could conceive of thousands of things he would rather do before he would start lifting weights just to pass the time. Now, in the age of DVDs, pushing a metal stick was the most exciting thing you could imagine? He had read once about a Soldier with a crap forest-guarding detail in Germany who had played Dungeons and Dragons 16 hours a day. He couldn't imagine finding another officer to play D&D with, or, for that matter, getting a junk detail that didn't require any attention, but still, he would rather do almost anything in the world than lift weights for fun.

"...And you eat and eat and you never gain weight," Deth concluded, "I've never seen you bust tape."

"Ah, well that's different," Packs said, "Do you want to light up? I don't think they're going to be here for a while?"

Deth glanced around the boneyard. It was a step up from the one they had tromped through Farmer Brown's property to no avail to find, but it was still a damn East Bumfuck, Oklahoma, cemetery.

"Yeah, why not?" Deth replied, lighting up a Lucky, "Here's hoping they don't get lost."

They left their positions of mild parade rest and leaned against the car. From experience, Deth wiped the grime from the area of the car he intended to lean against. "You want to know what the secret is to passing the tape test?" Packs asked.

Deth sighed. He was chubby enough that he never met the army's height-weight ratio, which was all ratified and written down in a book that probably hadn't been updated since World War II, when people had walked or ridden horses everywhere and had to go outside to the outhouse to piss at night. He did, however, always pass the tape test, a ridiculously outmoded and peculiar test whereby the circumference of one's belly had to meet a certain ratio with the circumference of his or her neck.

Deth found the whole thing more than a little demeaning, but only slightly for himself, since he always passed. He didn't care about exercise, but he wasn't out-of-shape. What he found really upsetting about the whole situation was that weight was completely independent of the quality of the Soldier. He had Soldiers who got the coveted 300 on their PT tests and couldn't pass weight or tape because they were built like brick houses. (Granted, those were the exceptions rather than the rule, and he understood that the army didn't want to underwrite a bunch of disgusting fatbodies.)

Still, Deth had noticed that, more than anything else, the tape test was really a method for enforcing the old boy's club. Since 1SG conducted the tape test, the joes that 1SG liked inevitably passed. (Or officers, who were not quite untouchable, but were not to be made fools of if it could be avoided. The Brannigans of the world choking themselves out during PT tests excepted, of course.) And when 1SG wanted to get rid of a guy, it might just so happen that he wouldn't pass weight or tape. It was somewhat ironical that being a meathead protected you from that. "Enlighten me."

"Don't eat."

Deth rolled his eyes. "Oh, thanks, Sergeant! I'll have to put a call in to the Army Times! 'Don't Eat and You'll Pass Tape.' It'll be their next cover story!"

"Nah, nah, that's not what I mean, and I don't recommend it for everyone. But what I do is, I just weigh myself every night. And usually I'm good. But if I'm ever overweight, I just stop eating."

"Huh? How do you mean, stop eating?"

"Just, no food."

"Until when?"

"Until the scale goes back down."

"Wouldn't you pass out during the day?"

"That's greatly exaggerated. Guys in Bataan went without eating. Guys in jail go without eating for sometimes days at a time."

"And yet, here we are in modern-day America."

Packs shrugged and shook his head like a bird. "I didn't say it was a good plan, I just said it was what I did."

Packs carefully squeezed the cherry out of his cigarette by pinching just above the filter and rolling the butt back and forth, gently. (Deth suspected he wouldn't have cared if he burnt himself, but nevertheless he took pains not to.) He stamped out the cherry, rolled up the filter like a dung beetle, and pocketed it to throw out later.

Deth, smoking unfiltereds, simply dropped his butt on the ground and stamped on it. "One of my classmates in OBC told me a story once," Deth said, "Apparently when she arrived at her unit..."

"She? They let females in FAOBC now?"

"Just started in '04. Won't be long until that stupid rule is repealed." Packs just grunted but gestured for Deth to continue. He probably had strong reactionary feelings about women in combat, but didn't want to get into it. "Anyway, when she arrived they put her in charge of doing the tape test for the females."

"Natch."

"Natch. So, Vu - that was her name - she gets a new batch of, I don't know, some low-density MOS, supply clerks or something, straight out of AIT."

All that "low-density" meant in regards to a Military Occupational Specialty was that there were fewer of them. For instance, a supply clerk in a chemical company, or a Field Artillery observer in an infantry battalion. AIT (Advanced Individualized Training) was the first school for an enlisted man after Basic Training, where the Soldier learned his or her MOS.

"So she tells the new kids to go into the other room to get ready, and when she comes in, they're all stark-ass naked."

"What?"

"That's the same thing Lieutenant Vu said! And so they said, 'Well, this is how Drill Sergeant always did our fat test in Basic.' And she said, 'Explain yourselves and do it exactly.' And so they told her about the 'internal fat test' that their drill sergeant used to give them."

Packs looked like he was about to slug someone. In fact, he punched a tree and bloodied two of his knuckles. "Did they get the son of a bitch?"

"Oh, yeah."

"See, that's the kind of shit...that's the kind of crap...fuck!" Packs fell silent.

Wordlessly, they began to stroll around the cemetery, ruminating on the terrible abuses of power that the army sometimes set itself up for. The cemetery was like any other they had ever seen, perhaps a bit poorer than some, but certainly not the worst. (Deth wasn't even sure if the one that had taken forever to find had been the worst. He had once seen one that hadn't seemed to have a date on a headstone more recent than the '80s and had apparently not been tended since then, either.)

Packs stopped, crouched down, and whistled in awe. "Would you look at that."

Deth rolled up behind him and glanced down. On the ground, flat, like the stump of a tree, lay a plaque. It was easy to miss. Every other gravestone was elevated at least slightly, and most at a minimum were crosses or humps. Even the lower ones that were just plaques like this usually had some kind of angle to it, just up enough off the ground to be noticed and read. This one was flat.

Also, it was made of wood. "Brigid Shaugnessy," Deth read, "You suppose they buried her in a refrigerator box, too?"

"Maybe," Packs said, the childlike wonder in his voice if anything rising, "How does that happen? I mean, I've seen pauper's graves before. Time was they didn't just cremate all the derelicts and John Does. Time was they dumped them all in a mass grave, like the Soviets. Potter's fields, they called them."

"Yes," Deth agreed.

He didn't recall where he had read the term, although he was certain he hadn't seen it in practice as Packs seemingly had. "But this..." Packs continued, like he had discovered a new species of insect, "Rich enough to get your own plot but poor enough that your headstone is made from wood? That's...that's something right there."

"That's Class with a capital 'C,'" Deth said.

Packs stood up and slapped his palms together as though they were covered with chalk. "That's exactly what I want when I die. No fuss, no muss. Just a chunk of wood that says 'Bela Packs.'"

"'Husband, Father...Lover.'"

"No. Just my name. No dates or anything."

"Crayoned in by a third grader."

"You laugh..."

"No, no, I couldn't possibly laugh at that request. You should update your will."

"Next time I deploy," Packs said vacantly, staring off into the distance.

After that, the funeral seemed like an afterthought. Deth couldn't stop thinking about that wooden gravestone. And, he suspected, neither could Packs.

16

Deth stared in bafflement at the five unopened beers sitting by Packs's side. The open can in his hand couldn't even have been half drained, and they had been sitting there on the hotel porch for twenty-odd minutes. Deth had never seen such a display of moderation on Packs's part.

Deth took another swig of his Mad Dog. "You're sick, aren't you?"

"I have a raging headache," Packs admitted.

"Migraine?"

"Only women get migraines."

"O...kay...do these non-migraines recur?" Packs shrugged. "Maybe you should see a doctor."

Packs rolled his eyes. "Doctors," he said as though it were a curse, "They always find something wrong with you."

"Like recurring migraines."

"I've never gone on sick call once," Packs declared proudly.

Deth raised an eyebrow. "Well, I asked a medic once why I was bleeding from the ears."

Deth never really believed movies when characters would do a spit-take, since they always seemed so phoney-baloney. However, he did one now, and as he had thought, he did not spurt the purple fortified wine forward like an upended whale, but rather choked and dribbled some onto his shirt and made himself sticky.

"Watch yourself, sir," Packs said, smiling at Deth's misery.

Hearing the word "sir," one of the other guests on the hotel porch approached and said, "Say, are you two...?"

"Firemen!" they both said, Deth getting over his choking fit enough to let out that one word.

The other guest wandered off, disappointed. When he had recovered, Deth spoke again. "Bleeding from the ears?"

Packs shrugged. "Hazard of being a redleg, I guess," he said, "And all the dust in the Sandbox. My Q-Tips started coming out black."

"Well, the Q-Tips are probably the reason your ears started bleeding."

"Are the Q-Tips why I have hearing loss? And tinnitus?"

"Quite possibly, yes."

"Well, I think it was the guns going off all the time. And not wearing hearing protection."

"You should wear earplugs."

"So it's okay to stick earplugs in my ear but not Q-Tips?"

"Pretty decidedly, yes." Packs shrugged. He was obviously still testy from his manly not-exactly-migraine. "That's really the only time you ever went on sick call?"

"Well..." Packs ran his finger around the inside of his collar, a gesture Deth had never seen him make before and one seemingly out of character. Deth leaned back in his chair. He could tell the distraction was helping to relieve Packs's headache, or at a minimum redirect his irritation outward at Deth instead of inward.

"Oh, do tell of your bout with malingering vaginitis."

"Malingering...I'll malinger you. Let me tell you about the only time I ever let one of those butchers at the TMC put his hamhocks on me. I got bit by a cold-blooded little shit called a sandfly."

"A bug bite? You went on sick call over a bug bite?" Deth told himself again he was helping to distract his PSG, but he couldn't deny he was getting some pleasure out of baiting the man.

"Let me finish," he said, holding up a long-suffering hand, "And I contracted a condition called d...leishmaniasis."

Deth smiled. He had heard of this before, even seen some Soldiers fresh home from the war with the so-called Jericho button lesions still littering their skin. "Dum-dum fever?" he said.

"Leishmaniasis," Packs reiterated with what even he recognized as false dignity.

"Tell me more about this bug," Deth said, "Was it as big as one of those giant camel spiders you always see online eating cats and shit?"

"In Eye-raq, the horrors come both big and small," Packs said like he was Socrates, "This was a smaller one."

"How big?"

"A sandfly is about as big as...a pimple."

Deth burst out laughing. Packs waited with ruptured dignity, though Deth could see he was no longer really worried about his masculine non-migraine head pain syndrome. "Okay," Deth said when he could finally breathe again, "So an itty-bitty little fly bit you and you got some Jericho buttons, and then you went on sick call for the first time in your life?"

"Oh, no," Packs said with as much dignity as he could muster, "I went a couple weeks without saying anything. Except I had one button here on my neck."

Packs pointed and Deth peered in, spotting a mortifying scar on the other man's neck. "Then I had to fly out to FOB Hammer to escort some, I don't know, some stupid gew-gaw that Big Smell didn't want to be sent by normal logistics routes. See, at Balad, it's just like being in garrison here back home, you can wear your soft cap and everything, the only difference is you have to carry your weapon. Outside the wire, though, you have to wear your Kevlar and body armor and everything.

"So I pulled all of this junk on to go fly on the bird. I didn't think anything of it, but there's a piece that chafes your neck. So I flew for a few hours with it chafing the nub on my neck, then I walked around a few hours at Hammer waiting to get picked up and all that other shit, then flew a few hours back. And by the next morning I had a great big dime-sized growth on my neck."

Deth fished through his pocket for a dime. He held it up a few centimeters away from the electric scar on Packs's neck. He could see that the man was only slightly exaggerating. "So you went on sick call."

"Oh, no," Packs said, shaking his head, "I let it go. It was just a pimple, right? Just a bug bite, like you said, and I thought the exact same thing. By the third day, my whole neck was as red as Farmer trying to run a mile and I could barely concentrate on my work. People were starting to notice, even Big Smell said something."

"So you went on sick call."

Packs shook his head again. "I took a knife and covered it with rubbing alcohol then lit it up with my cigarette lighter until it was red. Then I slashed across the button cross-wise." Packs demonstrated, drawing the invisible knife of his fingernail across his scar diagonally twice in an X pattern.

"And...?"

"It didn't leak or nothing. I figure that had to be the end of it. I even dug around in the wound trying to dig out...you know, whatever was in there. But it didn't leak or nothing."

"I'm guessing you didn't go to the doctor."

"Oh, no, after that I went. The redness had gone purple and I think I had a fever. I felt ridiculous telling the medic what had happened to me, but he just nodded and you know what he said?" Deth shook his head. "He said, 'Sergeant, I'm going to take care of this for you and you're going to hate me for it, but then you're going to love me for it. Now drop your drawers.'"

Packs made the motion of jabbing something from one hand into his clenched fist. "You got a shot in the ass?"

"Shot in my ass and two weeks worth of antibiotics that didn't do shit, so I had to go back and get the blue pills instead of the tan, and then it really started to fade. But you know what happened as soon as I got back to the office after that shot?"

"I'm not sure that I want to know."

"You don't, but I'm going to tell you anyway. That wound started to leak. And when it started to leak, it started to gush and, I'm not kidding, it was like the little Dutch boy took his finger out of the lesbian."

"I don't want to hear this."

Packs was on his bowed legs, making noises and illustrating the process with his hands and drawing the attention of the hotel guests who hadn't already left in horror at his story. "Sploosh! It just came pouring out, first the white stuff that's kind of like a pimple and kind of like snot. Then came the yellow stuff that's kind of clear but yellow and that didn't just come out all at once. No, that leaked all day like it was a drippy faucet that just can't quite drip. And after that came the red clear stuff like it was blood mixed with clear stuff. And then when it was just blood coming out, it was like the wound was clean, only, you know, the lump stayed on so long I had to go back to the doc to get some better meds. And even though all of that junk had leaked right on out of it, he told me it was still woody, and he pressed at it with those latex-gloved hands of his and he said, 'See, Sergeant? See how it's still like a chunk of wood in there?' And he gave me some better meds and now it's all pretty much healed up."

"That's the grossest thing I've ever heard."

"Well, it's not like I got shot," Packs said.

"If you did, I bet you wouldn't go on sick call." Packs nodded his agreement.

17

Up until the Compson funeral, Deth had thought that the funeral outside Little Rock where the undertaker had gotten lost was the most podunk he would ever have to endure. "This can't be right," Deth said, pointing at the name of the town on the map.

"What can't be right, sir?"

"This number," Deth said, "That can't be population. It's got to be elevation or something."

Packs glanced over the map. "Sure," he said pointing, "If you believe OKC's a million feet above sea level."

Deth glanced at the map at towns he more or less knew. Tulsa was 300,000 or so, OKC about a million, Lawton 100,000. No, there was no way any of those were elevation or square footage or anything like that. "Are you telling me this town's population is seriously 8?"

Packs shrugged.

"Well, 'town' might be a strong name for it. It might be unincorporated."

"It's on the map. Population 8."

"Well, don't forget, sir, the map could be old. Joe Bob might've come back from community college."

"Yeah, we should correct that," Deth said, crossing out the population number with a pencil and stenciling in 9. Packs glanced over his shoulder and smiled in amusement. "I mean, I've seen towns with double dig...here's one that's 62. But 8? That just seems wrong. How could you even...I mean, how does that even count? That seems more like a family than a community."

Packs shrugged. "At least we found the boneyard this time."

Indeed they had. So Packs was thinking of their "adventure" with Funeral Director Baines as well. What had been the name of that funeral? He couldn't remember. They all started to run together after a while. Eventually, the only things he remembered were the moments with Packs, like discovering the wooden "tombstone" or wearing the scarlet socks. Death, it seemed, had become his life now.

They had, after all, had no trouble finding this graveyard, which, as Deth had suspected, was closer to a family burial plot than a town receptacle for the dead. That had been the one positivity of finding the town, population 8. Deth promptly and irrevocably forgot the town's name.

The funeralgoers had been astonishingly polite almost to the point of a silence that ate at Deth's ever-running thoughts. Compson had been the name of the dead man, or still was, after a fashion, as it was certainly etched on his stone. Deth would never forget the name Compson, unlike the name of the town, or, perhaps, farmhouse, population 8.

No one had shaken hands with them, which was a welcome change from the usual humdrum or even comical conversations. In fact, Deth noted, no one, not even the next of kin, would meet his eyes. He was warier than he'd ever been, or, perhaps, as confused as he had ever felt. Usually he and Packs had to fight off the packs of admirers, secret military hero worshippers, and small kids who still dreamt of being Soldiers. Today there was none of that, just simple, what Deth would almost have described as tolerance.

"Did you see anywhere to eat?" Packs asked when the crowd had abated. Deth shook his head. "I'm going to ask the funeral director," Packs said, breaking ranks and walking up to the undertaker, who was starting to get into his car.

The man had scarcely said two words to them the whole day, and both of those had been to Packs. It had dawned on Deth what was going on, but he refused to believe that was the case, not today, not in 2006. He watched as Packs and the funeral director had an exchange. He thought he saw the vein on the side of Packs's head vibrating. If Packs went wild and turned on the funeral director the way he sometimes did on his own Soldiers when they weren't listening to him, well, it wasn't as though the funeral director was in the army.

He didn't have to take that shit and Deth certainly didn't want to get arrested.

He walked up firmly to join the exchange. "Sergeant Packs," he said loudly, "Is everything all right?"

"It will be, sir," Packs said with deadly quiescence, "Just as soon as this gentleman tells me where we can get a bite to eat around here."

Packs said the word "gentleman" as though it were the harshest insult in the English language, as though it were the word that Deth now suspected everyone around here considered him.

"And I told you, sir," the funeral director said, "We mightily appreciate you fellows coming out and we're very grateful for the flag, but it would probably be best if you just moved along."

"This is because I'm black," Deth said flatly.

The funeral director said nothing, did not even look at Deth, in fact. Now Deth saw that the vein on Packs's head was about to burst. He put his hand on Packs's elbow, but Packs immediately shook it off. "I believe you're mistaken," Packs said, his voice turning red, "My platoon leader is not black or white or yellow or red. He is green, as you can see. Now will you tell me where we can get a bite to eat around here."

The funeral director shook his head miserably, and Deth suddenly realized the poor man's impossible position. Yes, he was a racist, yes, the family members at the funeral might have been honorary members of the Ku Klux Klan. But they had made what they considered a magnanimous gesture in allowing Deth to handle their relative's flag. They had been...tolerant. And now the funeral director probably just genuinely didn't want Deth to get his ass beaten for trying to eat at a local dive where they would *find* a way to beat his ass, flag bearer or not.

It wasn't Deth's first brush with racism, nor even his hundredth, but it was definitely the most eye-opening. These people were torn. They hated him for his skin but loved him for the uniform he wore over it and somehow they couldn't see past either. "Sergeant Packs," Deth said quietly, "Let's just get out of here."

Packs wheeled on Deth, all the anger he obviously felt over the situation now directed at him, the victim. "Sir..." he said warningly, as though he were about to suggest a wall-to-wall counseling session.

"Let's just get out of here," Deth said, and, perhaps to reiterate his point or to indicate that it was an order without resorting to the tired cliché of saying "That's an order," he simply tapped the silver bar on his lapel.

"Yes, sir!" Packs announced boldly, as if to make a point to the funeral director that he took orders from a black man, loved it, in fact, wished he could take more orders from more black men all the damn time.

"Motherfucker!" Packs howled when they were alone in the car together and the funeral director had driven off, "Motherfucker cocksucker! I should have beat his ass! You know I could've, too!"

Packs pounded the steering wheel in a staccato rhythm with such fury that Deth was afraid he would snap it off the column. He waited until Packs's fury had abated.

"How aren't you pissed about this?" Packs was breathing heavily, his face purple with rage.

"I am," Deth said, "But I'm used to it."

"Used to it! How do you get used to...to...it's 2006, god damn it! This isn't fucking..." Packs punched the steering wheel again. He looked like he wanted to punch the window, and Deth was glad he didn't. He probably would have shattered it, and that would have been hard to deal with.

"Sergeant, you get angry about what people in a town population 8 think, you're going to be angry all the time."

"How are you not furious, sir? How are you not...why am I smashing up the car and you don't even care?"

"I care," Deth said, "I care and it cuts like a knife. But did you see that guy? I think he didn't want me to get lynched."

"Well, yeah..."

"He's not the guy to be mad at."

"Well, who do you get mad at then, if not him? The whole...fucking...society?"

Deth gave a grin. "Pretty much."

Suddenly, it dawned on Packs. "You're not mad because I stuck up for you. You're not mad because you saw how mad I got."

"Well, it's better than hearing you call somebody a fag."

"Oh."

"You told me once you weren't a racist, and when people feel the need to say that, it usually means they are a racist. But when somebody gets that mad about it, when they see the injustice in it, well, one at a time, I guess that's how you change this whole fucked-up society."

Packs started the car. "Let's just go find some chow," Packs said, "I'm hungry."

"Okay."

Dark was starting to fall. Packs turned to Deth. "I ain't a fucking liberal."

"I never accused you of being one."

18

"Yeah. Yeah, okay. All right, thanks." Packs looked up from the phone and snapped it closed.

"Well?" Deth prompted, when he didn't say anything.

"Would you believe me if I told you we're going home?"

"No."

Packs grinned. "Well, we are."

Deth lifted a single eyebrow, waiting for the other shoe to drop. A few seconds later, unable to keep up the façade, Packs let it. "Just temporarily, though. There's a full service at Ft. Sill National."

Deth slapped his forehead with both palms and groaned loudly. "Full service? I hate full service!"

"Could be worse," Packs mused.

"Yeah, I could be the one getting the full service, right?" Packs pointed a pretend gun at Deth and made a clicking sound with his tongue and teeth. "Well, at least we'll get to go back to post," Deth said, rubbing his hands together in anticipation, "I've been paying waaaaay too much for Mad Dog on the road. The Class 6 is calling my name."

Packs's icy, implacable, unchanging face alerted Deth to the fact that something was wrong. "What? What is it?"

"Well...odd as it sounds...Fort Sill National is not...on...Fort Sill."

"Fuck you talking about, Sergeant?"

Packs shrugged and pulled a map out of the sleeve in the Ford's passenger side door. He unfolded it partly, straightened it out on the dash and pointed. "There," he said.

"Elgin!" Deth fairly shouted, "We have to go to Elgin? That's close enough that...wait...is it...it can't be...is that within thirty miles?" Packs nodded, his smile finally giving way to a grim defeatist straight line of a mouth. "You mean we don't even get per diem?" Deth moaned loudly again.

"Better suck egg, sir."

"What does that mean?"

"Suck it up and deal."

"Yeah, I guess," Deth said, realizing what a child he was being after all, "Like you said, I could be the one getting the full service."

"You could be," Packs agreed.

They stopped at a place called Meers, famous, for reasons unclear to Deth, for their cheeseburgers. Although he grudgingly admitted that Oklahoman beef was far superior to any beef back home, he had tasted Meers burgers before and didn't understand what the fuss was about.

It was within the 30-mile radius of Ft. Sill such that they were theoretically not supposed to eat on per diem, the theory being that once you're within 30 miles of home, you ought to be able to eat at home or, in the case of Soldiers living in the barracks, at the chow hall. They had a workaround, though. Being as they were coming in from off the road, they just waited until after the chow hall on post, Guns and Rockets, closed. Mortuary Affairs wouldn't be able to nail them for it, even though neither of them ever actually ate at the chow hall.

"One last meal for the road, eh?" Deth asked as the waitress dropped two cheeseburgers that had to each weigh a pound in front of Packs.

"Yes, sir," Packs said with relish, and Deth suspected he would have said "sir" even if Deth wasn't an officer, "Better than family dinner, huh?"

"Family dinner?"

Packs released one hand from the giant burger he was holding and snapped his fingers as though recalling something. "That's funny," he said, "I talk to you about the war so much sometimes I forget you weren't there."

"Can you get me a combat patch by association?"

"Wish I could, sir, wish I could."

Packs ripped through half a cheeseburger, praising it to the high heavens as the greatest in all the world, which, although it carried some weight with Deth because Packs had been so many more places than him, he still had to disagree with. What was it about Meers that everybody loved so much?

"Family dinner," Packs said, remembering what they had been discussing, "Was something that Big Smell instituted. Every...what was it? Thursday night? I want to say Sunday, but Sunday was our half day off."

"You only got a half day off?"

Packs shrugged. "War's gotta go on."

"I thought Soldiers got a full day off a week on a rotating schedule."

"Not when you work for Big Smell and you only report to...MNC-I!" Packs shouted the last acronym in the manner of Brannigan.

"So, Thursdays..." Deth prompted.

"So, Thursdays, everyone on the LNO team...oops, I mean, 'Task Force Headquarters'...had to have dinner together. And Douchebag called it Family Dinner. Nobody wanted to do it. I don't think he even did, but I guess he got the idea somewhere and he started using it. That's the kind of guy he was. Do you know what FYSA means?"

Deth racked his brain for a moment. "I don't," he admitted, "But I'm new to the army."

"Well, I've been in the army fifteen years," Packs said darkly, "And I've known more acronyms than pussies in that time, and I ain'tnever heard of no FYSA. So one day Big Smell starts adding this acronym at the end of his e-mails."

"He e-mailed you from the same office?"

"Next office over. We didn't let him in the real office."

"Ah."

"So, no one said anything because it didn't seem to matter. There'd be a regular e-mail about something and then at the end it would say FYSA. So we just ignored it. Then he started dropping it into conversations and then he'd stand there and wait."

"Wait for you to ask what it meant?"

Packs nodded. "He was so excited at the idea of discovering a new acronym that nobody knew, and he was just creaming his pants with excitement that somebody would ask him. That he would get to, you know, explain something. Because he didn't know shit about his job, so the most exciting thing in his life was to explain what FYSA was."

"Did you finally break down?"

"No, we all loved it. We knew better than to ask, all of us. I warned BC and 1SG, and they told their Soldiers not to ask, too. Big Smell just walked around all day, dropping FYSA into conversations like it was going out of style. He would say it to the little Paki cooks, and they didn't care, they didn't speak that much English, they only knew 'one more spoonful' or 'two,' they weren't going to ask him what god-damn FYSA was, pardoning my French."

"Did you ever find out what it meant?"

Packs tapped the end of his second cheeseburger against his plate like he was putting out a cigarette. "That was the best part,"

Packs said, "Finally we looked it up when it finally, you know, appeared on the internet. FYSA is short for 'For Your Situational Awareness.'"

Situational Awareness was a junk term. Even Deth knew that. It just meant..."FYI?" Packs nodded. "He found a fancy new pretend-military way to say FYI and he wanted everybody to ask him about it?"

Packs shrugged. "That's the kind of guy he was. Imagine how many rockets didn't get fired because he was wasting our time with that shit."

Deth shook his head back and forth rapidly, like a dog trying to dry off after a bath. "I can't believe you never submitted that IG complaint," Deth said, "You wrote it."

Packs shrugged. "Schoolhouse rules," he said, "Nobody likes a squealer. He gets his ass kicked."

"So at these Family Dinners," Deth said, "Did you all have to like sit around the table and hold hands and pray? And did Big Smell sit at the head of the table?"

Packs leaned back in his chair, his cheeseburgers and mound of fries finally finished, and patted his belly as though he had a keg there instead of a six-pack. "Do we have any money left?"

Deth shrugged. Packs signaled to the waitress for another burger and fries. "It's funny you say that," he said, "Well, we didn't hold hands (I probably would've caved his face in if he had made us hold hands) but he did act like that. And he was real insistent all the time that it was Family Dinner. The rest of the time we avoided him like the plague. Waited until 1500 to go to lunch, that kind of thing."

"1500?"

"Well, 1455. Five minutes before whenever it closed. Or, if he was going at closing, we'd go right at 1100. But since he talked about damn Family Dinner so often when Father's Day rolled around, we did talk about whether we should get him a gift."

"Oh my God, you didn't, did you?"

Packs rolled his eyes. "Well, we definitely talked about it. And there's two PXes at Balad, you know, well, I guess one is on the Air Force side, so maybe they don't call it a PX. But it wasn't like we couldn't have found a gift if we wanted. And we knew what he was into."

"Which was?"

"Horses."

"Horses?"

"Horses. You know how I said he liked to think of himself as John Wayne or Clint Eastwood or some shit?"

"No, but I can easily imagine that."

"Meanwhile, he was more like Gilligan. Do you know Gilligan?"

Apparently they had finally hit a vein of pop culture that Packs was familiar with. "I know Gilligan."

"He wanted to be a cowboy, so he wanted to ride horses. Problem is, I gather, he was just as good at that as he was at everything else. So he bought a horse, but couldn't really ride it."

"This was in Lawton he bought a horse? Did he own a bunch of land or something?"

"Nope. And it's not like he owned a ranch back home or something, either. Anyway, I'm guessing about a lot of this stuff because we heard it all from him, which means it's mostly bullshit, but I gather that his wife, who is a sweetheart and probably should be a saint in Rome for being married to him, her parents take the horse. Because they do own a farm or something."

"So he didn't have the horse."

"Didn't have the horse, couldn't ride the horse, physically owned the horse, but still called himself a cowboy. He kept a picture of his horse on his desk. And if we ever got stuck talking to him, we'd get whole lectures on how to take care of horses. And, sir, you know me. I actually grew up on a farm."

"Horseshit?"

Packs smiled very slowly, getting what Deth was saying as the waitress put down his new plate in front of him. "Yeah," he said, "It was all horseshit. That's good, sir, you're good."

"I do my best."

"You know how sometimes the 1ˢᵗ Cav guys wear Stetsons?"

"Yeah," Deth said, "I did CTLT at Hood."

"CTLT? What's that?"

"Eh, don't worry about it," Deth said, "It's kind of like an internship."

"So, you know, then, that you can't just wear a Stetson."

"Sure, you have to earn it on a...what do they call it? Spur Run?"

"Spur Ride. Yeah, you've got to earn your spurs and then you can wear your Stetson. And the artillery units, 1-21 and them, they can go on Spur Rides, too. I went on one. I earned my Stetson."

Deth pressed his fingers to his forehead, impersonating Johnny Carson doing a routine that was old even when he was a kid.

"Wait, I'm getting a vision," Deth said, "Is it...it is...I think it's...Big Smell wearing a Stetson without earning one?"

"How did you know, sir?" Packs asked in mock surprise.

Deth must have been rubbing off on him. He had never known him to have the gift of sarcasm before. "So did you end up getting him a Father's Day present?"

Packs shook his head vigorously. "We couldn't figure out a way to get him something without him either taking it really wrong and getting really offended or taking it as though we really appreciated him. I mean, you want to slip in a little elbowing, but that guy, he'd either take it as the end of the world or not get the joke at all, you know what I mean?"

"I do know what you mean."

"You know, it's funny, his in-laws sent him...I told you his in-laws got the horse, right?"

"Because he couldn't keep it."

"Yeah, where would he have kept it? His garage? So the in-laws, I'm guessing they hated him just as much as we did, but who knows. Anyway, they sent him this package in the mail and he opened it up and started laughing and laughing about it all day." Deth was a little afraid to ask. "See, that's why we didn't know. We didn't know, you know, if we got him the complete Roy Rogers DVD collection or something he might take it really wrong or he might take it really wrong. But we didn't know. And you knew he wasn't going to get that it was with a wink and a nod. Nothing was a wink and a nod with that guy."

"What was it?" Deth asked, "What was in the box?"

"Horseshit."

19

Deth sank into his waterbed with a sigh. "It's been a long time, old friend," he said. The waterbed gurgled a response under him. "No, no," he said, holding up a finger to the bed's drainage valve as though he were hushing a lover with a finger to her lips, "Don't get used to it. It may just be tonight."

The bed didn't respond this time, being fully accustomed to his weight, so he squished his butt cheeks until it gurgled again. "Don't be upset, my darling," he said, "We may only have tonight, but we'll make the best of it. It's like the old song says..."

Before Deth could say what important lyric the old song may or may not have said, he was interrupted by the sound of his cell phone ringing. He twitched his lips to one side of his face like a disappointed bunny. "I hope that's not..."

He reached over and grabbed it, plucking it off the charger without thinking. It was not Packs. He put it to his ear. "Yello?" he asked tentatively.

"Deth?" It was a woman's voice. It rang a faint hint of a bell.

"That's me."

"It's Vu. I'm back in town, you old bastard. Why haven't you been responding to my e-mails?"

Deth glanced at his desktop in the other room. He hurried over and flicked it on, casting a cascade of Mounds wrappers off the keyboard and onto the floor. "God, Piera, it's good to hear from you," Deth said, finding it hard not to hold back his excitement or his nervosity, "Shit, you know, I've been on the road."

"On the road? What does that mean?"

"Doing...funerals, you know."

"You lost that many guys?"

"No, no. Not that. Old guys. Korea and The Big One. Or Vietnam now sometimes, too. I probably shouldn't have brought that up."

"Hey, I've never been to 'Nam," Piera responded, "My 'rents came over on rafts. I think they like Americans. And I am American. So, you've been putting old guys in the ground, huh? Where?"

"Oh, you know, all over Oklahoma and Misery and Arkansas. Almost got to Memphis once, but we weren't allowed to cross the border."

"So they don't have e-mail in Oklahoma or Missouri or Arkansas now?" He heard her clicking some buttons on her keyboard on the other end of the phone. "That's funny, my laptop's working just fine."

His computer had finally booted up. There, sure enough, were her e-mails. "You sent them to my personal account," he said.

"Sure, like ordinary people do."

"Christ, I'm sorry, Piera, I've only been checking my AKO account."

"You're a real company man now, huh?"

"Well, what about you? You're just back from Afghanistan, right?"

"Yeah, asshole, and I haven't had a drink in a year."

"I heard that was just an exaggeration."

"It's an exaggeration if you don't give a shit about the rules," she sighed loudly, "It's deadly sobriety if you're trying to be a good officer. Or a good Soldier, for that matter."

"What I hear you saying is," Deth said, quickly scanning through the half a dozen increasingly anxious e-mails she had sent him, "That you want to go to Gert's for a drink."

"Nah, nah, fuck Gertlestone's," she said, "That's an officer bar. I want to go to Hoffman's."

"That's..." Deth had to think, "I don't even know what that is. That's a dive."

"It's a dive with karaoke."

"I thought you said you were Vietnamese, not Japanese."

"I actually just said I was American, asshole. Now are you coming to the billets to pick me up?"

Vu was a compact little woman who looked like she could've ripped the hood off his car with one hand. Like all Soldiers, she wore her civvies a little oddly. At least she hadn't crammed herself into a cocktail dress like she was going slumming tonight. Instead, a brown t-shirt (army-issue, so its function as civvies was questionable) and jeans which didn't seem to fit. Deth, at least, had worn a colored t-shirt along with his jeans that didn't fit. She was wearing her ACU boots, too, with the cuffs of her jeans rolled down over them.

By way of greeting, she punched him in the shoulder. "You put on weight."

"Per diem. You look like you did, too."

She shrugged. "All those guys in the initial invasion didn't have D-FACs. God knows I've had to hear about it. Everything Over There's about how much it isn't like Tora Bora anymore. Well, fuck you, I like my make-your-own spaghetti on Saturday nights. Food is the only vice I get Over There. Well, I guess I've been smoking, too."

"Does that mean you're tying one on tonight?"

"Not only am I tying one on tonight, Deth," she said, putting her arm around his shoulder by way of his waist, "But I will probably be three sheets to the wind after beer three."

"You've lost your tolerance."

"I've lost my tolerance. You know, I tried to get drunk on O'Doul's Over There."

"How'd that work out for you?"

"I got a bladder infection. And not really drunk."

"Well, they're not really alcoholic."

"They have a certain level of alcohol."

"Like 0.5%."

"You gonna keep talking or you going to start driving?"

They stepped into Deth's car. Vu leaned her head against his headrest and put an unlit cigarette into her mouth. She closed her eyes. "You're not going to light that, are you?"

"Nope," she said, without opening her eyes.

"Good, because there's no smoking in my car."

"I know."

He started the car and pulled out of the billets parking lot. The billets always seemed a little off to him. He had never lived in them, even in OBC. The only time he had ever really gone there was to visit Vu, or his other OBC mates, and usually they came to his apartment anyway. They all hated the billets and would do anything to get out of there. So, in fact, he rarely visited them anyway. Sometimes he had to turn folks away from his place. One evening, after a solid six months of letting friends visit every night, he simply said that no one was coming over that night. They had never quite forgiven him for that, he sometimes still thought.

Vu had changed. He tried to get a good look at her while her eyes were closed, but it was difficult while trying to concentrate on the road. He couldn't quite make out what it was, but she was different. "So what's been going on since I've been gone?"

Deth thought for a moment. "You remember that instructor we had in OBC? The civilian?"

"The black guy in the purple suit?"

"No, the white guy who never talked."

"The one with the thing on his wrist."

"That's the one. Well, it turns out that he didn't have his wrist splinted because a Brown Recluse bit him."

"Oh no? Why were you even keeping up with him?"

"I wasn't. It was in the Constitution. He was a rapist."

"Ooh..." Vu said, making a tunnel with her lips, "So that was a love bite on his wrist."

"A rape bite, yes," Deth said, "But that's not the weird part."

"Advise me of the weird part, Bickham."

Deth turned his eyes off to the left to make sure no other cars were turning. He made his turn very gradually before speaking again. "So he had one of those windowless vans and he used to drive up to car washes late at night and snatch unattended girls then dump them off somewhere else. But here's the really spooky part: his wife did the driving while he did the snatching."

"You're kidding me." Deth shook his head. "So it was kind of a Mickey and Mallory kind of thing."

"If you like."

"Guess you never know about people."

"You really never do."

Deth stopped short at a green light just as it was turning yellow. The driver behind him was obviously upset he hadn't gone through. Although the other driver didn't honk, he was visibly waving his arms and pounding the steering column in anger. Deth could see it in the rearview, but Vu turned around to look over her shoulder with glee. "Don't look," he said.

"How are you such a shitty driver, grandma?" Vu asked, without opening her eyes, "I thought you've been on the road non-stop."

Deth stopped trying to suss out what was wrong with her and put both eyes on the road. "Yeah, well..." he said and trailed off.

Suddenly she sat up and looked him full in the face. "You let your NCOs drive you, didn't you?"

"Well, you're supposed to, aren't you?"

"Not all the time, dumbass. Don't you know whoever's in the driver's seat is in charge?"

"So I'm in charge of you?"

"No, dipshit, I'm in the TC's seat. I'm in charge of your car."

"So how is the driver in charge if the TC is..."

"You're supposed to drive yourself once in a while. You're scared of the wheel, aren't you?" Deth shrugged. He couldn't deny it. He knew Lawton was a podunk nowhere town and he didn't entirely hate driving in it. But going to Austin or Dallas or even OKC was a harrowing experience for him and he hated it. "When did you get your license?"

"What business is that of yourn?" He said "yourn" to be deliberately obfuscating. He half hoped she would pick up on it and ask him why he had said that so that they could talk about something other than his license. Of course, she didn't.

"Go on, then, LT, tell the truth."

"I got it when I was 22," he said, "About a month before I commissioned."

She goggled at him. "No, you didn't."

He shrugged. "My PMS said I had to have one before I joined the army. I don't know if that's in the UCMJ or..."

"Why didn't you have one before?"

Deth cleared his throat. He was uncomfortable with the poverty in which he had grown up. It had been more spiritual than physical. Although his parents had been divorced and money had always been tight, he had no doubt they could have easily afforded to pay the insurance to let him get a driver's license. For that matter, they probably could have afforded to pay for him to go to school, but instead, he had been compelled to get an ROTC scholarship. "I totaled the first car my dad tried to teach me in," he lied, "And then they wouldn't let me try again."

"So who taught you how to drive?"

"My faculty advisor," he said, which was true.

"A professor?"

"A...librarian."

"You're like an onion, Bickham Deth."

"I make you cry?"

"You've got layers," she said making a terrible impersonation of Shrek.

"What the hell was that?"

"Shrek!"

"No, it wasn't."

She punched him. He didn't let on that it had hurt. "I do a good Shrek."

"Sure you do," he said, making an exaggerated attempt to imitate her Scottish brogue or whatever it was that Mike Myers did.

And, like that, they were finally on a different subject.

Vu sat down across from him and took a pull from her beer. Her cheeks were rosy from exertion and her hair was sweaty. Deth breathed a puff of smoke up towards the ceiling instead of across the sticky table into her face. "You and your smoking," she said, waving it away as though it had gotten in her eyes anyway.

Vu had smoked nearly twice as many cigarettes as he had that night, but he gathered that, like Packs, she despised the scent of his unfiltered Luckies. "You and your caterwauling," he said.

"Caterwauling?" she asked in mock indignation, "I'll have you know that was Carrie Underwood."

"That wasn't Carrie Underwood," he said, "That was you."

She stuck her nose up in the air. "I'm sure you couldn't even tell the difference."

"You're right! I closed my eyes and it was like I was right there! In a shitty karaoke bar. With you singing off-key." She looked like she wanted to toss something at him but nothing came readily to hand. She reached across the table and slapped him in the same arm she had punched earlier. He knew it was the same arm because it still smarted. He decided to press his luck. "Doesn't even make any sense. Why would anybody think before he cheated if some girl ripped up all your shit? I'd just dump her ass."

"You're an idiot," Vu said.

He shrugged. "Maybe so."

"Why don't you get up there, then, you think you're so great?"

He shrugged again. "Karaoke is so bourgeois."

"Using words like 'bourgeois' is bourgeois." He said nothing and merely blew his smoke up towards the ceiling out of the corner of his mouth. "Who uses words like that anyway? What are you, a commie?"

"I'm not the one who rolls up in Hoffman's Bar and Grill looking like a VC comfort girl."

"Always with the racism."

"Hey, it's not racism if you're really with the VC. You kill any running dogs today, Charlie?"

Her attention had wandered to the ass of a guy playing pool at one of the two pool tables in the joint. He was bent over the table lining up his shot and Vu was clearly mesmerized by it. "He's probably enlisted," he said.

"I don't care," she cooed.

"You'll get in trooooouble," he said in a sing-song.

"He's not one of mine," she said, "It's fine. We're just two sexy-ass people who met in a bar."

"Look," Deth said, pointing after the pool player had shifted from his position, "You can see his Air Assault tattoo. Who gets an Air Assault tattoo? He's probably a 19-year-old buck private."

Vu was licking her lips. "He can buck my privates any time," she said.

Deth clapped his hands over his ears and started singing, "La la la..."

"Oh, grow up," she said, but he didn't stop singing. She came across the table to his side and began to push her breasts together to form superhero-style cleavage, whispering dark nothings, trying to get his attention, which only made him clench his ears tighter and sing "La lala" louder. She rubbed up against him until finally the waitress came and asked if they needed anything and they both, blaze-faced, said, "No."

When the waitress left, they burst out laughing. Vu returned to her side of the table.

"You really going to take that high schooler home tonight?" Deth asked.

Vu rolled her eyes. "I don't need that shit in my life," she said.

"When you finally going to shack up with some guy?"

Vu made a face like a redneck and gave an exaggerated "aww, shucks" yokel-laugh. "I don't see you picking up the Lizards, either," she said, finishing her beer and signaling for another, then adding to the waitress, "Make it a Jäger Bomb. 3%. I may as well be drinking O'Doul's again."

Deth shuddered involuntarily. The "women" of Lawton, known in the local parlance as Lawtonian Lizards, were legendary for their capacity to simultaneously be horrible and ensnare Soldiers anyway. Some of his classmates from OBC had left Ft. Sill for warmer climes with a native wife in tow. Deth was suddenly struck with the similarity to Packs picking up a Korean wife, although he had never heard a complaint against a juicy as a wife before they came back stateside. As Americans, Lizards were born entitled.

"Here," Vu said, pointing at a woman who had been sitting at the end of the bar all night, "How about her? I'll go home with Vin Diesel over there and you can go home with Drew Carey."

The woman Vu had pointed out was obese, and while he had known some overweight girls to carry it off well and even remain pleasantly voluptuous, this particular Lizard carried her weight scattered in large, malformed sacks all over her body. Her hair was stringy and seemed to be at least a little greasy, and he wasn't sure whether it was a result of natural bodily secretions or a significant portion of French fry grease. She had been laughing and clapping on her stool in a rather child-like manner for every karaoke singer that night, which somehow made her seem even more unpleasant than if she had been rude and ignorant. At least then she might have cultivated an air of mystery.

Oh, and she was missing several teeth.

"I think she's already married to Vin Diesel," Deth said, pointing back at Vu's preferred hunk of man meat, "Look, they're both wearing rings."

"Don't say that," Vu said, "Not my man. No, Vin, don't be married!" But it was too late. Deth saw how upset she was, even if going home with the man had been an idle thought. He had noticed the ring at once, though he hadn't been inclined to burst her illusions until she had started teasing him about the fat woman.

"Can't you just picture them making out?" Deth said, running his finger along his nose and then rubbing his nose oil around the rim of his glass to settle the foam of his beer down, "Big sloppy open-mouthed..."

"Enough!" Vu said, holding her hand out in his face as though to say, "Talk to the hand" like they used to in the '90s.

"Imagine what beautiful children they'll have," Deth said, unable to resist one last jab.

"You're a horrible, horrible person, Bickham Deth, and you're going straight to Hell."

"I thought Confucius say there is no Hell. I mean, Ho Chi Minh say..."

Vu gave him a disdainful look. "We're Catholic," she said, "You know we're Catholic."

"Is that one of those weird Catholic churches where all the signs are in Chinese or Japanese or something?"

"First of all, those are Korean churches," she said, "And, no, we just go to regular Ingy-speaky church. You know, after we get done using our credit cards to buy tickets to the opera, we hop into our Volkswagen and drive to church, carefully obeying all of the posted speed limits."

"Asians obeying speed limits? I'd like to see that."

"You're a retard," Vu said, "And a virgin."

"I'm not a virgin," Deth said, pointing with one finger while keeping the other four tightly wrapped around the handle of his mug, "My Uncle Manny popped my cherry in the toolshed when I was 7. I'll call him right now if you don't believe me."

"Oh, I meant you were light-on-the-right," she said, "You know that's what I meant."

Deth slowly swallowed his last sip of beer. He looked down into the bottom of the glass. A tiny squiggle decorated the bottom, the mark, perhaps, of the glass blower or the company who made the beer mugs. He could see it distinctly through the light yellowish urine color of the beer. He no longer had the heart for their light repartee.

Noticing, Vu immediately pounced. "Aww, did I huwtyouwliddlefeelin's?" He opened his mouth to make a rejoinder but said nothing for long enough that she realized she really had. "Oh, shit," she said, "Did I really hurt your feelings?"

He shrugged and leaned back. They exchanged a glance, a glance of true emotion that friends often try to ignore in such situations and that made them both uncomfortable. She shook her head, as though trying to shake off the stink of the awkward moment.

"Look, don't worry about me," she said, "I was the same..."

He held up a hand. "Please don't say you were the same way before you went, too."

She looked at him over the rim of her Jäger Bomb, which she was drinking like an ordinary beer instead of shotgunning, in the hopes of not having to have another awkward moment and infelicitously catching each other's eyes. "Okay," she said, "It's not a big deal, Deth, it's really not."

"Says you. Says everybody who's been. Everybody who hasn't, well, we know how big a deal it really is. It's a lot like being a virgin, like you said."

"That's not a big deal to girls."

"I'm not a girl."

"Well, you're certainly not a man."

He hissed between clenched teeth. "I know," he said, "I had hoped that war would make me one."

She rolled her eyes. "That's horseshit. You're going to come back from the war exactly the same man - yes, don't make me repeat it, I acknowledge you have gonads - that you were when you left."

"You're not."

She stared at him quietly for a moment. "What are you..." she started to protest.

"Well, you might as well just tell me what happened because I know you're not the same," he said, "Don't forget I knew you before. This is gay to say, but since we're in honesty hour, you were my best friend in OBC. Maybe the best friend I ever had. And I know what you were like. And you're different now. You don't even seem happy anymore and you used to be so...cheerful."

"This is because I helped you with that radio that one time, isn't it?"

"Well, you didn't have to."

She shook her head. Then, midway through not even taking a sip, she set the glass down, pushed it to one side, leaned over on the table and knitted her hands together. "Okay," she said, "You really want to know what happened Over There?" He nodded. She nodded a half a dozen times in response, as though picking up the baton from his nod. "I wasn't the first female officer they let in the Field Artillery, but I was pretty damn close," she said.

"I know."

"But that didn't change the fact that I have a box, so after I graduated from OBC, they put me in as the HHB XO for Brigade." The HHB was the Headquarters and Headquarters Battery. Unlike a firing battery which actually shot rockets (or guns) the HHB collected all the support elements for a unit, the staff, drivers, cooks, supply, and mechanics not assigned directly to line units. HHB Executive Officer was one of the few Field Artillery slots open to female officers, since it wasn't considered a "combat" position, whatever that meant in counterinsurgency operations. "And there I would remain until they could put me on the staff so that my precious little tits don't get in the way of any of the real Warriors. So what do you suppose happened the minute we hit the ground at Bagram?"

"Let me guess," he said, "Did it have something to do with not being allowed to use artillery in Counterinsurgency operations?"

"It's called COIN now," she said, "But, yeah, basically. They handed us rifles and sent us out on the streets."

"Doing infantry work."

"Infantry?" Vu said, splashing her drink and drawing some stares, "No, no, my dear boy, hardly infantry, hardly infantry at all. We were doing MP work."

"Which is different from infantry work in that...?"

Vu swallowed the rest of her drink. "A female lieutenant can lead a platoon."

"I see," he said.

"They sent us away from Bagram to a tiny little COB in the middle of nowhere, Ouroboros. You want to know what our mission was?"

"Sure."

"So do I. We existed purely for the purpose of existing. Our job was to defend ourselves and in doing so, justify that we deserved to be defended."

"That sounds...terrible."

"It was. But I'll tell you, Bickham, the freedom, my God, the freedom. To actually be out there, all but forgotten, doing what Audie Murphy did and all you have to do is not die? It's why we all joined up, isn't it?"

"That or college money."

She ignored him. In fact, she didn't even seem to remember he was there. She was staring distantly at the wall such that if Deth hadn't known it would've been rude, he would've turned his head to see what she was staring at. He knew she was just in a different plane, though, and that there was nothing on the wall but an old neon Budweiser sign with both of the E's dead.

"It was what I imagine World War II was like. Or 'Nam. Nobody gave a shit about us. We were supposed to round up villagers now and then, but there were no villages around us. We couldn't raise company on the radio, which was fine, because everything they told us to do was bass-ackwards. They couldn't get us or we'd ignore them if we didn't like it." She fixed him with a gaze, finally noticing him there again. "And since I know what a straight arrow you are, when I say 'didn't like it,' I don't mean we disobeyed orders, I mean I didn't do dumb shit to get my men killed."

He held up his hands in mock surrender. "I never claimed to be a straight arrow."

"You never claim to be shit." She sighed, back at Hoffman's Bar and Grill in Shitkicker, Oklahoma, instead of off in the oddly romantic and yet deadly Afghan countryside. Deth snapped his fingers at a waitress until she brought them another round of drinks. Up on what could only charitably be called a "stage," the immensely fat Lizard was singing "Strokin'" by Clarence Carter in the most unpleasant manner imaginable. "I killed a dog," she said.

"What do you mean?"

"The men adopted this dog, you know the kind I mean, malnourished and mangy and just looking like it was going to die so they, of course, brought it into the COB and tried to teach it to be a roving guard."

"Did it work?"

"Oh, it worked as far as being a roving guard goes. Which does not excuse the violation of General Order #1."

"Which is?"

"No fucking pets. Well, it's a bunch of things. No booze, no porn (you should remember that for when you go over, Deth.) But no adopting local animals."

"Are you sure about that? I see things on the news all the time about them bringing home dogs and..."

Vu was giving him a look like he was half-retarded. "I know it happens," she said, "That doesn't make it legal. Or right. I wish I'd been a better leader and put my foot down the minute they brought that dog into the COB."

She slid her still-frothy beer in a small rink from left to right between her hands as though it were an air hockey disk. In a few minutes, all the sweat on the glass would evaporate and she wouldn't be able to slide it anymore.

"Oh, who cares?" Deth said finally, "It was just a dog."

"The Taliban cared. Attacks on COB Ouroboros tripled."

"Tripled?"

"Taliban attacks tripled. Well, I say Taliban, what I really mean is Afghan. You're supposed to call them Taliban no matter who they really were. Because those fuckers hate hatehate dogs. Only thing they hate more is pigs. Well, and Jews, I guess. And women. But in terms of animals, there's not a whole lot more they hate than dogs. So when the local nationals noticed the little shit-eater that the boys adopted, suddenly we were persona non grata."

She bit into the knuckle of her forefinger and Deth watched, amazed that she didn't draw blood. Her eyes looked suddenly like she had been crying all day, though he'd been with her for hours and hadn't seen a drop. He suddenly noticed, perhaps for the first time, that she had one green eye and one brown eye. He was struck by the strange dichotomy and by the sudden funereal pall that had fallen over her. "Wooden got shot," she said.

"I'm sorry." He put out his hand and blanketed it over her own, the one she wasn't biting. She did not acknowledge it either to appreciate the empty gesture or to draw her hand away. She did, however, release her death grip on her knuckle and he saw that while no blood had been drawn, she had left deep indentations.

She held up the wrist of the hand with the finger she had just all but severed. With her other forefinger, she traced a line down between the two divergent bones of the forearm, around the area where someone's pulse is taken.

"Right here," she said, "He didn't die. I didn't mean to make you think he had died."

"Well, that's still upsetting," he said, "He got a Purple Heart?"

"Who gives a shit?" Deth felt his cheeks burning. "They shot that boy in the wrist," she reiterated, "Because of a fucking dog. He'll never have use of his hand again, and it's my fault."

"It's not your fault!" Deth said, "You didn't shoot him. And you didn't bring the dog on the COB. And Wooden was a big boy."

Vu took a long drink from her beer. "Some officer you are," she said.

It was the sharpest cut he had ever received. When she put the beer down, she wiped some invisible foam from her lips. She punctuated each sentence of the next few words she spoke with a harsh, down-pointing jointed finger plunged into the laminate surface of the table.

"I was in charge. I let them keep the dog. I put Wooden on duty that night. And, most importantly, I was in charge." She waited a few heartbeats for a response, but Deth had nothing. She took another drink, perhaps to brace herself. "You know, you always tell yourself shit happens, and that's all well and good, but then you go and you watch PFC Victor Wooden get shot in the wrist and you realize if you'd made different choices, if you'd, literally, just changed the watch schedule that night, or been more attentive, or, shit, paid more attention in OBC or maybe just if you'd tripped over a rock that night, things would've been different. And I have to live with that. It's nothing compared to what Wooden's living with, but..." She trailed off, allowing her hands to explain the unexplainable emotion for her.

"Come on, Piera," he said, "You're a war hero."

"War hero?" She shook her head. "You know who's a war hero? Talley's a war hero."

"Talley's a chump," Deth said, wrinkling his nose, "He sat in Kuwait his whole damn deployment."

"He brought every single one of his Soldiers home, safe and whole," Vu said, pounding out each word on the tabletop with her finger, "That's the definition of a war hero. I don't know what I am."

"I'm sorry, Piera." He didn't know what else could be said.

She smiled, but he could tell it was empty, a showman's smile, a vaudevillian's smile, the smile of one of those clowns that only reveal their real feelings when they're crying in the painting. "Forget it," she said.

Blessedly, the KJ spoke over the microphone. "...coming up next we've got Piera, Piera come on down..." The KJ didn't seem to speak in sentences, all of his words ran together, and he repeated phrases he had already spoken in different combinations ad infinitum. Deth suspected that if they would let him, he would talk like that all night. "...Piera's gonna sing a little Faith Hill for you, everybody, doesn't that sound nice, a little Faith Hill courtesy of Piera, Piera..."

As Vu sang, he thought he detected a little tremor in her voice, but he may have just imagined it. Against his better judgment, he flipped open one of the massive black binders containing the songs the KJ had available. The first half of the binder was alphabetical by song, which was all but unreadable unless you knew exactly the title of the song you wanted to sing, which almost no one ever did. The second half of the book, the more useful half, was alphabetical by artist and was littered with graffiti and beer stains.

Deth despised karaoke. Nevertheless, he jotted something down on one of the quartered strips of construction paper stuffed in the front of the binder, ignoring the lines carefully requesting name, song, and artist and writing his request on the back freehand. He went up to the bar to order two shots of Jäger (Vu's favorite) and made like he was waving hello to her while he secreted the slip of construction paper into the KJ's woven reed basket.

The KJ looked thankful. Pickings had been slim for him at Hoffman's that evening. He unfolded the slip of construction paper and bobbed his head in time to Vu's song. Deth sat back down. When Vu was finally finished, he did no more than point at the shot of Jäger and she gratefully drank it. He saw that between the singing and the shot, some of the vigor was starting to return to her face. "Oh, I forgot to tell you," she said, as though mentioning an article she had spotted in the Constitution that morning, "How I killed it."

"Piera..."

"No, no, no," she said, "You'll wonder forever."

"Okay," he said, "How'd you kill it?"

"I took it outside the fence, threw some wire over a tree branch, wrapped a loop around its neck, and pulled the other end until it hung."

"That sounds...monstrous."

"Better that dog than another one of my men. Besides, I told them the Taliban had done it. They went batshit for a while, grilling the villagers, but then the locals saw the dog was dead and everything went back to normal. I can still see that dog hanging from the tree, struggling to bark, like she was going to get out of a wire noose. Tough old bitch. Guess I had to admire her, but General Order #1 is General Order #1."

Deth had to give props to the KJ, that was the second time that night he had interrupted a supremely awkward pause in the conversation with his old friend. "...okay, coming up next we've got Bickham, Bickham's coming up here right now to sing you a little 'Born in the USA,' a nice patriotic tune coming right at you from Bickham, everybody here he is, give it up for Bickham..."

Deth swallowed the non-existent dregs in one of his old beer mugs to brace himself.

"You're singing?"

"Only for you, Piera, only for you."

20

On the plus side, the full service team was made up of Soldiers from their platoon. In newly pressed greens that some of them hadn't worn since graduating from Basic, they looked fresh and excited. The O'Hara funeral would be a chance for them to get out of sweeping the motor pool and do something fun and unusual in a uniform they never got to wear. Deth remembered that feeling. He envied them.

"Sir!" SSG Phillips fairly shouted, saluting Deth. Deth returned the salute, reminding himself to act in real time and not one-third time. The military courtesies done away with, Phillips grabbed his hand and pumped it. "How you doing, LT? Long time no see."

"Sergeant Phillips," Deth said, nodding.

"What do you say, Sergeant?" Phillips said, turning to Packs. Packs looked like if he'd had his 'druthers he would've decked

Phillips. The two had never gotten along, and Deth was intrigued to note that absence had apparently made the heart grow harder. Seeing that Packs was not going to return his smile or even utter a word of greeting and perhaps considering the game won, Phillips simply addressed Deth without taking his eyes off Packs's sturdy frame. "Did you hear about Sergeant Emerson, sir?"

Deth was taken aback. He didn't know Emerson, he only knew he was a very senior E-7 who was destined never to grab that brass ring of First Sergeanthood and was simply biding his time 'til retirement. The man was in his forties but made elderly by the army and crippling alcohol addiction.

Deth had never yet met Emerson when the man wasn't drunk, which included, perhaps disproportionately, instances of him being drunk on duty. Deth had arrived at the battalion in the middle of the night, the result of some misunderstood orders and his desire not to be sent to Leavenworth for failing to report before midnight on his start date.

SFC Emerson had met him, technically on duty, at the Battalion Staff Duty desk, with a giant 40-oz 7-Eleven plastic cup at his side. Having never met the man before, Deth had no idea that he had been slurring because of drunkenness rather than Southernness (and he was damned Southern.) Ever after he had seen that Big Gulp cup in Emerson's hand, and he had quickly realized that he had been a fool to think it had ever been anything other than 40 ounces of vodka with a little Coke thrown in for food coloring. Emerson's assertion that he bought a new one every day was belied by the ever blackening bottom of the cup which he laid on ashtrays as he chain-smoked and the hoods of HMMWVs and tracks while he pretended to supervise their maintenance.

"Sergeant Emerson retired," Packs said, breaking his self-imposed oath of silence, "I went to his party before I got st...assigned to funeral detail."

"Yes, that's true, Sergeant," Phillips said, now looking at Deth and addressing Packs instead of the other way around, "He's dead now, though."

"Booze?" Deth mouthed silently, praying that the men couldn't see him ask the question.

Packs and Emerson had been mates. Perhaps Emerson was a bit older, but they had come up together, Emerson always in the FDC (Fire Direction Center) while Packs had been running his launcher and, later, his platoon. Phillips had obviously brought the matter up to upset him, and he had done so in front of the men. Deth couldn't abide it, but he wasn't sure what to do about it, either. Packs would probably sort it all out later, anyway.

"No, sir," Phillips said, graciously not mentioning what Deth had guessed, "Heart gave out. I guess without the army, he just...didn't have anything to live for anymore. Some people are like that, you know. No outside interests."

Deth couldn't deny he was a path-of-least-resistance kind of guy, maybe not well suited to command. But this kind of dick-measuring, especially amongst NCOs, was decidedly out of his wheelhouse. "Uh..."

"We got a while yet," Packs broke in, "Before the funeral. I suppose First Sergeant told you all to be up and in uniform before PT?"

The men all nodded. It was only 0900 now, which meant they'd been that way for four hours, and the funeral wasn't even until 1330. Deth had been wondering why First Sergeant had asked him and Packs to report to Mortuary Affairs to meet the full service team four hours before the funeral, but now he understood. It was just the way 1SGs all over the army worked. When a general wanted to take a brigade run at 0600, it was as inevitable as the tide that every intermediary would knock fifteen minutes off the report time until 1SGs were ordering their men to stand to at 0400.

"All right," Packs said, "Let's hit up the D-FAC. I've never said this before and I'll probably lose my pumpkin patch for saying it..." Packs tapped the badge on his chest that indicated he had once been a drill sergeant. It proudly proclaimed "This We'll Defend," the motto of the army, and a snake that always made Deth think it ought to say "Don't Tread on Me." "...but eat slow," Packs concluded, "Take time to have two cups of dishwater."

The men groaned, not as one, but clearly of one mind. Packs wasn't a hardass, a "smoke" as Deth had heard the PSGs in the non-13M units called, but he wasn't a fainting lily with the men either. In any case, Deth was surprised to see Packs accept their griping with good humor. "What is it?" Packs grunted.

Tentatively, Figueroa stepped forward as the boldest member of the junior enlisted. "Come on, Sergeant," Fig said, "Don't be cheap."

Packs was suddenly struck by a look on his face that suggested he would be happier to snap Fig's neck like a breadstick than anything else in the world right now. Deth saw Packs's hands starting to scrabble at his rank insignia, as though he were about to rip it off and declare it time to go behind the shed as two men without rank. Deth recognized the mounting ire and stepped in front of his PSG. "What's all this 'cheap' business?" Deth asked, "You expecting me and Sergeant Packs to pay for all your breakfasts?"

"You want to come over later and fuck my sister, too?" Packs asked.

"Come on, sir," Fig said, "We know you've got the credit card. What about the money you're getting for all eight of us? You and Sarge gonna eat eight steak and eggs? We wan' go to Denny's."

Deth knew it didn't add up, but at least he had gathered what the men were upset about and had headed off disaster with Packs pummeling into a wall-to-wall counseling session with Fig. No possible outcome of that could've been considered positive. Deth was about to speak when Packs put a beefy hand on his shoulder.

"I'll field this if you don't mind, sir." Deth gestured as though they were actors on stage. Packs stepped forward and leaned into Fig's face, not closely enough to invade his personal space, but close enough to intimidate everyone else present. "Why don't you learn some shit before you talk some shit?"

That got some hoots and catcalls. The men detested Packs as a general rule for being an authority figure, and more specifically for not letting them get away with dumb shit, but every single one of them loved to see someone get put in their place, as long as it was someone *else*. It was practically part of the Army ethos.

"In case you didn't notice, this is a local funeral, *Specialist*," Packs said, using Fig's rank like a particularly obscene euphemism for shit, "That means no per diem. But even if we did get per diem, you couldn't use it within 30 miles of a post where you have D-FAC privileges or draw subsistence pay. Otherwise the army might be paying for you to eat twice and then the whole damn Treasury would just explode."

The men were laughing and slapping Fig on the back and repeating the word "explode," except that most of them pronounced it "asplode." Fig was scowling, but Packs had had his fun. He saw no reason to continue to demean the kid. "Come on, Guns and Rockets is right over there," Packs said, gesturing towards the D-FAC.

Deth surreptitiously checked his wallet. Since he lived off post, he drew subsistence pay and therefore had to pay every time he used the post dining facilities. Consequently, he rarely ate at Guns and Rockets, except occasionally after PT when something pressing would keep him from going home, or after a late morning piss test when he could no longer go home. He had five bucks and some change, and while he couldn't remember offhand exactly how much breakfast at the chow hall cost, he knew it was less than that. Breakfast, despite being the best meal available at an Army chow hall, was always the cheapest.

"What if we paid?" Fig said, after Deth had been sure the matter had been settled. Packs turned back. He had already made it about ten steps towards the D-FAC.

"Well, we've got the van and gas gets paid for no matter what," Phillips chimed in, "And the men do need to get out of the billets more."

Packs glanced from face to face. "I can't make anyone go to Denny's who doesn't have the money and isn't willing to pay," Packs said, "If just one of you doesn't want to, we eat at the D-FAC."

Deth wasn't sure what Packs's game was. Putting it that way was certain to get them all to agree to pay, even the buck privates that didn't have a dollar left over after borrowing from a payday loan joint to pay their Ferrari payments. Making it so that whichever individual volunteered not to go first would be blamed for the whole outing being cancelled ensured that no individual would step forward. It was like group punishment in reverse.

"That's not just chow, that includes gratuity," Deth pointed out, "I'm not going to have you stiff a waitress because you didn't really want to go out." Now the men were snickering at him. He narrowed his eyes. "What is it?"

"What'd you say, sir?" Simmons asked, "'Gratuity?'"

All of the men echoed, in varying levels of falsetto and with varying degrees of disparagement in their voices, "tooity" or something like that. Deth raised an eyebrow. "You don't know what a gratuity is?" Deth asked, gobsmacked.

"Tooity," the men echoed like parrots or cockatiels.

Sometimes, the capacity of joes to be either ignorant or to hide their intelligence behind a veil of ignorance to go along with the group astonished Deth. "A tip," he explained, "You need to tip the waitress."

"Well, shit, sir, why didn't you just say so?"

The O'Hara funeral went off without a hitch, which was good because they were under much closer scrutiny than usual. The garrison commander was there, as was the Third Corps Artillery commander, and every bird colonel who was anybody. Unlike for most of their funerals around Oklahoma and Arkansas, SGT O'Hara had been active duty.

Deaths of active duty service members were thankfully rare at Ft. Sill. Having an occasionally analytical mind, Deth had to say to himself that with only (if "only" was the correct or human adjective to use in that case) 4000 dead in Iraq, and something like a million people having cycled through, give or take, and discounting double tours, deaths were statistically an anomaly at .000004%. That didn't change the media's obsession with combat deaths, which made them seem like an inevitability.

Deth's own mother was convinced he would die for having joined the army. There was no point bandying about statistics with five zeroes and a decimal place in them, she was simply convinced he would die. He hadn't even been allowed to play with guns as a child, and while joining the army had been more of a financial decision than anything else, he had to appreciate the subtle and lopsided rebellion of it.

All other things being equal, the death of someone you knew was rare enough that the death of someone at the same post as you really struck home. O'Hara had become a cause célèbre, and even Deth couldn't deny it seemed to strike impossibly close to home, math be damned.

All that is to say that, sheep-like or not, his platoon performed admirably under exceptional scrutiny. O'Hara's coffin was brought into Ft. Sill National on a caisson pulled by horses, which was the sort of magnificent military flourish that made Deth disagree with Packs about wanting only a cheap wooden tombstone.

In a full service, the music did not come from the invisible aether (a.k.a. a boombox hidden behind a gravestone.) Instead, there was an actual bugler (or "buggler" as Deth insisted on calling it or "buggerer" as Packs insisted on calling Fig.) The army didn't really keep that many buglers on staff anymore, and most of them were playing in band performances, so Figueroa was the designated "musician."

Of course, not knowing how to play a bugle meant that Fig had to fake the fingering while the pre-recorded music played. Deth had always been intrigued by the little stereo that was perfectly shaped to fit into an otherwise ordinary bugle. All Fig had to do was flick the toggle on the stereo, point the bugle skyward, and pantomime.

Packs, then, instead of being a one-man show, was now reveling in his opportunity to conduct drill and ceremony in the big time. While the two of them (with Packs doing all of the actual work) could easily fold a flag, at a full service funeral, it took six men and the orders of a seventh to do it. The result was heartbreaking, and when

Deth received his flag from Packs to give to the widow as usual, he risked a glance at the generals and saw that they were moved. They had done good.

"We done good," Deth confirmed later, when the mourners and even the caisson had vacated the cemetery and they were leaning against their old familiar sedan smoking.

"Phillips did a good job training them," Packs agreed, "Except Simmons almost folded it backwards. Too bad I'm going to have to kick his ass later."

"Who, Simmons?"

"No, Phillips."

"Why?"

"For what he said about Emerson."

"Ah," Deth said, nodding, "I had forgotten about that."

"I didn't," Packs said, "Emerson may have been a lush, but he was an NCO in the United States Army and deserving of respect."

"So is Sergeant Phillips."

"Barely."

The rape van pulled up alongside them and Phillips stuck his head out of the passenger's side window, smiling broadly. "Looks like you ain't rid of us yet, sir, Sergeant!"

"Sergeant Phillips, what are you talking about?" Packs growled, tossing his cigarette to the ground and stamping it without revealing the anger obviously pulsing through him.

"We got another full service in Joplin." Phillips reached up into the invisible air outside the van window and tugged at it, as though it were the horn of a tractor trailer. "Toot toot!" Phillips declared, "We'll meet you back at the billets so everybody can change."

Packs already had the government-issued cell phone out and open before the van had puttered off. He spoke no more than five words during the entire four minute conversation with Mortuary Affairs and then merely nodded to Deth by way of acknowledging Phillips's rectitude. They climbed into the car. "I hope we can shake them soon," Packs said, "If I've got to do this grind I'd rather do it without a sideshow."

"I don't know," Deth said, "It's nice to be around the men again."

"You and me I trust to show a little dignity," Packs said, "These are military funerals, after all. With this barrel of monkeys, it's only a matter of time before they make fools of themselves and make you and me look bad. Oh, speaking of foolish monkeys, I dug this up while I was at home."

Packs patted the inside of his dress jacket. He found what he was looking for, a glossy 5x8 photo, and handed it to Deth. He knew at a glance, without being told or even reading the name tape on the Soldier's chest, who it was. The Byzantine forehead, the pained look of attempting to think, the bulk without definition, even the eyebrows you could hide a wallaby behind.

"Big Smell," Deth whispered as though he were Indiana Jones picking the right cup in the den of the Holy Grail.

"Notice anything off about that picture?" Packs asked, pulling the car into gear.

Deth scanned the photo. He had been so hung up on the man's mongoloid looks he hadn't looked any deeper. Then he saw it. A watermark of Santa in the background, and below it, in semi-broken English, the inscription "Merry christmas From Tikrit, iraq, love, Dave brannigan."

"A Christmas card?" Deth asked, perplexed, "A freaking Christmas card? Who sends a Christmas card from a war zone? Who gets a Christmas card made in a war zone?"

"Guys with too much money and time on their hands and not enough warring to do," Packs said.

"That's an interesting capitalization convention he's using there," Deth mused, "Wait a minute, you never mentioned being in Tikrit. I thought you were in Balad."

"We were," Packs said, "But 42nd wasn't. Take a look at the combat patch he's wearing."

Deth looked again. It was decidedly not their unit's. He scratched his head. "Are you saying he..."

"...went to Tikrit," Packs said, "Put on a fake patch, and got a bunch of Christmas cards taken to send home. We each stole one from his pile, so, sorry Mrs. Brannigan or whoever didn't get theirs."

"Why would somebody do that?" Deth asked, "Fake being in a different unit?"

"A more prestigious unit, you mean? Stationed in Saddam's hometown? I can't imagine why someone who earned an Air Medal would have to fake stolen valor."

21

Phillips had changed into a t-shirt that said "Mortaritaville" with a mockup of Parrothead paraphernalia and a map of Iraq. The other members of the full service team were looking out of sorts in ill-fitting polos and t-shirts. "You got the card, Sergeant?" Phillips asked Packs.

Packs jerked a thumb over his shoulder at Deth. "L.T.'s got it," Packs said.

Phillips turned his gaze to Deth. "Where we headed, sir? Denny's?"

Deth shook his head. "Not the one in town," he said, "We've got to get at least thirty miles out before we can use the card. Although if you men want to eat here, I think the D-FAC's still open..." There was a near-universal hooting, jeering, and scowling. "All right, just to be clear, drinks do not go on the card, but if you want, we can go somewhere where you can drink. But you're buying your own. We're going to pass through OKC, so there's some pretty good restaurants there. Where do you men want to go?"

Deth waited. All of his men were smiling the exact same shit-eating grin at him. They all had something in mind but none of them wanted to say it. Fig, of course, rarely had qualms. "We go to Hooters, sir?"

Deth raised an eyebrow. "Why?" he asked, "The food's shit there."

"Food ain't why you go to Hooters, sir." The men started laughing like horny high schoolers. Deth folded his arms. He was younger than quite a few of these men. He recalled, at the tender age of 22, having to go over the finances of a near-30-year-old specialist and, without any real authority to order any changes in the way he spent his own money, trying desperately to point out that if he didn't buy Mountain Dew and hot dogs at the shoppette every day, he could probably afford to feed his family with commissary food. Actually, the commissary was shit now. Wal-Mart was cheaper a lot of the time.

"Is that what you men want?" Nodding. All of them. Even Phillips had a big stupid grin plastered on his face. "All right," Deth said, shrugging his shoulders, "Don't say I didn't warn you. Sergeant Packs and I will take the sedan. Sergeant Phillips, you follow us in the van. We'll lead the way."

"Follow Me!" someone shouted, apparently someone who had gone to basic at Benning.

That set off a whole other round of giggling. When they were buttoned up safe in the sedan, Deth turned to Packs. "Some of them are older than me," he said.

Packs nodded. "Army's great, keeps you immature," Packs said, "Except your hair."

Deth nodded. His PMS at ROTC had been grey as a mule at the age of thirty. Packs was all salt and pepper, what there was left of his hair, and he was only in his forties. Just the other day, Deth had squinted in the mirror all morning trying to figure out whether one of his hairs was grey from stress or had just been bleached blond from the sun. Unable to tell, he had simply plucked it out and not worried about it any further.

Musing on Phillips's shirt, Deth asked, "What's Mortaritaville? Just Iraq?"

Packs snorted, but didn't take his eyes off the road. "You mean Hollywood's shirt over there? Showing off what he's seen when he ain't seen shit?"

"Yeah, I guess."

"No, it's not Eye-raq. It's LSA Anaconda. Balad. Where I was."

"Well, why do they call it that?"

"Shit, sir, we got mortared every day. I think it was ten, eleven times a day when I was there."

"Why? Is it that important?"

"Not really. There's a lot of logistics there. Hajji's got nothing better to do, I guess."

"Well, mortars don't have much range. Why couldn't you guys stop it?"

Packs shook his head. He didn't seem upset at the question so much as at the answer. "Anytime you saw a guy with a goat within a hundred meters of the fenceline, he was either a guy with a goat or he was a spotter for the mortars. Anytime you see a kid with a soccer ball within a hundred meters of the fenceline, he was either just a kid with a soccer ball or he was a spotter for the mortars. So our choice was to shoot every raghead that came within a mile of the place or not shoot any of them. And you know what happens whenever you shoot an innocent kid or whatever, his whole family suddenly becomes terrorists and then you just made the problem worse. Which is just as well, because it's not like they ever hit shit. It was better just to take the mortars all day than to turn the whole town into a terrorist rathole."

"What was it like getting shelled every day?"

Packs shrugged. "Nothing much to it. Usually you don't even notice until the announcement goes off."

"Announcement?"

Packs cleared his throat and imitated a robotic-sounding woman. "This is the command post. There has been an indirect fire attack. All personnel are released. All personnel should remain vigilant for UXOs. All clear, all clear, all clear. Command post out."

He reverted to his regular voice. "I always admired that lady for staying so frosty under pressure. She sounded exactly the same every time."

"It was a recording, wasn't it?"

Packs was smiling. Deth folded his arms. "I'm just yanking your chain, sir. It really wasn't that big a deal. Every once in a while you'd hear a boom-boom. We didn't even have to wear our Kevlars walking around the LSA. The explosions were usually distant. Most of the time you didn't notice anything. One time, though, hoo-ee, it knocked me right out of bed."

"Yeah?"

"Yeah, I could've sworn it hit one of the cans next to mine. That's what we called the little, you know, aluminum buildings where we slept. I even stumbled out, naked as a jaybird, to check."

"No you didn't."

"I did! Everyone else was in PTs, but I didn't care. What the fuck did I care? I just grabbed my flashlight and went. Nothing, though. I think it hit the CRSP yard, which was pretty close, but I still couldn't believe it made a bang like that. And at 0300, too. You'd think Hajji could be a little more considerate."

"So you were never in that much danger Over There?"

Packs shook his head. "Cakewalk," he said, "Except for that RPG I told you about. You know what was funny, though, was Big Smell kept walking around after that mortar hit the CRSP yard long after everyone else had gone back to bed. I think he was looking for it. I think he wanted to pretend he had been within 30 yards of it."

"Why? Oh, for a Combat Action Badge."

Packs nodded. "In fact..." He snorted, unable to contain a laugh. "Well, you know, General O was a redleg before he became a general officer."

"Oh, yeah? I didn't know that."

"He was. So the BC one day, well, see, he was off-schedule with Big Smell, so this was when he was getting ready to leave and Big Smell wasn't. So he put in loddy doddy everybody for CABs. Every last one of his Soldiers."

"Did they see a lot of action?"

"Not a bit of it. Most of them never left the FOB. But if you look at the regs, it says that if you engage the enemy, you're eligible for a CAB. So since we were shooting rockets into combat..."

"...And General O was a redleg..."

Packs nodded. "He signed off on it. Believe it or not. And the BC didn't put any of us in the LNO section in because we never fired any rockets. I thought it was hilarious, but Big Smell was steaming. He would've killed for that CAB, and he couldn't even take it out on BC, because BC was already back in the rear."

"I'll bet he took it out on you."

Packs shrugged. "Occupational hazard. I'll tell you what, though...well, this isn't actually very funny. It's actually kind of sad. There was a big explosion one day. This was way after that mortar that hit near the cans. This was a big one, though, biggest I ever heard. And you know, we heard it every day, so much so that you usually just tune it out.

"Except we were all at the office. So we saw this happening in real time. Big Smell was in the little office next to the main one, where we made him sequester himself. We all turn and we see this blur going by. Big Smell running by the door.

"So, I follow him after a minute, shaking my head. Outside the building I go, and he's just trucking. Now, I've told you before how in shape Big Smell is."

"Not at all."

"Not even a little. I don't know how the man ever passed a PT test. Yes I do: falsifying records. So he's puffing and fuming, his big old limbs flying every which way like one of those dolls at a car dealership."

"Wacky Waving Inflatable Arm-Flailing Tube Man?"

"Sure. That's what he looked like."

Without taking his hands off the wheel, Packs made an approximation of how ridiculous Big Smell looked running. He waggled his elbows and his free leg like a lunatic. Deth laughed just looking at him, without even imagining it. Then, when he imagined a grown man, a man in a position of authority and (theoretically) respect doing it, he guffawed. "So he went running towards the mortar?"

"Yes, sir. He wanted to be first on the scene so he could say he had been within thirty meters when it went off."

"Too bad he couldn't have taken a chopper to it. Get an Air Medal and a CAB all at once."

"Yeah."

"I'm guessing he never got his CAB."

Packs took his eyes off the road long enough to fix Deth with a somewhat depressing look. "Sir, it was worse than that. It was pretty bad. He came back a while later and he looked shaken, which, for someone like him, is saying something. To actually, you know, be ashamed of yourself. He was the most shameless son of a bitch I ever met."

Deth leaned forward in his seat, felt the safety belt suddenly restraining him as it seemed to do at random intervals, and leaned back to allow it to relax its death grip again. "What happened?"

"It wasn't a mortar. It was a VBIED. They drove right up to the checkpoint and set it off. It's just that it was a checkpoint on the other side of the LSA, so it sounded like a big mortar to us."

"Did anybody get hurt?"

Packs nodded grimly. "The terrorists died. But who gives a shit about them? They killed two of our guys and a friendly Eye-raqi who just happened to be trying to get through the gate. One of the mechanics at the civilian motor pool, I think. There were intestines on the ground, that's what Big Smell said, and I guess I've got to hand it to him, at least he was ashamed of himself. But he also said that the MPs had already gotten there and put up a perimeter."

"So he would've faked being in the explosion if they hadn't?"

Packs shrugged. "I like to believe the best about human nature."

"No, you don't."

"No, I don't, but I guess maybe I like to believe Dave Brannigan has just a little humanity in his soul. Otherwise...it's too scary. Like looking into a...pit."

The Hooters loomed in front of them. Shaking his head, Packs pulled in. The van pulled in after them, and all of the Soldiers looked unconscionably excited. "Why do they want to eat at this place, anyway?" Deth asked shaking his head.

"Sir, most of these guys don't get out of the billets. Ever."

"Why not?"

Packs shrugged. "It's just what you do, I guess. So when they do get to leave, if they want to eat at a stupid place like Hooters, hey, at least they're not getting the clap from some juicy girl in downtown Seoul, am I right?"

"Good thing Lawton ain't Seoul."

Deth snorted awake in the middle of the night to the sound of loveplay. He blinked, glanced around the room, squinted his eyes to make out the big red lights of the alarm clock. Suddenly the wall next door shuddered again.

Deth made a hammer with his fist and banged on the wall. "Knock it off in there, you two!"

"Sir?" Packs's voice drifted through the wall.

Deth narrowed his eyes. He had never pictured Packs as the philandering sort. In fact, Packs had often joked that he always called his wife ahead of time before coming home from any trip and advised her just to get the other guy's slippers out from under her bed. "Sergeant Packs?"

"Yes..."

"Who's in there with you?"

A choked voice replied, "Sergeant Phillips, sir!"

"Is this a Don't Ask Don't Tell thing I should be worried about?"

"No, sir," Packs responded, "We're just doing some wall-to-wall counseling."

"Is that right, Phillips?"

"Yes, sir," Phillips dutifully responded.

"Do it on the other wall. Wake Fig."

As Deth settled back down into bed he heard the tell-tale sound of Phillips's head bouncing off something hard again, but this time it was distant enough that it must've been the far wall. "Talk to me about Emerson being dead!" he heard Packs yelling, "In front of the men!"

Oh, yeah. He had forgotten about that. The whole thing disappeared from his mind as soon as his head hit the pillow.

22

The Ashburnham funeral turned out to be the worst funeral of all time.

Not of Deth's experience.

Not in American history.

Of all time.

Until the day he died, Deth would always remember the name Ashburnham, and he'd remember the poor National Guardsman's funeral as the greatest debacle in military history. In comparison, Little Big Horn didn't seem so bad.

The cemetery outside Joplin, MO, was nicer than the O'Hara funeral at Ft. Sill National had been, but the setup was much the same. For one thing, there was more shade there than Oklahoma could usually muster, and the grass was much lusher. The gravesite sat to the side of a small embankment which divided the cemetery from a copse of trees and kept the whole area cool and largely free of wind. Upon arrival, Deth had been thinking that, if anything, this funeral would go off even better than O'Hara's.

"Okay, Specialist Fig," Deth said, "You're kind of our designated buggler, so why don't you set up..." Deth glanced around and found a nice spot where Fig would have plenty of shade and be off in the distance, sort of the way a lone bugler should look for a funeral. (Not to mention far enough away that spectators wouldn't notice the hunk of black machinery blocking the bugle's mouth. It didn't usually worry him, but when he had the room to play with, he wanted to be sure of its invisibility.) Deth stepped to a spot that seemed good. "Here," he concluded.

"Roger that, sir," Fig said with a grin, running up with the phony baloney bugle.

"Roger doesn't have a last name," Packs said as Fig ran past him to his appointed spot.

"And as for the rest of us...have you scoped out a good spot, Sergeant Packs?"

"I have, sir."

"All right, let's run through it once or twice."

The pavilion was already set up and thankfully none of the guests had arrived yet, so they had a chance to practice on the exact spot where they would be performing the ceremony. "Train as you fight" was one of Deth's favorite mottos, and it always called to mind the time during an ROTC Field Training Exercise that parents had been invited and one of the MS-IVs had coyly stated,   "Train as you fight. With your moms and dads watching and taking pictures."

Deth surveyed the scene. Only one real street led into the cemetery and up to the pavilion where CSM Ashburnham's funeral would take place. After that, it petered out into a sort of a grey packed dirt road. They had pulled the van and the car off the road in an area where they would hopefully be inconspicuous.

"Well," Deth said, "The good thing is we know which way they have to come in. They're going to be coming in from that way..." Deth pointed towards the mouth of the paved road. "...Which means that the coffin will have to sit this way."

Deth showed what he meant for the men. With a two-man team, if the blue field of stars pointed the opposite direction of what they had been expecting, all Packs and Deth had to do was switch places. With a full service, each man had a specific place around the coffin, so switching the field meant reversing everyone's roles, which could be a pain. Thankfully, since they knew which way the hearse was coming, they wouldn't have to deal with that at all.

If it had just been him and Packs, Deth wouldn't have bothered to practice even once. With Phillips's less experienced crew, he wanted to run through it at least twice. When Simmons damn near folded the whole flag backwards the first time, Deth decided that twice had just been upped to thrice, and Simmons was off the all-important foot. "Sergeant Phillips, why don't you take the foot?"

"Yes, sir."

"Okay, Fig!" Deth shouted from afar, "When we all turn and salute, that's your cue."

"Should I actually do it, sir?"

"Don't waste the battery!" Phillips shouted, "Just point it to the sky and pretend!"

Phillips took a particular delight tootling "Taps" out of the side of his mouth during the walkthroughs, even though it didn't at all synch up to how long Fig was actually pretending to hold up the bugle. Some of the men waited for Phillips to stop tootling and the others waited for Fig to lower his instrument and all of them burst out laughing when they saw how confused they all were.

"Let's just do it with the music," Packs growled.

"I wouldn't, Sergeant," Phillips said, "I don't know how much battery power we have left. Better save it for the show."

Upon reflection, Deth recognized that all the signs had been in the tea leaves of their inevitable and catastrophic failure, though he had failed to properly read them. He had always been more of a fan of entrail-reading, anyway.

Ashburnham didn't come in on a caisson as O'Hara had. That was more or less to be expected. Caissons were not commonplace enough to let every vet's family be able to find, let alone afford for their funeral. O'Hara had been a bit of an exception as an active duty service member.

Deth hadn't really expected there to be a caisson, so he was able to deal with that relatively simply. Not to mention it didn't affect anything they had to do. What did affect what they were doing was that the hearse came from the opposite direction of where they had been expecting. Somehow the hearse was coming from the packed clay trail instead of the paved road. "Shit," Packs muttered, "Everything's reversed. Change your lineup."

The men, not expecting this, scrambled to change their positions in the honor guard so that when they rolled out to march up to the coffin, they would be in the right position. Having practiced in the exact opposite way, they took an educated guess.

"Simmons, you in the right spot?" Packs growled under his breath as the follow-on cars began to discharge their passengers.

Simmons gave Packs a look like a deer in headlights. "Forget it," Packs said, and then, using his parade order voice, "Atten-tion!"

The full service team snapped to, rigiding their backs. "Present," Packs whispered lustily, "Harms!"

The team saluted the hearse as it passed, as usual drawing the pleasure of the crowd for saluting their father/uncle/whatever when they were, in fact, only saluting the flag draped over his casket. The funeral director thankfully came up behind Deth and tapped him on the shoulder. "That's the next-of-kin in the front row center, red hair, in the veil," the funeral director said quietly.

Deth glanced over. The widow seemed young, but, then, Ashburnham was National Guard, not one of these old "I was a corporal in the '40s" vets they usually buried. In fact, he might have died very young, judging by the number of Guardsmen attending his funeral.

The Guardsmen who were in attendance were wearing ACUs. It seemed odd to Deth to wear ACUs to a funeral, but then the National Guard was a whole different world. A light colonel in ACUs with one of those weird Missouri standing bear patches on his shoulder caught Deth's eye in particular.

The light colonel looked on at them, not quite sternly, more like a father figure. At least, he did at first. Then the mistakes started, and they wouldn't stop coming. It became like a flood and Deth could judge the failure of his team by each glance at the colonel's face to see how much more his mood had darkened.

It started when they had all turned to salute as Fig lifted the faux bugle to his mouth and "Taps" began to play. It started out beautifully. "Dun dundun!" the stereo within the bugle announced once loudly. Then it allowed for a second, "Dun dundun," and, had Deth been paying closer attention, he might have noticed that it was already struggling.

Then, somewhere between the seventh and ninth note of the eternal and hallowed song, the stereo slowed, flickered, and died. "Duuunduuuuuundewwwwwww..." and then it just trailed off.

Every eye of every mourner, even the ones that had been watching the service team or chatting in a low murmur with a neighboring family member suddenly turned and locked on SPC Figueroa, the ersatz bugler. "Motherfucker," Deth said out loud, and wished he hadn't.

Fig's eyes were as wide as MLRS backblast plates. He slowly lowered the bugle from his lips to his chest as he was supposed to do after completing the song. But he had not completed the song. Covered with flop sweat despite the cool morning and aware of all the eyes on him, Fig seemed totally lost as to what to do. Then he made a ridiculous decision and fell over floridly as though the non-existent sun had pierced through the clouds and struck him with a sort of heatstroke that made him flop around like a fish to avoid the mud and grass.

And then, like that, all eyes were back on Deth and his men, in mute, angry expectation. "Order harms," Packs stage-whispered, though clearly he would've preferred to say, "Son of a bitch!"

The men moved silently and sternly to fold the flag with exacting precision, to make up for the obvious failure of their bugler. Deth saw on their ashen faces the dozen curses they were each running through their minds for Fig. The poor specialist, lying on the ground now as though he had passed out when the stereo had very distinctly run out of batteries, would be in for it later. Deth was never sure if things like the blanket party in *Full Metal Jacket* happened in real life, but if it did, it would probably befall Fig later tonight, if not the instant they got back to the billets.

Then, suddenly, snapped out of his reverie, Deth noticed that Simmons was at the foot of the coffin beginning the fold. The hearse's unexpected entry point has messed up their preparations and now the one man he didn't trust to be at the foot was there. And, as Deth had feared, he had already messed up the fold. And not just in a slight, unnoticeable-to-the-average-civilian way.

Simmons had somehow folded the blue field face up during the half fold. That wouldn't have been the end of the world, they could have still flipped the flag and folded again so that the blue field was showing and then all would have been right with the world. But in some kind of one-in-a-million tragedy, not only had Simmons been put on the spot, but he had managed to make the only fold of the flag which would be utterly impossible to miss as wrong. In the quarter fold, the blue field disappeared entirely, and Phillips, at the other end of the flag, had missed the mistake.

Deth's lower lip quivered with a mixture of terror and rage. Terror that he would not only develop a reputation for being a terrible honors team leader, but more importantly that they would disrespect Ashburnham in front of his friends, family, and the leadership of the Missouri National Guard. And rage, justified rage, that Simmons could've made the one mistake that would sink the whole ship.

Deth breathed deeply. Okay, he reasoned, the people in the crowd had not seen anything yet. The backs of three of his men blocked the view of the mourners from seeing what was going on up on the dais. That meant all was not lost yet. He just had to signal them to start over.

"Simmons," Deth hissed as quietly as he could. He had to hiss six more times before Simmons actually looked up at him. "You're doing it backwards!" Deth mouthed.

Simmons shook his head. "I know what I'm doing, sir!" he insisted.

Now Deth just watched with abject horror as the men spent the few minutes allotted to them to fold the flag folding it completely backwards. He wanted to reach out and throttle Simmons for fucking up and Phillips for not noticing and the others for just going along with it, and Figueroa for collapsing like a buffoon, and himself most of all for fucking the whole thing up.

It took until they had fully finished fucking up until they realized that they had folded the flag wrong. Instead of a blue triangle with an exacting number of stars on each side, they had a ridiculous-looking red-and-white striped paper football which even someone who didn't know the difference between marines and Soldiers would recognize as wrong.

Deth said nothing. He didn't have to. Simmons was looking at the boondoggle he had created as though it were an illegitimate child he would now have to support. His jaw worked in a funny fashion, like he had no idea what to do. And he didn't. Nobody did. "Unfold it," Packs said, "And do it right."

Deth couldn't have said it better himself. There was nothing else for it. The mourners were already shifting in their seats. They might not know much about how this was supposed to go, but they already knew it was taking too long. The light colonel, who had gone from respectful to bemused to peeved to furious now looked as though he were cataloguing a list of arcane and medieval tortures to visit upon each of the members of the full service team, but Deth most of all.

It was excruciating watching the men unfold the flag with the slow deliberation with which they had folded it wrong. And then to start all over again, and no one in the audience was fooled anymore. They sat and stared with stony silence. Even the Catholic priest seemed pissed, and everyone seemed furious to have their time wasted. Finally, after what seemed a never-ending stint in purgatory, Packs snuck three highly polished brass shells into the flag and handed it to Deth. "It's fine," Packs whispered barely audibly, so that Deth would not waste any more time checking each corner of the flag.

Deth nodded his silent thanks to his PSG. He was almost half-tempted after the fifteen-minute debacle to simply blow through the delivery ceremony and get his men off the stage as soon as possible. He took a deep breath and told himself that if there was nothing else he could control, he could control this, and CSM Ashburnham at least deserved this last dignity if nothing else.

Deth knelt down before the red-haired woman the funeral director had identified as Mrs. Ashburnham. "On behalf of a grateful nation," Deth said, "I present to you this flag, as a symbol of the sacrifices and service of your husband."

"Father," the apparently Ms. Ashburnham said, sounding so sweet and blameless in her correction that it cut him far deeper than if she had grown fierce and accusative.

Deth hoped his eyes didn't go too wide. Why hadn't he just said "loved one?"

"Father," he agreed, his mouth suddenly the Kalahari. One last mistake for the road. Inwardly, he cursed the damn mortician as he rose to salute the flag, but he knew after all that there was no reason why a next of kin couldn't be a daughter just as well as a wife. It was his own fault for not asking. He was struck by the memory of the second-worst funeral he had ever conducted, when the Hendersons and kin had fallen all over each other like the Hatfields and the McCoys for their loved one's flag. He had, up until that very moment, always considered the Henderson funeral to be the very worst funeral anyone anywhere had ever conducted, but he knew in that instant that Ashburnham now had snatched that dubious honor.

Phillips grabbed up the flopper Fig and judiciously marched the men straight to the van. Packs and Deth stared longingly after them. Phillips had been wise enough to park the van in a copse of trees so that the mourners would not notice when they pulled out. The sedan, however, was right in the middle of the field, where everyone would see them hurrying away in shame. "We ought to run," Deth said.

"Suck egg, sir," Packs said, "Don't worry, I've got more ass than anyone can chew."

They stood grimly, as though awaiting the executioner. Phillips, Simmons, Fig, and the others being gone left the two heads of the platoon in the unenviable position of being the sole source for the mourners to vent their displeasure on. Deth had braced himself for jeers, catcalls, even impassioned women clutching at him and slapping him. In a way, the cold, deliberate stare of every mourner passing by cut him deeper than any passion he could have imagined. Each of them seemed to reflect and amplify every nasty thought he had about himself. Had they said something, he would have accepted the criticism, but the silence ensured that he could only invent his own, which was far worse.

Then, when the rest of the cemetery was empty, the lieutenant colonel in the ACUs stood to in front of them. They both saluted, and he returned the salute, a bit tired. His hair was grey and he wore glasses. He looked like nothing so much as Geppetto, or a lovely old memory of your grandfather. Deth knew instantly it would be far tougher to take an ass-chewing from someone who so genuinely seemed to have cared about Ashburnham than from a crusty old drill sergeant or some uppity prick.

"I don't have to tell you CSM Ashburnham deserved better than this. He served with distinction in the National Guard for thirty years," the colonel said, and his voice did not belie his paternal appearance, "I want you boys to promise me something."

"Yes, sir," they said together like contrite pre-teens.

"Don't let this happen again. I don't want anybody else to have to go through this."

Deth hung his head, so it was Packs who said, "Yes, sir." The light colonel nodded and accepted their parting salute before stepping off less smartly than in seeming physical pain reflecting his emotional state.

"That wasn't so bad," Deth said.

"That was the worst chewing out I've ever had," Packs said.

"Yeah, I guess you're right. It would've been easier if he had yelled at us."

"You know what the really fucked-up part about that is, sir?"

"More fucked up than Fig pretending to fall over?"

"The fucked-up part is that that colonel and sergeant major is you and me in twenty years."

23

Deth was distinctly aware of the lastness of everything they did that evening. The last time they would ever pass through OKC on their way back to Lawton. The last time Packs would caterwaul a country song just to get Deth's goat. The last steak dinner. The last gas station stop.

In the wake of the worst funeral he or any living man had ever been forced to put on, he had fully expected to finally get recalled to Ft. Sill. There would probably be a chewing out, then it would be forgotten, but most importantly he would be back with his men where he belonged. Seeing the men from his platoon, even the losers like Fig, had sorely aggravated this desire in him.

The look on Packs's face as he spoke on the cell phone to mortuary affairs, possibly to Mortuary Affairs himself, was one of unchecked, childlike wonder. It was not the face of a man being chewed out.

"What is it?" Deth had asked when Packs had stood, motionless, the just clasped-together phone still in his hands, "Did we have a negative report?" Packs nodded dumbly. "Damn. I was hoping that light colonel wouldn't rat us out."

"He didn't," Packs said, his voice distant.

"What do you mean?"

Packs finally locked his eyes on Deth, with all the suddenness of a man snapping out of a daydream. "Do you remember that time you wore scarlet socks to the graveside?"

"Someone complained about that?"

"Yeah."

"Is Colonel Fink pissed?"

"Mortuary Affairs said it was too stupid to even report to battalion. But he is pulling us off the road."

"We're off the road?"

Packs nodded, just once, very lightly.

Deth did a victory dance, far more lascivious than any ecdysiast's and far more boastful than any touchdown-scoring quarterback's. He repeated "wa-hoo-oo, wa-hoo-oo" in a robotic sing-song, exactly the same way each time, as though he were incapable of coming up with any other word with which to express his profound and long-frustrated joy. Then he stopped when he saw that Packs, while not doing anything nearly as ridiculous, was not expressing his pleasure in any fashion.

"What is it?"

Packs cocked his head. "Did you volunteer for a radar section?"

Deth blinked his eyes. "Yes," he said, remembering, "A while ago. Before..." he made an all-encompassing gesture, "This."

"Well, they picked you. Radar school is a six month course. If Mortuary Affairs had kept us on the road you would have had to wait for the next one. But on account of the complaint...you report tomorrow."

"Six months of radar school?" Deth said, "And then..."

"You're going to war."

Deth sat down. There was no stool, no stump, nothing there. He simply sat down, from standing to the ground in a single motion that bruised his coccyx. If there hadn't been another man standing there, he might have cried. The dance of joy had been mechanical, something that he had been storing up in his bones daily over every long funeral, waiting to explode outward. This, though, was profoundly different. This was like losing his virginity. It was like something he had waited his whole life for had finally come true and there were neither words nor motions to do anything with it.

"Downrange," Deth said. Packs nodded. "Over There." Packs nodded again. "The Sandbox." Packs nodded a third time.

Which brought them here. To the last gas station they would ever stop at together. Well, there might be another someday, but in a way, this felt like the end of the line. It was surreal. He found himself dawdling at the coffee station, but Packs didn't seem to be in any hurry, either. Perhaps the NCO also felt the sense of an ending of all things.

"Guess you'll finally win that Medal of Honor you always wanted, eh, sir?" Packs said, surprisingly being the first to break the ice.

Deth plucked a sugar packet from its cubby hole, shook it, found it unacceptable for some reason, and put it back to rifle around for another. "I don't need one of those," Deth said, "Just going's good enough for me."

"Come on, sir," Packs said, "You don't have to prove anything to me. I know you've dreamed about getting that first MOH of the war."

Deth laughed. Having finally selected sugar and cream, Deth filled his coffee cup to overflowing so he could stand there for a little while gradually bleeding off a little with his lips until he could fit a lid over it. "I'd be lying if I pretended I hadn't dreamt about being Forrest Gump," he said, "Well, the Vietnam part, anyway. I just don't see myself ever getting into that situation in the real world. Besides, there's only one award I care about..."

Deth turned away suddenly, blushing, but Packs had already heard. "Oh, so you do want a chest full of metal after all? Just like Major Brannigan. Major Deth and Major Brannigan, we'll be telling stories about the both of ya."

"It's not that," Deth said, "It's just...ever since I saw you get your St. Barbara's Day Medal at the ball I've wanted one, too."

Packs raised an eyebrow. St. Barbara was the patron saint of the Field Artillery, through a complex series of logical leaps involving a tower, a bolt of lightning, and the propensity of 18th and 19th century cannons to explode. The Medal of St. Barbara, though, was not a military award, it was a purely honorary thing handed out by the Field

Artillery professional association for perceived devotion to the branch. In other words, battery commanders got it after their first command, and first sergeants (or PSGs about to make 1SG) got it.

"You're a real redleg, aren't you, sir?" Deth shrugged. That made Packs smile. "I ever tell you about the time Big Smell stole a St. Barbara's Day Medal?"

Deth slapped him on the shoulder, somewhat more effeminately than he had intended to, in retrospect. "You just made that up," he said, "You're making fun of me."

"No," Packs said, shaking his head, "It's 100% true." They walked towards the cash register. There was something of a line, but feeling wistful as Deth was, he didn't mind waiting. "So, you know you get your St. Babs after your first command. It's not a rule, in the same way that giving E-7 and above Bronze Stars is 'not a rule.'"

"You've got a St. Barbara."

Packs shrugged and pretended to be flustered. "Well, it's different for NCOs. Sometimes we get it before we make First Sergeant, but, you know, we'll have been in for ten, fifteen years. But you ever seen a lieutenant with a St. Babs?"

Deth scowled. He had, in fact. Vu had gotten a St. Barbara's before she went to Afghanistan and had pretended to him like she hadn't even really cared about the award. As a matter of fact, if he was being honest with himself, knowing Vu, she probably really hadn't cared about getting one. He was the only Field Artillery nerd. Vu had only chosen FA as a branch so she could blaze a path for women in the combat arms. Most of his other peers from OBC had either been there involuntarily or had been branch detailed, meaning that they would serve in the FA for a set number of years before being transferred automatically to the branch they had really always desired. Deth was the only FA officer in his cohort that he knew of who really loved the smell of cordite and wanted to do nothing else with the rest of his career. Sometimes he even dreaded in a weird way the idea of becoming a general and having to slough off his crossed cannons.

Packs interrupted his train of thought with a, "So, Colonel Fink had intended for BC to get his medal after his first full 18 months of command." Deth nodded. 18 months was the expected duration of a battery command. If you were relieved after 12 months, it meant you were a piece of shit. If you were kept on for 24 months it meant you were shit-hot and the battalion commander didn't want to lose you. For the middle third, 18 months was the rule of thumb. "Except BC was already going to hit his 18 months right when they decided to send him to Eye-raq. Which ended up being a twelve-month deployment that got extended to fifteen months, so, shit, I guess he was in command for 33 months?"

"Shit-hot."

"You betcha. Anyway, Colonel Fink made the mistake of giving the Big Douche the medal. He told him to award it to him Over There. You know, because he outranked him."

"Urgh..." Deth said, "I think I can already see where this is going."

"Thing is, though, did I ever tell you how he got to be major?"

"By mistake, I would assume."

They paid for their coffees and walked out to the all-but-empty fuel pumps. The place was so deserted Deth didn't feel bad leaning against the hood of the car while they chatted. "Worse than that," he said, "So-called 'Major' Brannigan had a break in service of about five years. He quit after his initial enlistment..."

"Obligation."

"Whatever you officers call it. He went out and tried to make it as a door-to-door salesman or something. Anyway, I didn't witness this part, but I guess this is what they say happened. He was just as bad at that as he was at everything else, so one day his boss shit-canned him in the middle of the day, didn't even wait until a Friday or something. So he goes, drives to a café, and drinks coffee all day until it's time to go home. Then he just walks in to see his wife and says he's been thinking it over and he wants to go back in the army."

"That really happened?"

"That's what Emerson says. Used to say." Packs scowled, thinking about his lost friend.

"Sorry."

"You didn't know, sir. So anyway, Big Smell comes back in the army with a five-year break in service but when it comes time to process promotions for his year group - surprise, surprise! - he comes up on the promotion list. He gets major having never had a command."

"Same thing happened to my old BC, Captain Crane. Well, except Crane told them about it and they changed his year group so he could get his command."

"Not Big Smell. So the man having never had a command never got..."

They said it together. "A St. Barbara's."

"Exactly, sir. So, lo and behold the St. Barbara's Day medal that Big Smell was supposed to confer on BC on St. Barbara's Day that year we were in Eye-raq just up and disappears. St. Barbara's Day came and went and never was it presented to our illustrious commander. And who should Colonel Fink ask about it but me?"

"What'd you say?"

"I said I'd get to the bottom of it. So I confronted Big Smell. You know what he told me, sir?"

"I suspect you're about to let me know."

"He told me that he had given it to one of those guys in one of the batteries and that," here he adopted his rowdy Brannigan impression, "'You know how those guys are, Sergeant Packs. We'd probably better have Colonel Fink send us another one from the rear. You know, just to be safe.' So I asked him who, exactly, had it and he said Sergeant Burns."

Packs shook his head at the memory. "What Big Smell didn't know was, I knew Burns. We came up together, him and Emerson and me, back in Steel Rain. So I go up to 'im and I says, 'Hey, Burnsie, did Major Brannigan ever give you that St. Barbara's medal we've been saving up for the BC?' And he just hangs his head in shame and he says, 'Bela, that Big Dumb Fuck came up to me when we first got here. And real rat-like, he says to me, "'Ey! Sergeant Burns! You still got that thing I gave you?" And I'm like, "What 'thing,' sir?" So he says, "You know, that thiiing." And we went on like this for about fifteen minutes until he finally told me he meant the St. Barbara's Medal and I told him to fuck off because he'd never given me anything.'" Packs leaned in towards Deth as though he were confiding an important secret that even here in this deserted gas station on the long lonely Oklahoma highway had to be protected."Sir," he said, "I got the same...exact...fucking...story from every senior enlisted and every officer in both batteries. I just about asked BC himself."

"So he was running around like a chicken with his head cut off trying to find where he lost the medal?"

Packs snorted, which seemed to involve a goodly amount of coffee going up his nose, to which he did not react."Sir," he said, "I guarantee you the son of a bitch *stole* the medal. When he gets to his next unit and starts showing up to balls and dining-ins wearing a St. Barbara's Medal, who's going to gainsay him? Who's going to look it up? It's not like it's a military award. They'd have to call the FA Association and somehow prove no one had ever given him one."

"Then why did he keep asking...oh. To make it look like he had lost it and didn't know where."

"The man was dumb as a post, but when it came to dicking people over, he was a fucking genius."

"Well, I'll be damned," Deth said, stretching out his arms and punctuating his thought with a sharp, high-pitched whistle.

Packs just gave him a glance and raised an eyebrow. "Well, Big Smell spent the whole deployment chasing after medals, didn't he? I guess he finally got one."

As they finally got bored of watching the stars, they climbed into the sedan. Buckling up, Deth asked, "Sergeant Packs, do you mind telling me these stories all the time?"

Packs shook his head. "Hell no, sir. Did you ever read the UCMJ?"

"Cover to cover."

"Seriously."

Deth shook his head. "No, of course not. Who would read the UCMJ except to look something up?"

"Did you ever read any manual?"

Deth rubbed his chin. "I've read parts of manuals," he said, "6-60, 6-40..."

"But not head to toe?"

"Not if I can avoid it."

"You know why that is?"

"Because they're boring?"

"Partly. But you still know the UCMJ, right? And you still know how to calculate safety and MET data. That's because you don't learn in the army from reading manuals. You learn from telling stories. You could pass right over the section about Soldiers not using umbrellas in the reg, but if I tell you about the time I kicked Fig's ass for opening an umbrella in front of me, you'll remember it."

Deth laughed. "That's true."

"No, I don't mind telling you stories, sir. That's how Soldiers learn. Just you remember when you're a general sometime about the old E-7 that took the time out of his day to teach you how to be a good officer."

"Heh. If I ever make general, I'm making you my sergeant major."

"Oh, I'll be long dead by then, sir, long dead. You ever read *Slaughterhouse-5*, sir?" Deth was so startled by the question he nearly shook the coffee out of his paper cup. He looked intoPacks's eyes. "Yeah, I know how to read," Packs said, just barely showing his teeth.

"Yeah, in high school."

"You know how it's all out of order? All, um..."

"Disjointed?"

"Disjointed, yeah. All the great movies and books about war are like that. You know why that is?"

Deth thought about it a moment. "No, I guess I don't."

"It's because war isn't a straight line from grid square A to grid square B. War is a series of stories we tell ourselves and each other. That's all it is. There's no way to understand war in a straight line. And if you try, it's just a textbook. It's not really war. War is just a jumble."

Deth nodded. "Why don't you let me drive home?" Deth asked.

He held out his hand and Packs reluctantly placed the keys in his palm.

That was the last time they spoke, except to shake hands when they left the motor pool. The next day, Deth reported to training.

24

Deth carved a small, perfect triangle out of his steak and held it up. For a moment, his anticipation would be everything. The steak wasn't particularly good, nor was it particularly well prepared. It was pink inside and juicy, just the way he liked it, but in a few minutes it would go the way of all cheap breakfast beef and go dry. For right now, though, for this one, perfect instant, the steak was calling to him like a lover.

He bit into it, and instantly was back on the road with Packs. Sometimes he stepped outside when it had just been raining, and the air or the temperature or the humidity or something was just exactly right and he was instantly back in his childhood home on a rainy day, or maybe a breeze came from the east and he was transported, as though he were really there, back to the beach house his parents had taken him to each family vacation. Right now he was having a similar experience. Some marbling or texture or flavor of the beef had fired some half-forgotten neuron perfectly, and he was laughing at an overfull table at some Oklahoma steakhouse with Bela Packs.

He felt a twinge of sadness. He'd been so busy with radar school he hadn't seen Packs in months. If he hadn't been wearing his PT uniform he would've reached for his cell phone and possibly texted the old man right then. But he never carried his phone during PT, and though technically he wasn't necessarily doing PT, per se, he had still left it in his car due to habit.

The bell on the door to Sunrise and Shine rang and Deth looked up, almost wondering if karma had sent his erstwhile platoon sergeant back to him for a chat. Instead, he was almost as surprised to see Vu standing there. "Well, well, well," she said, shaking her head in time to her chastening words, "Lieutenant Deth. Skipping out on PT to eat breakfast I see."

He rose and stood at perfect attention. If it had been the movies, he would have saluted her, but even as a joke he couldn't bring himself to do so indoors. "Yes, ma'am. Same as you are, Captain Vu, ma'am."

"Knock it off with the 'ma'am' stuff," she growled between clenched teeth.

"You've gotten so feisty since your promotion."

"Coffee," she said, signaling to the lone waitress on duty at 6:20 in the morning, who nodded and moved not terribly fast to fetch her some. Vu sat down across from him. "Call me feisty again. And what the hell are you eating? Steak and eggs?"

"Yeah."

"No wonder you can't pass a PT test."

"I can certainly *pass* the APFT. I just don't *excel* at the APFT."

"How is it?" she asked.

He shrugged. "Not the greatest steak in the world. But we're still in Oklahoma so any steak is better than most places'."

Without preamble, she reached over and ripped off a small hunk of his steak – it was that kind of cut –and popped it in her mouth.

"Help yourself," he added helpfully.

She chewed and shrugged, expressing with her shoulders essentially the same sentiment he just had with his words. "You shouldn't be eating this garbage," she said accepting her coffee and proceeding to order steel-cut oatmeal and some fruit dish or some shit. "Or skipping PT."

"Captain Pot," Deth said, nodding, "Lieutenant Kettle. Nice to meet you."

Vu's eyes narrowed. "Was that another Asian joke?"

"Heh?"

"Pol Pot?"

"What's a pole pot?"

She shook her head. "Nevermind. And I've got a reason to be here. The brigade commander is having a breakfast meeting after PT."

"Fuck," Deth muttered, clanging his cutlery, "I'd better make sure to be out of here." He checked his watch. "Well, I've got to be out for final formation anyway. Which I take it you're not worried about?"

She shrugged. "Brigade is a whole other animal. They trust us more."

"And look what you're doing with that trust."

"Shut it." Vu's bowl of bland grain arrived with a side of fresh fruit. She didn't even pour sugar on the pauper's meal before digging in. "How's radar school?"

He shrugged. "Every school in the army is exactly the same. The nice thing is hardly anyone seems to give a shit, so I'm on track to be Distinguished Honor Grad."

"Wow. That must be a sad little school to have you as DHG, considering how you did in FAOBC."

"I did fine in OBC. I passed."

"Don't you ever aspire to do more than coast through life?"

"Yeah, I aspire to be the brigade commander's pet and get the HHB command."

A volley of shredded oats flew by his face, just barely missing his eye. Behind the lunch counter, the cook scowled, as though knowing something had just happened, but not quite sure what. The waitress was busying herself in a well-worn romance novel, and didn't notice the new splash of manila Vu had added to the décor. Likely the mess would still be there the next time Deth stopped by the diner in a few months. It was that kind of place.

"Boy, you'd think for someone who did so well at OBC, you would've hit me," Deth said, rolling his eyes. "I didn't even duck."

"Yeah, well, I've got other things on my mind now. Like my cook who drank bleach and wandered out into the street."

"Dare I ask why he drank bleach and wandered out into the street?"

"I guess he was trying to kill himself. But not terribly hard."

"I know. You'd think a cook would have ready access to a stove to stick his head into. Or a knife. Shit, there are tons of ways to kill yourself in a D-FAC."

"Like I said: I think he wasn't trying very hard."

Deth pierced the yellow heart of his sunny side-up egg and used the yolk as a steak sauce, now that his cut was going dry. "So is that what being brigade HHB commander is like? Cooks killing themselves and red tape?"

She shook her head mournfully, not disagreeing with him, just disappointed in the situation. "That's about the long and short of it. Aside from a handful of cooks and mechanics, I'm the lowest ranking and least senior person at brigade. And I'm supposed to be in charge of the lot of them. It's like herding mice."

"You mean cats."

"You ever try to herd mice?"

"No."

"It's a lot harder than herding cats, I can tell you that."

Deth shrugged in non-disagreement. "Aren't you glad you agreed to be one of the first female redlegs? This is what you can look forward to in your career. You're in combat arms but not allowed in a combat unit, so it's all going to be HHB positions and staff job after staff job after staff job."

"Curse your dirty mouth hole, Bickham Deth." She hunched over a bit. "Yeah, I knew it was going to suck. But how do you turn down the chance to be a pioneer at something? Bringing the military out of the knuckle-dragging Bronze Age? How was I supposed to say no to that?"

"I wouldn't count on the military running out of knuckle-draggers just yet."

"Oh?" she asked, taking a spoonful of raw oats, "Somebody been hassling you at radar school?"

"Nah," he said, shaking his head, "I just meant in general."

Vu narrowed her eyes and jabbed a finger into his chest. "No you didn't. You meant someone very particular. I can read you like a book, Deth."

He laughed. "All right," he admitted, "I did mean someone in particular. I'm just not entirely sure he's real."

"The fuck do you mean by that?"

He waved his fork in the air, trying to compose his thoughts. "There's just this guy my old platoon sergeant used to talk about. Except, I don't think he can possibly be real. I mean, the more I think about it, the more I think my left arm was putting me on."

"Like a shaggy dog story?"

He shrugged. "Or like Private Snuffy. Every time something goes wrong, it was Snuffy. Or every time somebody sleeps with somebody's wife it's Jody. I mean, there's no way that one person can be as bad as all that. He must've just been telling me a whole lot of different stories and attributing them all to the same guy." He shook his head. "Yeah, there's no way MAJ Brannigan's one guy."

Vu wore a smile as wide as all of the outdoors. "You mean David Z. Brannigan? Daffodil Dave? Big Smell?"

Deth's eyes widened. "You know him?"

Vu laughed out loud. "Yeah, I know him. And unless your platoon sergeant told you he shot John Wilkes Booth, it's all true."

The waitress stopped by to re-fill their coffees, interrupting the flow of the conversation. Deth checked his watch in a sudden panic. He'd have to leave real soon if he wanted to make it back before final formation. But he couldn't pass up this opportunity to hear about Big Smell from someone other than Packs. Surely at least some of it had been exaggerated? "Really? How do you know him?"

"I had to work with that cumrag. Did you know he had this cockamamie plan to fire artillery without clearing the airspace first?"

"I heard about that! And he really went chasing after incoming mortar rounds to get a CAB?"

She nodded. "I've heard a million things about that buffoon. Everyone in the battalion knew him. Who was your platoon sergeant?"

"Bela Packs."

Vu nodded, wiping her face with a napkin, though, considering she was eating dry oats, of what he couldn't guess. "Oh, yeah, SFC Packs. He's a good NCO. Not an exaggerator, either. He tell you about Daffodil Dave getting into a slap fight with MAJ Steele?"

"Yeah, he did!"

Vu chuckled. "How about the Southern Pride-themed military ball?" Deth shook his head. "You want to hear about it?"

He shrugged. "Sure."

"How are you on time?"

He checked his watch. "I've got time for a quick one, but then I've got to go."

Vu nodded and leaned forward, clenching her fists together on the table like she was about to dicker a deal with a mob boss. "So this guy had a break in service. He's not even supposed to be an O-4. But what are you going to do, right? So after his S-3 gig he's made battalion XO. But guess what he calls himself?" Deth shrugged. Vu rolled her eyes and took a long sip of her black coffee before continuing. "He called himself the DCO."

Deth shook his head in disbelief. At brigade levels and higher the commander often had a Deputy Commanding Officer, his immediate second-in-command, as well as an XO, who was more like the chief of staff. At battalion level and lower the XO filled both roles.

The only meaningful difference Deth could think of was that DCOs were almost always generals and colonels, while XOs were commonly majors or lieutenant colonels. That, and it sounded vaguely more important. It occurred to Deth that someone with a yellow oakleaf on his chest calling himself a DCO was a bit like someone with a small penis buying a big red sportscar.

"So, in his capacity as 'DCO', Daffodil Dave decided to pick me as the OIC of the Fall Ball. Directly." An OIC was an Officer In Charge, essentially meaning whoever'd been given an unwanted hot potato.

"Um...shouldn't he have asked your BC? Or for volunteers?"

Vu nodded. "That *is* how the chain of command works, Lieutenant Deth. But, no, he came straight to me. It came time for the planning committee of this ball to meet. The committee, for whatever reason, consisted solely of FRG ladies."

"Wives? And he assigned you because...?"

Vu nodded. "Because I'm a woman. I'm 90% sure. So I'm at this meeting with nothing but wives, and I have no idea why they're there, but I don't speak up, you know, to be polite. And I watch on in horror as they're talking and they decide that the ball would not be formal, it would be a theme party, and not just any theme party, but a Southern Pride-themed country-and-western hoedown."

"In what sense then was it still a military ball?"

She shrugged. "I tried as nicely as I could to point out that perhaps not everyone in the battalion would be excited by the idea of a white trash line dance in place of a formal military ceremony. I didn't specifically point out that a Southern Pride theme might not necessarily sit well with the African-Americans in the battalion, but I hope it was implicit. None of these wives - did I point out they were wives and not Soldiers? - none of these wives agreed with my perspective and so I was stuck, it seemed, planning a country bear jamboree in place of an even marginally respectable battalion event." Vu took another sip of her coffee.

"What'd you do?" Deth asked.

"I brought the matter to my chain of command - see how that works, the chain of command? - and both my First Sergeant and my BC agreed with me that the whole thing was a terrible idea, and that no one would want to go and there might just be a few dozen EO complaints tossed in to boot. I asked them if I should speak to the battalion commander, and my BC agreed that it was a good idea, but

I should write everything down, maybe do a PowerPoint, and give the colonel a good brief. I must've spent three hours putting that damn thing together, which I never should have done in the first place, then I showed it to my BC for review, then made an appointment through the S1."

"Went through all the proper channels, in other words." She nodded. "You must've still been nervous as fuck, though."

"Yeah. Who wants to be a lieutenant telling their battalion commander they're all fucked up? I spent most of the day having a panic attack and trying not to vomit. But, at the end of the day…" She shrugged.

"Duty," Deth suggested.

She nodded. "So, I was confident I was doing the right thing, that I had gone about it in the right way, and that the colonel would recognize that and address my concerns. Finally I went to wait for my meeting and I sat down outside the colonel's office. That was when Daffodil Dave walked out of his own office."

"Oh, Christ," Deth said, "What'd he do?"

"Exactly what I was expecting him to do. He locked me with a deadly stare from those piggish eyes of his. My heart sunk. 'What are you doing here, Piera?' he mumbled."

Deth's eyes widened. He'd listened to Packs telling stories about Brannigan for so long that he'd stopped noticing the goofy voice Packs had put on for Brannigan. It sounded oafish, loutish, and only semi-human. Deth had always assumed it had just been Packs exaggerating for effect. But now Vu was doing the exact same voice, so close it was shocking, in fact. Was this really what this guy sounded like?

Vu went on. "'I'm here to see the colonel, sir,' I said.

"'Why are you going to see the colonel?' he asked.

"'I have an appointment with him, sir,' I said.

"'An appointment about what?' he asked.

"'About the ball,' I said.

"'About the ball? What do you mean? I'm in charge of the ball. If you have anything to say about the ball, you talk to me about it. I'm the commander of the ball.'

"Commander of the ball?" Deth asked, unable to hold in his laughter. She nodded, her eyes closing as though she had a headache. "This guy is completely obsessed with imaginary command authority. What did you say?"

"I told him he could sit in on the brief if he wanted.

"'No, he's not waiting on you, Piera, he doesn't even know you're here,' he said, to make sure I knew I was a piece of shit, 'Why don't you just show *me* what you've got?'

"And that was it. I knew that all my concerns, my carefully prepared brief, all the concerns of my BC and first sergeant and everyone else with half a shred of sense would never get to the colonel. Daffodil Dave began to read the brief and not at all to my surprise dismissed it all out of hand.

"'You know,' he said, 'This could be seen as going behind the committee's back or trying to jump the chain of command. You could present these concerns at the next committee.'"

"Uh..." Deth said, "You weren't the one jumping the chain of command. In fact, if he yanked you out of a scheduled appointment and refused to let you see your battalion commander, he was the one fucking up the chain of command."

She opened her hands before him in agreement. "Yup. So I told him that dealing with spouses is difficult because you can't exactly order them around and the reason I had arranged to meet with the commander was to show I was a team player and avoid insulting the spouses. I am a lady and an officer, you know. The truth is I thought spouses had no place on the fucking planning committee and that they had no concept of military protocol or equal opportunity laws and the whole thing was fucked from day one. But you know what Daffodil Dave said to me?"

"I can guess."

"He said, 'Well, uh, you know, I hand-selected the planning committee. They're all there because of me.' Hm. Really. Couldn't have guessed that one. 'You need to stay in your lane. You're not a planner, you're an executor.' Really. Is that why I'm on the *planning* committee, then?"

"Is that why, in the army, officers are planners and NCOs are executors? Maybe he didn't really consider you an officer."

"It gets better. He said, 'You're making this way too hard. This is supposed to be easy. Let me relieve you of your concerns about the planning. We'll take care of that, you'll just execute.'

"I told him, 'Yes, sir, that's why I just want to make sure the colonel is fully informed about our plans before he makes a final decision about the ball theme.'

"'You still want to see the colonel? Even after I've just addressed all of your concerns?'

"Addressed my concerns? What the fuck did he address? So I said, 'Yes, sir, I still want to see the colonel.'"

"Ha!" Deth said, slapping his hands together. "That must've pissed him off."

"He turned and looked at his computer and began typing. He was looking, I suppose, to see whether I actually had an appointment with the colonel. He seemed visibly upset that I did. I guess he was hoping that I was really out of line and trying to be a crazy upstart instead of just doing my duty as an officer. But that didn't stop him from stonewalling me.

"'Don't worry,' he said, 'I already know what the colonel's going to say. I'm trying to save you the frustration of talking to him.'

"Yeah, frustrating. That's what it would be like talking to the colonel instead of you, you fat dipshit. I tried one last time. 'I just want him to have all of the information before he makes his decision, sir,' I said.

"'Well, I'll brief the colonel for you. I'll make sure he hears your concerns,' Daffodil Dave said."

"How re-assuring."

"Of course. Anyway, the S1 said I should file a formal complaint against him for being denied access to my chain of command."

"Did you do it?"

She shook her head. "What would I have gotten out of it? It's no good blowing the whistle, Deth. Puts your career on the line. Besides, as soon as the colonel caught wind of the Southern Pride hoedown shit he shut the whole thing down. I think the last vestige was that we had a few hay bales as decorations in the ballroom. Which I was fine with."

"Fucking Brannigan. Well, I'd better get out of here." Deth stood up and pulled his wallet out of his IPFU jacket pocket. He tossed down enough money for his breakfast and Vu's, though she quickly snatched it up and attempted to stuff it back in his pocket. "Get your hands out of my pocket," Deth growled.

She stood up and embraced him. "This one's on me. When are you headed overseas?"

"Couple of weeks."

"Call me. We need to go to Hoffman's one more time."

He nodded and took a step to the door. He glanced down at his watch. No time left. He had to go, like, time now. "Hey, do you know whatever happened to Brannigan?"

She laughed. "Yeah. He works for post. Taking care of toilets or something."

"Really?" She nodded. He nodded in agreement. "Seems apropos."

25

Packs's conception of an airport belied his rural upbringing. Growing up in West Bumfuck, Egypt, he had never had much occasion to go down to the sorts of airports that the crop-dusters used, which were sometimes still just dirt runways carved out of cornfields. He never thought of an airport that way. But after joining the army, he had flown all over the world and had at least made footfall in every major airport, Seoul and DFW more than a few times.

He had never lived in a big city, but he had very cosmopolitan thoughts about what an airport should be. The airstrip at Lawton, therefore, was something of a novelty for him. Parking was like a hazy dream. He never had to walk farther than two parking spaces (maybe three at Christmas) and across the one-lane road where drop-offs occasionally took place.

The front doors were automated, or at least some of them were, but they reminded Packs more of a country grocery store's sliding glass doors than a proper airport's. There was one clerk at one counter to sell tickets and take baggage for the one airline that flew out of Lawton to its solitary destination (DFW.) And not only that, but the same clerk who took your baggage hurried out to the tarmac to load it and then hurried back in to man the security checkpoint.

Packs always had to laugh at the shoestring staff that Lawton Regional used. He never doubted that one day he would walk to the baggage carousel (actually just a counter with a shuttered window where someone pushed bags onto the floor) and find one of the pilots manning it.

The waiting area, such as it was, consisted of one TV (not a flatscreen) and a bunch of hard orange chairs that didn't swivel and had been designed for maximum ergonomic comfort sometime in the 1980s. Lawton Regional also had precisely two amenities. One was an arcade with games that would have made even a sixteen-year-old Bela Packs embarrassed to play, including one that apparently starred the rock band KISS. The other was a lunch counter that Packs had deliberately avoided on his every other trip here, fearing the mayonnaise used in the chicken salad to be made up of maggot eggs and the coffee to likely be urine mingled with rust.

Still, there was no avoiding it. The options were to take one of the hard plastic orange torture chairs, stand by the KISS arcade game, or sit down at the decrepit lunch counter. Besides, Deth was already sitting there, coffee in hand. Packs spotted him before he spotted Packs. "Hey, sir, how's it going?"

Deth smiled and looked up at Packs before standing and taking his hand eagerly. He looked different somehow, nervous perhaps, or perhaps the few weeks of pre-Iraq training had really made an impression on him. Or perhaps it was just that Packs wasn't used to seeing him in ACUs, since they had almost always worn greens when they had been on the road together.

"Sergeant Packs, damn good to see you," Deth said, "Can I buy you a cup of bat piss?"

That earned the young officer a look of death from the blue-hair behind the counter, but what was she going to do? They were the only customers, despite the few dozen-odd Soldiers and hangers-on milling about in the lobby of the airport. "Preferably something bottled, please," Packs said, "A Coke, maybe?"

Dust puffed out of each of her joints as she went to find a can of Diet RC Cola and laid it down before Packs, holding out her hand expectantly. Deth put some change into it.

"You look good," Packs said, reaching out and fingering the new piece of Velcro that stood out from the rest of Deth's uniform on his chest, "Captain, huh?"

Deth shrugged. "Frocked," he said, "For now. Few months and they'll start paying me."

"Couldn't have happened to a nicer fellow."

"Well, you taught me everything I know."

"Ain't that the truth."

They sat awkwardly for a while, their once easy rapport evaporated, gone to dust like all the veterans they had buried that long winter into spring. Finally, Packs checked his watch.

"What time is your flight?"

"1430."

"Well, it's 1545 now."

Deth shrugged. "Welcome to the army."

Packs shook his head and cracked the tab on the soda he hadn't ordered. He could still remember like it was happening the hours and minutes before his first deployment. He had sat with Yu-Ni, embracing each other under a blanket, and watching their favorite show, *Raymond,* on DVD. They had been told to report at 0945 but to wait for a call, then the first call had said 1115 but to wait for the next call. Then it was 1300, then it was 1430, and by the time all was said and done, he didn't even report until 1745. They had just sat there, watching episode after episode, terrified that the next minute together might be the last and not wanting to break their embrace until they had to. When it had finally come, it hadn't been so bad after all.

Yu-Ni told him later she hadn't been able to watch *Raymond* at all during the deployment. He hadn't either, had turned it off any time it came on AFN. "So you're flying out commercial or military?"

"Military, if you can believe it," Deth said, "They're supposed to drop a C-5 Galaxy here that I guess can actually carry a launcher. You ever been on one?"

"Take earplugs."

"Earplugs, really?"

Packs laughed. "You've never flown military. It ain't like flying commercial. You know how commercial, you sort of think they could make things more comfortable for you if they tried?"

"Yeah..."

"Once you've flown military, you'll get a whole new appreciation for how nice they make it for you. I don't give any stewardesses a rough time, I tell you what."

"I wish everyone was like you."

"So do I. But then I wouldn't be special."

Deth shook his head and tried to add enough sugar and cream to his bat piss to make it palatable. The attempt, Packs saw, was relatively futile. He wasn't much caring for his Diet RC Cola himself, either.

"So you're finally not going to be light-on-the-right anymore," Packs said, landing a punch on the shoulder in question and being delighted to see the officer flinch in a pain he would not admit to.

"So it would seem," he agreed with a wan smile.

"I guess when you get back you'll be the one telling me stories."

"Oh, that's all well and good," Deth said, "But no story will ever top the raccoon story."

Deth took a sip of his mop water.

"What's the raccoon story?"

Deth furrowed his brow. "The Greatest Joe Story Ever Told," Deth explained with such reverence that Packs could almost see the capital letters emblazoned in fire in the theater of his mind.

Packs shook his head. Deth threw his coffee cup down with such force that it nearly shattered the saucer and took about ten seconds before it stopped vibrating. Silently, the blue-haired counter attendant refilled it.

"You telling me I never told you the raccoon story? All those months on the road? You never let me get a word in edgewise?"

"More like you wouldn't stop harassing me asking me about Over There, but, sure, sir, if that's how you want to put it."

Deth eyed him shrewdly. "You really don't know this one?"

"Is it really the greatest joe story of all time?"

"It's better than that. It's like a crazy joke, but it was all real."

"Well, don't hold out on me, sir."

"Well, you know what every joe story has to start with..."

They said it together. "No shit, there I was..."

Then Deth picked it up from there. "...sitting in the BOC."

"This was before I started OBC. I was blackbirding with III Corps HHB. Or was it snowbirding?"

"Blackbirding," Packs said, "Er...no, wait, were you coming from or going to?"

"Coming...going to."

"Then it was...well, whatever, you were attached to the unit because you didn't have anything better to do."

"Right. And I counted myself lucky. Half of my classmates had to sit in holding pens at the OBC company HQ. It was like purgatory. I was delighted when III Corps HHB picked me up, ridiculous of a unit though that may have been."

Packs shook his head. A battalion level HHB was stuffed with pogues to begin with, and the higher you got, the more head-up-in-the-clouds they became. He could just imagine what a Corps HHB was like. All Good Idea Fairies and no god-damn common sense.

"We were on top of a hill in West Range, you know the one, the one that if you've ever been to Ft. Sill, you've set up your BOC on top of." Packs nodded. "At the bottom of the hill was our 5-ton with our supply guys. So I was acting OpsO because they didn't have one, hence why they asked me to snowbird...er...blackbird. The BC, Captain Crane, figured put enough NCOs around me and I couldn't do any damage."

"Just like all officers."

Deth ignored the crack. "It was around this time that we all began carrying those ICOM walkie-talkies. So my call sign was Hardcharger 5, and supply's was Hardcharger 44. Around 1700, I got a call on my ICOM. I heard PFC Greene's voice coming through, and he sounded terrified.

"Greene was a fellow who claimed to have been in the can. That's what he called it - the can. But considering that he was 19 and from Bel Air, Maryland, if he had ever been in the can at all, it had been juvie, and it had probably been white collar. Nevertheless, he never missed an opportunity to teach us how to make shivs or fifis."

Packs shook his head. He didn't have to ask what a fifi was. He had known a joker like that in Iraq, too, one who had claimed to have been in jail, although his guy had probably actually been in jail. He had shown them how to make a faux vagina out of a latex glove, a bath towel, and a rubber band. He had always insisted that you use Blue Magic hair gel instead of Vaseline to lubricate.

Packs was ashamed to admit he had, indeed, tried a fifi once. It was better if you tucked it between your mattress and your box spring.

"'Hardcharger 5, Hardcharger 5, this is Hardcharger 44!' Greene said.

"Being the OpsO, and not knowing what the hell I was doing, I was a bit busy running the BOC and although I knew damn well Greene didn't have anything important to say, I wasn't going to blow him off. So with a little bit of a grin I answered the call.

"'Hardcharger 44, this is Hardcharger 5,' I said.

"'Hardcharger 5, this is Hardcharger 44,' Greene said, and I could hear his panic rising to a crescendo, 'I don't want to alarm you, but there's raccoons down here!'

"Everyone in the BOC who was listening started cracking up, myself included.

"'This is Hardcharger 5, roger. What are you calling for?' I asked.

"'Well, uh...can we have permission to shoot them if they start threatening the 5-ton?'"

Packs nearly bent double in laughter. Deth was on the cusp of explaining, but he didn't have to, not to Packs. Firstly, no one was carrying live rounds on a field exercise. And secondly, harassing the wildlife was about the one thing you could do to get banned from the field permanently by range control.

Deth continued. "So everyone in the BOC is cracking up. I've got tears streaming down my face. But I call him back.

"'Negative, 44, you can't shoot them, and you're only carrying blanks, anyway,' I said, then I figured I'd have a little fun with them, 'You've got knives though, right? Maybe you should get out and fight them.'

"'Roger that, Hardcharger 5.'

"I almost said, 'Roger doesn't have a last name,' but I was laughing too hard so I just put the ICOM down and started to get back to my work. But Sergeant Krell was standing there with his arms folded.

"'Uh, sir,' Sergeant Krell said, "You know, you'd better call them back and let them know you were joking. It *is* Greene down there.'

"I looked around. I wasn't sure where Greene's NCO was. Probably on guard duty somewhere else, being as they were low-density MOSs. Greene was down there with Rubio, and neither of them were particularly bright bulbs. I scrambled to grab my ICOM and ring up the 5-ton.

"'44, this is 5,' I said.

"'This is 44,' came the reply.

"'This is 5, you're not actually to use your knives on any wildlife, understood?'

"'This is 44, roger.'

"I wiped my brow in relief and had a good chuckle over it. As the night wore on, Captain Crane returned to the BOC. We had conducted a good day of training and it was finally getting to be that time, so I started looking around for a chemlight to light my way to my hooch. We had boxes and boxes of chemlights. But for some reason I couldn't find any.

"'Where the fuck are the chemlights?' I asked no one in particular.

"Now, Specialist Dykstra was sitting nearby, probably getting in out of the cold, and he looked up at me just like an innocent little baby.

"And he says, 'Oh, you don't know, sir?'

Deth let that sink like a thud. "Captain Crane and I slowly turned to look at Dykstra.

"'Greene and Rubio came up a while ago and took all the chemlights,' Dykstra explained, 'To fight the raccoons with.'"

Packs's eyes were wide. He had to admit, he had never heard such a story before. Deth looked so animated telling it, too.

"Captain Crane and I slowly looked at each other. Suddenly, Captain Crane jumped up and dashed out of the tent. I fumbled around, looking for my rifle and my Kevlar. I finally stumbled out the door once I had found them and looked down the hill at the 5-ton. There were hundreds and hundreds of chemlights strewn all around the 5-ton. It looked like a god-damned airport runway. Captain Crane was flying down the hill. I just stood there, astonished, and wandered back into the BOC.

"Captain Crane came back in a few minutes later.

"'What happened?' I asked.

"'They were crouching in the back of the 5-ton, hiding like they were under attack,' Captain Crane said, 'They had been breaking chemlights and throwing them at the raccoons all night. And they couldn't understand why the raccoons weren't running away! And then as I came up to them, they stopped me and said, 'Stay back sir! They's coyotes around here!'"

Packs buried his face in his hands. There was no way to laugh that hard and maintain one's dignity. Deth didn't seem to care. He seemed to be laughing as much at Packs's reaction as at his own story. In a few moments, they were both in outright tears and the old blue-hair behind the counter was staring on in wonder.

"You're scaring away..." she started to say, but it was patently untrue as several of the other waiting greensuiters and occasional civilians who had been waiting for their planes had started to wander in to the lunch counter to see what the fuss was all about. She insisted on taking their orders before any of them could protest. It was a banner day at the Lawton Regional lunch counter.

When they finally recovered, it was impossible for Packs to hide the grimness on his face. Deth was surprised, but somewhat moved. "So you're finally going to get your big wish," the E-7 said.

"Yeah, I guess so."

"What are we up to now, OIF VII?"

"Oh, they discontinued that number bullshit."

"How is it now?"

"It's by year. This is OIF 06-08."

Packs punched Deth, but not very hard as he sometimes had in the past. "Dates are still numbers."

"Dates are still numbers, sir," Deth corrected him wanly.

"...sir," Packs echoed.

They looked away from each other. It was awkward. They had never really known what they had been to each other. Brothers, in a way. Father and son in another. Peer and mentor in another, and yet, fundamentally, they were just a platoon sergeant a platoon leader. There was nothing else in the world to compare that relationship to. It was part of all of those and part of none. "Well, sir," Packs said, jumping to his feet and offering his beefy hand, "Good luck Over There."

"Don't take any wooden nickels, Sergeant Packs," Deth responded, taking it.

26

The day Bickham Deth returned from Iraq, Bela Packs met him at the airport. He was the first off the plane. The baggage handlers who brought him out of the hold turned him over to Packs's custody. Packs saluted the flag-draped coffin with a three-second delay that would have made Deth jealous.

"Welcome home, sir."

27

Deth would've hated being buried at Ft. Sill National. Packs knew that like he knew the girth of his own cock. But Deth had no wife and his parents didn't know any better. Packs could've told them, could've told them they were doing the wrong thing by their son, that he would've done anything to be buried up north somewhere, or maybe he probably wouldn't have wanted a burial at all but would've preferred to be cremated.

Packs reflected on the day they had seen the little wooden plaque that stood in place of a tombstone together. He had so offhandedly mentioned to Deth what his own wishes were when he died. He had never asked Deth what he would have wanted, though he knew it wouldn't have been Fort Sill National. He had hardly ever let the poor kid get a word in edgewise, always talking his ear off.

He could've told Deth's parents he would've hated this, would've hated the caisson and the honor guard especially, but who would that have helped? Funerals were for the living, not the dead.

Just as he had insisted on picking up Deth at the airport (he refused to refer to him as "remains," not even in his own mind) he had insisted on conducting the funeral. LTC Fink had simply nodded, sipped a Dixie cup full of the bourbon he kept in his desk and offered Packs a taste. Packs had been tempted, but he refused. "You know you can't do it alone," Fink said.

"I know," Packs said, "I need an O-3 or higher." Deth had been formally promoted during his time in the Sandbox.

"I want our whole battalion there in formation," Fink said, "I'll see if post can scrounge up an officer. You understand I'm only letting you do this because it's you?" Packs nodded. "You're sure you wouldn't rather be in formation with your platoon?"

Packs shook his head. "He'd want me to."

"Maybe," Fink had agreed.

Now, standing by the coffin, he reached into the paper bag he had carried here from Fluffy's Quick Stop. "I can't believe I bought this for you, sir," Packs said with a laugh, "I never buy shit." He drew out the bottle of Mad Dog, tasted it, and puckered his lips. "You can have the whole bottle," he said, pouring it out at the foot of the coffin.

"Sergeant Packs!"

The voice made him grind his teeth. It sounded so jolly, so happy, so...dumb. Packs stood rigidly where he had been, hoping the voice had been a phantom, or that if it really belonged to who he thought it did, that person was just saying "hello" and would walk on by if he ignored him long enough. "Hey, Sergeant Packs," the voice said again, closer this time, "Pouring out a 40 for your LT?"

Packs turned with all the speed and precision of an M270 compared to an M270A1. There, realer than real, in living color, stood MAJ David Brannigan. He was smiling as only he was capable, a crooked, lopsided smile that seemed to light up the whole cemetery with a new brand of dumb. "Sergeant Packs," Brannigan said again, "I'm your partner. Grounds and sanitation said they could spare me."

Suddenly Packs had a terrible premonition. He'd never really had one before, couldn't account for it, but he saw a whole lifetime unfolding out before him. Even though someone had had the good sense to shuffle Big Smell into sewage detail now, he saw the man keeping his head down and getting his O-5 right at the eighteen-year mark. Seniority was so much more important than competence for officer promotions, right up to O-5. Then the man would have a battalion, an actual battalion, full of actual Soldiers who would be submitted to his madness, his whims, his self-centeredness and his obsession with medals at the cost of everything else. "Packs?" Brannigan said, starting to sound a little worried, "You DO remember me, don't you? Major Brannigan? Task Force Commander? DA Select? We served together in Eye-raq."

Even though he didn't really care about Phillips, Packs saw him dead, because LTC Brannigan had sent him to a FOB with no life support. He saw Fig and Simmons and Early going outside the wire on a ridiculous mission because Big Smell wanted a CAB. And he saw Deth designated to be a battery commander, should've been a battery commander, would've been one of the brighter and better ones, dead because...

He slugged him. Big Smell staggered backwards, clutching at his now-bleeding nose. "The frick, Packs?" Brannigan roared, clipping his curses even after being punched in the face.

"You go back!" Packs yelled, pointing his beefy index finger at him, "You tell them I'll take anyone but you. You tell them to send me a real officer. Bickham Deth deserves better than you! The army deserves better than you!"

Brannigan looked like he wanted to throw the full fury of his massive soft body into a fight. But he was obviously daunted by Packs's dominant physicality. Unsure what to do, but motivated by passion and revenge, he made a cup with his left hand and gave Packs a limp-wristed, open-handed slap in the face. It scarcely even stung. Packs didn't budge an inch. "You go back, sir," Packs growled, "I won't have you sully this solemn affair."

"I'm going to report you for...!"

"You're not going to report me for shit, sir. Or they'll get you for retaliation against a whistleblower."

"Whistle...?"

But Packs already had his cell phone open. "Colonel Fink," Packs said, "I'm afraid garrison wasn't able to provide anyone acceptable. Would you be willing to fold the flag with me, sir? Yes, I do think that's what Captain Deth would've wanted. Thank you, sir."

Packs snapped the cell phone shut sharply. Brannigan was still staring at him with astonishment. "Look, Sergeant Packs," Brannigan said, a note of desperation in his voice, "Why don't we forget any of this happened. You struck me, I struck you, we could call it even..."

Packs shook his head. "Rank wasn't involved in that, sir. That never happened. But I am going to submit that IG complaint. I should've done it before but I was a coward."

"IG complaint? What IG complaint?"

"I was worried about my career. Nobody wants to deal with a whistleblower. It makes you look like a malingerer. Makes you look soft. Nobody wants you anymore. But I was wrong. You have to call out war crimes when they happen. You have to stamp out incompetence or it just grows and grows."

"War crimes? Incompetence? You haven't got a thing on me."

"I've got manifests from every chalk we sent men to FOB Normandy on after the general ordered you not to." Brannigan blanched. "Disobeying a lawful order," Packs said, "Endangering the lives of your Soldiers. Dereliction of duty. It's not all I've got, but it's the worst of it. And I've got you on the MTOE as Task Force Commander. DA Select. In your handwriting."

Brannigan's lower lip quivered. His eyes were like Bambi's. Fink, who had already been in the crowd, approached them. "Sergeant Packs," Fink said, calling for his attention.

Packs turned and saluted sharply. Fink returned his salute. "What happened?" the light colonel asked.

"Garrison didn't send us someone who could bury Captain Deth."

"Oh, they sent a lieutenant?"

"Even worse, sir."

"That's fine, Sergeant, I've done my share of funerals. Well, who's this, then?"

Packs glanced over at Big Smell. "Oh, no, sir, Major Brannigan just wanted to speak to me about a complaint I filed against him. I advised him it was inappropriate for us to speak outside of an official setting."

Fink was obviously looking at the blood trailing down from Brannigan's purpling nose and staining his Class A's. The chalk outlines were still visible on Brannigan's uniform where he had marked where to put his medals and insignia. He had never wiped the chalk away. "I see," Fink said flatly, "Well, let's see if we can't do right by our young officer."

"Yes, sir."

Hours after the funeral, which all present had agreed would have been most satisfactory to Deth, Packs stood, leaning against the hood of the sedan they had seen so many miles in together, staring at the headstone. What the odds were that mortuary affairs would somehow produce the same exact vehicle for this funeral, Packs didn't know, but he suspected the hand of Providence or Fate had reunited it with him.

"How many hours did we spend just like this, hanging around in a boneyard waiting?" Packs asked the implacable headstone, "Do you think it added up to days? A week? Probably days. Probably not a week. I don't know." Packs finally opened the pack of Lucky Strikes he had bought just for the occasion. He took one and laid the rest at the foot of the stone. "This tastes like ass," he said after lighting it.

He glanced to the tombstone for an answer, but none was forthcoming. He sighed. Felt the weight of his years in the army pressing down squarely on his shoulders. It wasn't about to get easier. Going through an IG complaint was going to be a long, arduous process that would probably find his career tanked at the other end once he crawled through that pile of shit. He'd never make First Sergeant after all, it seemed. But maybe he would do a better service to the army by taking Big Smell off the street than he would have as a First Sergeant.

"Ever since I was a raw recruit, all I wanted to be wasFirst Sergeant," he said to the silent standing stone, "I wanted it as bad as you wanted to be deployed."

He didn't have anything schmaltzy to say. Nothing about how they had been best friends or how he had been the best officer he had ever worked with. Besides, neither of those was true. They had been friends (maybe) and good friends (but it had remained unspoken) and Deth had been an all right officer with some potential. He had lost Emerson, whom he had known for almost twenty years, just a few months ago, and it was hard to deny that he had been both a better friend and a better Soldier than Deth.

Packs wasn't really sure what he felt. He never liked it when people died, even shitheads like Gauge, who had gotten high in

Germany and wandered onto the train tracks. Packs had logged a lot of hours on the road with Deth doing funerals. Maybe it was that. Or maybe it was the special bond of a PSG and a PL, a relationship which there was nothing else quite like in the world. Or maybe it was just a moribund, underdeveloped sense of irony that told him the master of funerals should have lived to see his own. Or maybe it was happiness that Deth had finally gotten his wish and seen combat before he died. Maybe it was all of those, and a dozen more feelings combined.

"Well, I'll be seeing you, sir," he said, "Don't take any wooden nickels." Packs pulled open the door of the trusty sedan and then stopped. "Oh, I almost forgot," he said, "I went out and bought these last night. I wore them for you."

He tugged up his pantleg and revealed a scarlet sock.

THE END

Author's Note

Thank you for reading *Broken-Down Heroes of the Western Night*. Whether you liked it or not I hope you'll take a moment to leave a review on Amazon or your favorite book review site. Reviews are vitally important to me as an author both to help me market my book and to improve my writing in the future. Thank you!

Acknowledgements

My thanks go out to Kayleigh Marie Edwards, without whom this novel would still be sitting on my hard drive.

Without the support of my life partner Amy Lower I would be terrified to put this or any other work out there, and I owe her everything.

Finally, for those of you who have been wondering, almost none of the characters in this book are based on real people. With only one exception (which you wouldn't believe if I told you) they're all amalgamations of dozens, possibly hundreds of service members I've served with and/or heard stories about. So don't go looking for yourself in here. That being said, I owe a heartfelt thanks to the many NCOs, officers, and Soldiers who informed this book and made my brief military career anything resembling a success.

About the Author

Stephen Kozeniewski (pronounced "causin' ooze key") is the author of several books utterly unlike this one. During his time as a Field Artillery officer he served for three years in Oklahoma and one in Iraq, where, due to what he assumes was a clerical error, he was awarded the Bronze Star. He lives in Pennsylvaniawith his girlfriend and their two cats.

Printed in Great Britain
by Amazon